SORCERESS ENRAGED

LISA BLACKWOOD

SORCERESS ENRAGED

A Gargoyle and Sorceress Tale / Book 5

Lisa Blackwood

Sorceress Enraged

Gargoyle & Sorceress Book 5

Copyright © 2017 by Lisa Smeaton

http://lisablackwood.com/

COVER DESIGNED BY: Heather Hamilton-Senter

EDITED BY: Perry Constantine

PROOFREAD BY: Tracy Vandervliet

Special Thanks to Stan H for his eagle eyes.

PRINT ISBN: 978-1-990608-51-3

EDITION: 10/27/2021

❀ Created with Vellum

Sorceress Enraged

While Lillian and Gregory have their hands full trying to track down Commander Gryton and prepare for an imminent invasion, Corporal Anna Mackenzie has her own set of problems. And surprisingly, it doesn't have anything to do with the fact that she'd been converted into a gargoyle by a well-meaning cub.

No. Her new gargoyle nature is something she'll come to grips with...eventually. Having that same gargoyle cub abducted by an evil demigoddess? That's another story altogether.

Anna has never failed to accomplish something once she's put her mind to it, and her mind is now firmly set on seeing the young gargoyle freed at any cost. And if the evil demigoddess gets in her way...the Lady of Battles will be in for the fight of her immortal life.

Never had the sound of the ocean crashing against the cliffs failed to soothe him, but the restlessness of an unknown future had drawn Draydrak here to the edge of his self-imposed prison, and this dawn the seas failed to calm his rising unease.

Soon, the Divine Ones would call upon him to serve. He felt it in his soul. Yet, for the first time in his existence, he wasn't sure if he was strong enough to succeed. Or even if that was his wish. He was weary of his role.

As this planet's sun cleared the horizon, its light stretched across the sky in a white-gold glow. The perpetual beauty of the act wasn't lost on him. It represented hope's ever-renewing promise.

New beginnings.

The one thing beyond his power to give himself. And not unlike all the mortals upon the mortal plane, he craved the one thing he himself could not have.

A hundred thousand times each moment his power

bestowed the gift of new beginnings upon all the souls of the universe. Many mortals feared it, fought it, terrified to accept his embrace, his greatest gift, not understanding that it was merely a new beginning. Hope. The promise of life eternal as ordained by the Divine Ones at the beginning.

The one thing forbidden to him.

Death.

But Lord Death could not succumb to his own power, even though he would willingly embrace it for the chance to absolve his greatest mistake and end the rivalry with his sister.

In the past, he had tried. Even falling upon his four swords to no avail. His magic was tied to his twin's and hers to his. Once, long ago, when he and his twin had first started their war, he had attempted to kill her and send her back to the Divine Ones for healing.

To the woe of all the Realms, the Battle Goddess would live as long as her twin existed and Draydrak could not die.

Their war had threatened to destabilize all of creation until the Avatars had been reborn into the Magic Realm and they had shown him a way to imprison his wayward sibling.

Thus, the duality curse had been born, trapping both twins in their respective temples.

Draydrak had gone willingly. His twin had not. Even trapped within her temple, she still sought to continue the war, raising armies and setting them loose every few thousand years.

The Avatars returned each time to put an end to her

rebellions. Until this time, when his twin had found a way to manipulate even them.

War was coming again, and this time he wished an eternal ending to this on-going strife. He wanted a new beginning for them all, especially his sister. She needed healing only the Divine Ones could grant.

But first, he needed to win the coming war and find a way to strike a fatal blow that his twin would not be able to escape.

"Dray?" The ocean breeze tried to steal the words of the speaker, but Thayn was too determined to let anything, even an innocent breeze, interfere with his plans. "Might I have a word with you?"

Thayn was always there to draw him from his melancholy thoughts. Draydrak shifted his weight and glanced over his shoulder to an outcropping of rock where the gargoyle elder perched.

"Of course my old friend," he said as he turned to face the much smaller gargoyle. Boulders crumbled under Dray's hooves as he turned his back on the ocean and the ever-seductive call of renewal the rising sun represented. "Speak."

The gargoyle's ears flicked forward and back, betraying some small hint of uncertainty. At last, he said what was on his mind. "My Lord, the entire council felt the arrival of two new gargoyles in this realm. But they are unlike any to come before them."

Ah. His gargoyle legion had felt the arrival of his twin's newest experiment.

"I am aware," he confirmed. "They are my sister's doing."

"Of course, but do you wish us to raid the Battle Goddess's lands and capture these two?"

There was a hint of excitement in the old gargoyle's expression.

Dray hated to dash his general's hopes, but he feared these two were not born of Divine will, were instead firmly his sister's creatures, or would be before long. Although, that was yet to be determined. Perhaps they could still be reasoned with, persuaded into doing what was right.

"No, I'll not waste gargoyle lives on such an endeavor until I've learned more about them myself." Draydrak paused and glanced back toward the rising sun. "If I find them worthy of saving, then I will act, but if they are just more souls turned by my sister's corrupt power, then I will free their souls to return to the Divine Ones."

"But, my Lord, one of them is female. A female gargoyle, surely this is what the Divine Ones prophesized long ago."

Ah. Of course, his gargoyles would wish to believe the coming of the first female gargoyle would mark his own mate's arrival as the ancient prophecy said.

"I am sorry my old friend, I very much doubt this is Divine will."

The gargoyle huffed out an amused snort. "It's not for myself I ask, or even the rest of the gargoyle Legion—the dryads suit us well enough. I had hoped for your sake this would signal the beginning of the prophecy."

Dray's lips curled back from his fangs as he grinned down at Thayn. "Foolish old gargoyle. I am too set in my ways to want a mate. Besides, what female would be brave enough to court death?"

"The female the Divine Ones chose for you, I would assume?" The gargoyle replied with dry wit.

Draydrak chuckled and gestured at his own body with all four of his arms. Once he'd made his point, he folded his arms and allowed his wings to expand to catch the ocean breeze.

But it wasn't his physical form that he was worried about. It was within his power to take other shapes for short times. No, his true fear was rooted in what had happened to his sister. She had once been loyal to the Divine Ones. At least until the day her mate, the Shield-bearer, had decided he wanted the power over life and death and was willing to kill Draydrak to secure it.

When Draydrak had killed his twin's mate, her grief over losing him had twisted her soul until she became the darkly obsessed being that now wanted to rule all of creation so every living creature would feel the sorrow she now felt.

That's what love had done to his twin. He would avoid such a fate at almost any cost. So far, the Divine Ones seemed to concur, for they had not used their Avatars to birth another demigod into the universe to become his mate.

"Well, then, if you're not going to order the gargoyle Legion to invade your sister's territory, what are your orders instead?"

The old gargoyle wasn't going to give up just yet.

Dray had no time for a foolish prophecy or an equally foolish romantic old fool. No, he would deny fate, prophecy, and even meddling elderly matchmakers.

"Continue training the young ones as you have been,"

he said, but then surprised himself by adding, "And send more gargoyles to scout along my sister's domain. I will see what I can learn about her two newest projects and discover if they are slaves or willing servants. If the latter, and should they attempt an escape, I want some of my army near to collect them and bring them here."

And just like that, he felt Fate tightening her clutches. Still, he didn't take back his words. Rescue mission or assassination attempt, foiling his sister's plans for these two would be a worthy use of his time.

PART ONE

$\mathcal{A}$nna had been following a river for most of the morning when she spotted what looked like a path cutting along one side of the valley. Her first thought was that it was a game trail because she hadn't seen any signs of civilization since she first arrived in fantasyland last evening.

Last night she'd found a spot to shelter beside a fallen tree and used her night vision goggles to scan for signs of hostiles. There'd been nothing but wildlife. Deer and wolves were plentiful. So too were the sizeable hairy mountain goats. She'd even spotted a big cat-like shape on the opposite slope.

Fantasyland looked a lot like the Rockies. Well, if one removed roads, towns, and people.

This morning she'd started out near dawn and traveled alongside the stream she'd landed in yesterday, eventually coming to the river she now followed. Not once in the fifteen-kilometer hike had she seen another human or other fae. Which made her wonder if the locals knew better than to venture in the direction she was headed.

She hiked for another three kilometers and then spotted something that made her halt and crouch low. After a moment, she rose from her crouch and then slowly traversed the rocky ground until she reached a large outcropping. She used it to hide.

Peering through her scope, she scanned the terrain ahead. A break in the thinning greenery was what had first caught her interest. The view through her scope confirmed it was too uniform for a game trail.

Someone had built a road to cut through the mountain pass, and a road almost always went somewhere. It had probably been running alongside the river all along, its location hidden by the thick tree canopy. Now that the vegetation was sparser, she could clearly see the pale line of the road.

This one led out of the valley and began to snake its way up toward a pass in the mountains. The higher the road climbed, the sparser the cover. Fewer trees and shrubs meant less cover to hide her movements.

While that was unfortunate, it wouldn't stop her. This road led in the direction her magic said Shadowlight lay. She thanked whatever god was responsible, for as long as that magic tugged her closer to him, she knew he was still alive.

If he was alive, she could rescue him.

She scanned the rough road again before rising from her crouch behind the cluster of boulders. It would be too dangerous to use the road even if it would make her route marginally quicker. Anna hadn't seen any patrols, but that didn't mean there weren't any.

Jogging cross country might take a little longer than following the road, but it was better than getting captured.

After hoisting her pack, she adjusted it and then checked her gun. Once everything was in order, she broke into a lope.

"Hold on, kid. I'm coming for you."

Anna stayed close to the road for the rest of the day. The sun was just beginning its descent when the road reached the narrow pass she'd seen earlier. The trees were thinner here, the ground rockier. Staying close to the western side of the pass, she hid herself using shadow magic.

She marched two more kilometers before the pass dumped her into another valley. Instincts screamed a warning, telling her this one wasn't empty of habitation. Glancing around, she slipped between the cliff wall and a section of rock that had fallen from above.

After Anna had inched her way up the rock pile, she peered toward what she'd only glimpsed before. Blinking against the glare of the setting sun, she studied the mountainous city carved out of the northern slope of the valley.

This, then, was the road's destination. Midway up the slope, pillars cut from a blood-red stone rose out of the ground and flanked the road. Studying the rise of the land through her scope, she saw where the road merged into a staircase two-thirds of the way up the mountain.

From her present vantage point, it didn't look like the slope on either side was scalable without climbing gear.

Not good.

If she wished to go farther, she would need to call upon her gargoyle shadow magic after dark and attempt the climb with the hope no one discovered her. There was no way she was turning back now. Her eyes drifted higher to study the fortress or city or whatever one called an evil overlord's abode.

Regardless of the dangers, she was going to infiltrate that place.

Shadowlight was somewhere inside.

Beyond the fortress's tall, impenetrable outer walls, she saw the high peak of what must be a temple. That was Shadowlight's most probable location if Daryna's intel was accurate. Anna would have a better idea once she scouted around. First, she had to get inside without getting caught.

She scowled at the sun. To gauge by its position above the horizon, it would be at least another forty-five minutes before it was dark enough for her shadow magic to hide her entirely.

Crouching down behind her present sheltering outcropping of rock, she pulled food and water from her pack. She'd eat and then cross the valley floor and see if there was any other way inside besides the front door.

CHAPTER TWO

The human-gargoyle hybrid had been this way already. She'd done a fine job of covering her tracks as she'd followed the lay of the land until she'd come to the road. The human had possessed the wherewithal to know not to walk the road in broad daylight, but she'd followed it as she tracked the young gargoyle's location unerringly to the Battle Goddess's fortress.

When she'd first exited the pass, she'd waited until full dark to call her shadow magic and start the last leg of her journey. She moved with stealth and cunning, hiding her presence from the sentries that patrolled these lands. He'd have to have his captains discipline the men sleeping at their posts. A human, even a half-gargoyle one, shouldn't have slunk unnoticed past his guards.

Still, anger didn't manifest at the realization. Perhaps he should discipline himself while he was at it. This human had once managed to use one of his own daggers against him. A lucky toss, perhaps, but she'd still bloodied him.

Overpowering her now and taking her to the Battle Goddess might be wise, but he was curious just how deep into their territory this female would manage to infiltrate. He could always capture her later.

And this little exercise might make an excellent example of what the young gargoyle's Kyrsu was capable of. It might even please the Lady of Battles to learn that, although human, Shadowlight's future second in command could overcome her birth handicap and grow into a truly formidable ally.

Commander Gryton grinned up at the night sky as he followed Corporal Anna Mackenzie into the heart of the Battle Goddess's territory.

Anna inched past another set of guards, slowly placing one foot in front of the other without so much as shifting a pebble. So far, she hadn't given herself away. Not yet.

She wasn't sure how much longer her luck would hold, but it only had to last for a few more hours, just long enough to rescue Shadowlight. Once free, they would follow Daryna's instructions and hope for the best. Anywhere was better than here.

When she'd first reached the gate and beheld the biggest set of stone doors she'd ever seen, she'd had to wait for shift change before attempting to enter the city. But luck had been with her, and she'd arrived not long before new soldiers had come to relieve the ones on duty.

All the guards were dressed similarly to Tin Man in heavy

body armor. The rattle of their armor and weapons helped disguise Anna's soft footfalls. Still, she didn't relax as she made her way farther down a cobblestone street and crossed paths with an increasing number of enemy combatants. After all, gargoyles could hear something as soft as a heartbeat and these guards might have senses just as developed.

She took the first side street she found, a narrow alley with almost no traffic. She needed to find a place to hole up for a few hours where she could wait for the nocturnal citizens of this fortress to sleep. She'd heed that much of Daryna's warnings and instructions.

As Anna made her way farther down the narrow alley, the smell of manure grew stronger. Realization struck, and she followed the odor to a large stable complex. The building would be as good a place as any to lay low for a while.

It surprised her that they kept horses here. It probably shouldn't have, since the weapons and armor all were medieval-looking. But the presence of horses surprised her. How could a primitive, horse-riding culture be a threat to all Earth?

But she knew the answer.

Magic.

It all came down to magic.

Anna entered the stable and soon found a ladder leading into the loft. After glancing around once, she started up the wooden rungs. Once she was safely out of sight, she released her hold on her shadow magic.

Weaving her way between stacks of hay bales, she situated herself in a back corner. It wasn't until this moment that an uneasy thought presented itself. What if those weren't horses down there in the stalls?

The pooka and the unicorn could pass for horses easily enough.

Fuck.

Her finger eased against her rifle's trigger as she waited for some sign that she'd been discovered. But after thirty seconds, and there was still no dreaded outburst from the creatures below, she decided they were just animals. The sound of their chewing, the rattling of buckets, and the occasional nicker as the horses talked to their friends further away in the paddocks all helped to soothe her nerves. With luck, the animals had just been bedded down for the night, and no one else would come until dawn. So far so good.

The first hour passed without incident except the horse in the stall below her took a piss and Anna's eyes and nose burned from the powerful ammonia vapors.

She silently cursed her heightened gargoyle senses for the first time.

At least no one would smell her over that pungent odor.

The contented sounds of horses lulled her, and she soon drifted into a light sleep. Approaching footsteps on the stone cobbles outside awoke her sometime later. Anna's eyes snapped open, and she rolled onto her belly, crawling forward a few feet until she could glance between a gap in the loft's floorboards and watch the stable's west-facing door. After a moment it swung open enough to admit a hulking figure in full plate armor like what Gryton wore, but since it didn't have as much bling as Tin Man's, she assumed this was a soldier of lesser rank.

He eased through the door and glanced around the empty lane and then whispered something to another unseen person behind him.

Anna's index finger touched the trigger as she peered through the scope.

"The grooms have left for the night," the big male whispered to the person behind him.

"Good. I don't have all night."

The second speaker was female.

"In a hurry?" The male challenged, masculine pride evident in his tone.

"The arrival of the gargoyle disrupted my routine. I need to feed before I report for duty."

"Ah, I wouldn't be a very good subordinate if I let my captain go hungry, would I?"

The female stepped forward and shoved the male against the wall with enough force to raise dust. "Stop talking, or I'll find a better use for your mouth."

Anna scanned the female and noted she also wore armor, but hers was of a slightly more ornate design than the guy's.

This was likely one of Tin Man's senior officers. More importantly, the female knew about the gargoyle, which had to be Shadowlight. This female would lead her to wherever the kid was being held.

Anna's magic told her Shadowlight was somewhere below her present elevation, which probably meant he was housed in a dungeon of some kind. And it would be a whole lot easier to find by following this female than it would be for Anna to poke around on her own and risk discovery.

So far, the two below hadn't sensed Anna's presence or noticed the faint glow given off by her ward-spelled weapons. And soon it looked like they would be too involved to notice her, but she wasn't taking any chances and remained still with her rifle pointed at them.

The female was aggressively stripping the male of his armor, and he was returning the favor. Anna's eyebrow arched to her hairline. It looked more like mutual assault than any kind of foreplay, but neither one was complaining.

The female hauled open the door to the empty stall behind them and then shoved the male back into the clean straw lining the floor.

"Vaspara, you spoil a male," he said with a throaty chuckle.

The stall's one window allowed enough moonlight in to illuminate the two. The female, Vaspara, appeared human. The male, not so much. He was taller and broader than an average human. Something was odd about the texture of his skin. All she could ascertain in the semi-darkness was that it didn't look quite normal. But the telltale giveaway was the short pair of horns curling around his head and the spikes growing out of his shoulders.

Nope. Not human.

It was too dark to make out much else, but she thought she saw the white flash of fangs at his mouth before the woman leaned down for a kiss.

Anna scanned the stables once more to make sure someone hadn't come to check on the noise.

Eventually, the fantasyland porn stars finished up with

groans and snarls. Seriously. Snarls. Anna had another reason to curse her enhanced gargoyle senses, but then a wave of coppery stink obscured the scents of musk and sweat. And this wasn't just a few beads of blood from a scratch.

She glanced back at the two, half expecting one of them to be dead. But nope. Both soon rolled to their feet and began to dress. It looked like the male had a few scratches, but the female was the one with the big bite on her shoulder.

She moved like it didn't hurt her at all. Once they were dressed the male turned back to the female with a fanged grin. "Anytime you need me, I'm always happy to serve." He purred. "I do love a good roll in the hay with a succubus."

"It's Captain. Do I need to discipline you, soldier?"

All playfulness vanished from the male and he came to attention. "No, Captain Vaspara."

"Good." She turned and marched from the stables. The big male was swift to return to wherever he'd come from as well.

Once Anna was confident the way was clear, she eased down the ladder and silently picked her way to the stable door. She listened for a full minute but didn't hear anyone outside. After calling her shadow magic to cloak herself, she eased the door open just a little and squeezed through the narrow space she'd made.

Outside, she scanned the area for more activity. There were guards out in the yard in front of the stables, and she heard a few others patrolling somewhere behind the building, but they were the only ones she sensed close by.

At the opposite end of the cobbled yard, a torch-lit walkway led off to some other part of the fortress. Vaspara was almost out of sight already. If Anna wanted to find Shadowlight quickly, her best bet was to follow the captain.

Anna didn't fool herself. Walking the city at night, when most of its nocturnal residents would be most alert, wasn't a good plan, but after what she'd seen and heard she didn't want that female, that succubus, alone with the kid.

Nope. No sitting and waiting for dawn while that demoness did God only knows what to Shadowlight.

Dragging in a deep breath, Anna left her hiding place and set out to follow the female to wherever Shadowlight was being held. She didn't fool herself. This was extremely dangerous. If she got caught, Shadowlight might never escape from the Battle Goddess's domain. As much tactical sense as it made to sit and wait until dawn when the enemies' senses would be dulled, she couldn't just leave a child to be abused, either.

Anna wouldn't fail. If she had to give her own life to protect the kid, she would. One way or another, Shadowlight was going to gain his freedom.

CHAPTER THREE

Her initial assumption that Shadowlight was being held in a dungeon proved correct. She had followed Captain Vaspara deeper into the sublevels of the city, and eventually to the dungeons where she'd managed to get within a couple hundred meters of the kid's cell. Unfortunately, she couldn't just sneak in, grab him, and sneak out again.

For one thing, there were two guards parked at either side of his door, with others stationed where branching tunnels intersected with this passage. She'd counted six different checkpoints leading out of the dungeon. The only reason she'd gotten this far was that she'd followed close upon Vaspara's heels and slipped through each of the checkpoints before the soldiers closed ranks again.

The constant strain of maintaining her cloaking shadow magic was starting to wear upon Anna, but no one had sensed her yet. Then again, no one was looking for an enemy soldier to be foolish enough to infiltrate this place.

That advantage would only last while Shadowlight was still in his cell. As soon as she broke him out, if she managed to break him out, the enemy would swiftly discover it, and the hunt would be on.

She doubted her shadow magic was up for hiding her from anyone actively searching for an escaped gargoyle.

The second problem was the chains.

When Captain Vaspara had entered Shadowlight's cell, Anna had heard the rattle of chains accompanying the kid's rumbling growl of warning.

Even though Anna knew she wouldn't like what she found, those two sounds together had been enough to cause her talons and her fangs to lengthen. Those weren't the only changes. Her joints had ached and throbbed until she'd feared she might shift into a fully-fledged gargoyle there on the spot.

She'd held her shit together. Barely. Then backtracked fifty feet to an empty room she'd spied on the way. With her back against the wall, she glanced around the room to confirm it was indeed empty. Breathing slowly and steadily, she clapped down on instincts that were still urging her to attack.

Shadowlight needed her calm and logical, not a rage monster on a killing spree.

Although, that might be needed later to escape this place.

Anna looked around her hiding place. Its surfaces were covered in what looked like a century's worth of dust, which suggested it hadn't been used lately. That suited her just fine.

Conversation drifted down the hall and Anna heard Captain Vaspara addressing Shadowlight.

"Come now, you must be hungry," Captain Vaspara said in a reasonable voice. "I brought you some food."

Shadowlight's answering growl sounded more like a 'fuck you' than a 'thank you.'

Anna fingered her rifle's trigger.

Eventually, the succubus gave up trying to talk to the young gargoyle and slammed the heavy door back in place. The demoness left orders that no one was to feed the gargoyle until she returned later.

Anna narrowed her eyes. Captain Vaspara was apparently trying to gain the kid's trust, but he was too smart for that. He was brave. She allowed herself to feel a little pride on the kid's behalf.

Then reality intruded. It didn't matter how brave he was, courage wouldn't help him out of those chains. His rescue depended on her finding a way to free him.

Communicating with him was the first hurdle she needed to overcome after she came up with a plan. In the past, he'd been able to read her mind. At least until Gregory had started his training sessions. Now she was able to hide her presence and her thoughts.

That same training also allowed her to speak with Shadowlight over a distance. But could she do it without betraying her presence?

She didn't know the answer to that. She wouldn't risk it. Not yet. Once she had an escape plan mapped out in her mind, only then would she attempt to reach him.

As long as Shadowlight wasn't in immediate danger, she

would wait until daylight when more of the fortress's citizens would be asleep.

Right. That gave her a few hours to come up with a plan.

Making her way deeper into what she thought was actually an old guard's room that had later been transformed into a storage area, Anna studied a row of barrels sitting along one wall. There was a narrow space between them and the wall so she wedged herself into it, safely out of sight of anyone who might happen to glance into the room as they passed by in the hall.

She kept her shadow magic in place as well, just in case.

A little over three hours later, she heard several pairs of footsteps and the now-familiar voice of Captain Vaspara.

"Any trouble from him?" Vaspara asked.

"No. He was pretending to sleep, though, so he's likely waiting for a chance to strike."

"I'd expect nothing less from a gargoyle, even one as young as him," Vaspara acknowledged.

The rattle of a latch sliding back was followed by the heavy scrape of the cell door opening. A low growl echoed down the hall.

"Young one, I've brought you some food and drink." Only Shadowlight's low growl answered Vaspara's words. "You haven't eaten in over a day. You must be hungry."

Shadowlight continued to growl.

That's my boy, Anna thought while a wolfish grin crossed her lips.

Eventually, the female captain gave up and exited Shadowlight's cell.

"If he isn't taking food by tomorrow night the Battle

Goddess has instructed me to use magic to gain his cooperation. Until then, no one else is going in there. Understood?"

"Yes, Captain Vaspara!" The words were accompanied by the stomp of boots against stone and the rattle of armor as they gave their version of a salute.

Anna waited to make her move until dawn, or at least what passed for morning here. This planet's day wasn't the same twenty-four hours as Earth's. As best she could figure, it had a twenty-eight-hour day. Enough to notice, but not enough to handicap her significantly. Although, she supposed the planet had a different gravity than Earth, too. When she'd first arrived, she'd just assumed her weariness was a result of the altitude up in the mountains.

Nope. Nothing so mundane. Alien planet. Complete with super unfriendly magic-wielding aliens.

Huh. And some people whined about jetlag. Try portal hopping to another planet.

While she waited, Anna checked over all her weapons. One in particular, since it was still relatively new to her. When she'd broken into the workshop where Lillian and Gran had been wards-spelling all the weapons, she'd spotted a rack of the new 272 semi-automatic sniper weapons used during some of the sessions with the joint fae-human training units.

The rifles still hadn't been deployed for regular use, hadn't even been given an official designation yet as far as she knew, though the humans on the team were already calling it by the unimaginative moniker of C20.

Taking an unfamiliar weapon into a fight was an excellent way to get killed, so she'd practiced with it on the trail. The suppressor and her own shadow magic had done a good job of silencing the report.

She'd checked the rifle and her other weapons a half-dozen times while she'd waited. When she gauged it was four hours past dawn, Anna left her hiding spot and peered through the crack between the frame and the ancient wooden door.

Unfortunately, this time she didn't have the rattle of the guards' armor or the stomp of boots to disguise the creak of the old hinges as the door opened.

Gritting her teeth, she slowly opened the door a few millimeters at a time and poked the muzzle of her rifle through. She shifted only enough to verify she had a clean shot at both guards.

If her attempt to communicate with Shadowlight blew her cover, she'd need to take out the pair of guards quickly and quietly. It was a risk, but one she had to take.

Here goes nothing.

She brought the pad of her finger against her rifle's trigger and exhaled slowly.

"Shadowlight, if you can hear me, respond but don't give away that you are talking mind to mind, or whatever the fuck you want to call this mental voodoo."

"Anna?" His voice filled her mind. Emotions flowed along with that one word. Hope, fear, suspicion, and desperation were the most palpable. She also knew he wanted to believe it was her, but he expected a trap.

"It's me, kid. Daryna sent me to rescue you. If she hadn't, I would have found a way to find you."

"It really is you." Excitement and hope blooming fully formed in his thoughts.

Their conversation didn't distract her from studying the two guards. If either showed even a hint that they sensed her communication with Shadowlight, she was taking them out.

So far, they showed no signs of suspicion.

"Kid, I'm going to get you out of there. I've got explosives to blow the latch on the door, but that will announce my presence rather loudly, and I don't know if I'll have enough time to free you from the chains. Tell me how they're attached. I have an idea."

"They're bolted to the wall by some magical means. I can't tear them loose."

"Okay. Don't worry about that. How are they attached to you?"

"Manacles around my wrists."

"Nothing around your neck or ankles?"

"No."

"Good." Hope flared, and she had to calm her mind. She didn't want her insecurities to leak across her link to the kid. Or, worse, to the guards. *"I've seen Gregory shift to human form before. Are you capable of that? Because if you are, then you might be able to slip out of those manacles."*

"Gregory is an Avatar. He has many powers that a regular gargoyle doesn't. But even so, most gargoyles have the ability to shift forms for short times."

"Do you think you can?"

There was a long pause followed by a wave of uncertainty. *"I'm not yet fully mature. Lillian is older than me and only learned to shapeshift recently."*

"She only just learned about magic a few months ago, right? She didn't even know she had the ability," Anna reasoned. *"You're pure gargoyle and already command a good bit of magic."*

"I'll try, but if I can't, then what do we do?"

Anna shrugged even though she knew he couldn't see it. *"Shoot the guards, blow the door, more explosives where the chains are attached to the wall and then run like hell. Once we're free, we'll find a way to get those manacles off later."*

"We might not escape."

"No. There are no guarantees other than I won't leave you behind."

"I don't want you to get captured." Worry tinted the young gargoyle's thoughts.

"That's not on my wishlist, either, but I'm not leaving without you. We're doing this one way or the other."

"I'll try to shapeshift," he promised.

"Good, but don't stress if you can't. I'll still break you out."

"Should I try now?"

"Sure kid. Everything's ready on my end," Anna said, sighting the first guard through her scope. *"Let me know if it works."*

"It might take me a few minutes. I need to access my father's memories."

"Take all the time you need."

If at all possible, she'd take the two guards down silently, set the charge and then pick off any guards that came running toward the sound of the blast. Once Shadowlight was free of the cell, they'd use shadow magic to hide and make their way back to the surface, using the route Anna had plotted out in her head.

That was the plan. She just hoped Fate was on board with it.

"Anna, I found my father's memories, I'll try."

"Okay. Keep me informed."

But with Shadowlight merged with her through the magic of his shared blood, he didn't have to tell her it worked, she could feel his sense of pride at mastering another ability.

"Good job, kid. Are you able to get the manacles off?"

"Yes."

He was practically bouncing with happiness.

"Good. Don't move yet, I don't want the guards to know what's about to hit them."

And they didn't. She made two clean headshots through their helmet's open visor. The guards hit the floor with the loud clatter of armor against stone. She shoved the door aside and made her way to Shadowlight's cell while scanning up and down the hall for newcomers.

"Crouch low against the far wall," she instructed as she shaped the C4 and set the charge. When she was done, she moved down the hall and covered her ears. *"You clear?"*

"Yes, but I'm not sure if I can shapeshift back to my gargoyle form again so soon." There was a hint of uncertainty in his voice.

"Don't worry about it. Can you still call on your shadow magic to hide?"

"Yes."

"Good. That's all we need. Because we're screwed if we have to

fight our way free of this place. There are enemy combatants all over the fuck.”

“Gran says you shouldn’t swear.”

“I won’t tell her if you don’t.”

Happiness radiated along the mental link and he promised, *“I won’t.”*

“Good, you ready? It’s going to be loud. As soon as the door blows, I want you out of there and on my six. We’re going to run thirty feet down the tunnel until we reach the stairs. Don’t stop for nothing. Stay behind me. I will be shooting at anything that moves. Anything comes up from behind, just tap me on the shoulder. Understand?”

“Yes.”

“Good. Here goes.”

CHAPTER FOUR

The blast from the charge deafened her for a few precious seconds, but she held her position, rifle pointed toward the stairs. Their location was exposed, enemies able to approach from two directions, but it couldn't be helped.

Anna was glancing back at the cell's blown door when an adolescent boy burst out of the cell and sprinted toward her. He moved wicked fast, but it was still a surprise to see a scrawny boy and not a massive gargoyle running toward her even though she knew he'd shifted forms.

She glanced forward again. *"Grab my pack. Move when I move. We get separated now, we're screwed. There won't be a second prison break attempt."*

Together they ran back the way Anna had first come. She'd memorized the route in her head, going over it several times during the night so they wouldn't get lost as they ran.

They made it to the stairs by the time the first guard came running toward them.

His helmet's visor was up, and though he had some form of defensive magic in place, it did him no good. He died as swiftly as the first two guards had.

Three more guards appeared and died just as quickly. Then Shadowlight slapped his hand down on her shoulder. She twisted and took out two more guards approaching from behind.

She and Shadowlight bolted up the stairs, breaking through the doors at the top just as more guards came rushing to their comrades' aid. Anna took out as many of them as she could and kept moving. Shadowlight snatched a sword from a fallen enemy's hand without releasing Anna's pack.

They ran, never slowing or stopping unless they needed to dart into a side room to avoid a larger company of soldiers than Anna wanted to fight. Once the way was clear again, she and Shadowlight continued their mad dash to the surface.

When they emerged into the sunlight, Anna blinked back tears at the brightness but kept moving. They darted between what shadows they could find now that the sun was high in the sky.

They were about halfway to the main gate, but unless some miracle occurred, they weren't going to make it that far. Soldiers swarmed out of buildings and alleyways faster than ants in defense of their nest.

There were just too damned many of the enemy and not enough shadows to hide in even though Anna hugged the walls of buildings or sought the shade cast by the few trees growing in the fortress.

Changing directions, she headed for the stables. That dubious shelter was closer and perhaps by the time they reached it Shadowlight would be able to shift back to gargoyle form. He'd have a far better chance of escaping on the wing than on foot.

His chances doubled if she stayed behind and provided cover fire while he made his escape.

"Where are we going?" he asked. "The gate is the other way."

Anna reached back and dragged Shadowlight along when he slowed.

They kept running, ducking under the trees, around horse-drawn carts and what looked like honest-to-god human peasants. There was other, less human-looking, foot traffic as well. But thankfully it thinned out a bit as she and Shadowlight moved farther from the central keep.

At last, they managed to get clear of the densest concentration of soldiers, and they weren't now being chased. At least that she could see. It didn't mean there wasn't someone following.

Anna sprinted around the side of another building and into a narrow alley. There they paused to catch their breaths. Her eyes darted to the kid and away again. It was disconcerting.

She was used to seeing the big, black-skinned wall of muscle that was a gargoyle. Even a child like Shadowlight was still taller and bulkier than her. She wasn't used to seeing this scrawny little teen even though she knew Shadowlight was a child.

Fuck. Fuck it. Evil overlords should just leave kids the fuck alone.

At last, she asked, "How you holding up?"

"I'm fine," he whispered.

Crap, he even sounded younger. More victim than warrior.

"I'm sorry, kid. Ready for another run? There's a stable up ahead. I hid there last night. We might be able to hide long enough for you to shapeshift back to gargoyle form and then fly out of here under cover of shadow magic."

Anna glanced up and down the alley and then out into the rustic cobblestone yard beyond. The stable was just a short sprint across that open area.

"The yard is too damned open, but the stable is the best place to hide. If we stay here, guards will find us."

"Then we must go," Shadowlight said.

They darted out of the alley but only made it halfway across the yard before a thread of warning and instinct raised the hair at the back of her neck. A foreign power crackled along her senses and rushed around them like an unnatural breeze.

"Shadowlight! Look out! It's a trap." She shoved him toward another alley leading away from the cobbled yard, but it was too late.

Guards poured out of the mouth of the alley, blocking any escape that way. But it wasn't the guards that made her blood run cold; it was the tall, armored form that exited the stables with his arms folded as he took in the scene.

She'd recognize that armor anywhere.

Fuck it all to hell. Tin Man was here.

Last she'd seen him, he'd been back on Earth.

"Corporal Anna Mackenzie, surrender before you get the youngling killed."

"No!" Shadowlight snarled as he sidestepped Anna and charged Commander Gryton.

"Shadowlight stop!" But he didn't heed her words and kept on going.

The power crackling along Anna's senses shifted, chasing the kid. When it caught him, it transformed into a raging wall of flames between Shadowlight and his target. Tin Man wasn't done yet, though, and the fire swiftly spread until it encircled the human-form gargoyle, trapping him inside.

"Shadowlight!"

Anna could only watch in rising horror as the fiery walls began to contract, the circle shrinking slowly inward.

CHAPTER FIVE

Gryton smiled at the human-gargoyle half-breed while he maintained careful control of the fire ring surrounding Shadowlight. He'd been secretly watching the human as she'd hidden practically in his soldiers' shadows. Not once had they suspected an invader was within the fortress, one who had managed to infiltrate all the way into the dungeons. If nothing else, Corporal Anna Mackenzie had shown him weaknesses within the Battle Goddess's kingdom.

Though, not many souls would be foolish enough to attempt to exploit those weaknesses. More interesting was how close they had come to success. The only reason they hadn't escaped the fortress was because Anna didn't yet possess the ability to shapeshift into gargoyle form and Shadowlight didn't presently have the strength to shift back into his true form. Had luck been with them, Gryton was confident they would have escaped the fortress.

Well, had he not already been tracking the human female since early this morning, that is.

"You won't kill him," Anna challenged him, still not ready to admit defeat, he saw. "Not after you went to such trouble to capture him. You need him alive."

Well, that was true, Gryton admitted. Grinning, he clarified, "You are correct. I won't kill the child, but he'll have some nasty burns. The kind that would kill a human, but gargoyles possess a powerful gift for self-healing. He'll recover, eventually."

"Tin Man, if you hurt him, I swear I'll see you dead."

Gryton's grin grew broader at her use of a nickname. None ever intentionally annoyed him, at least not twice, but this human had no fear. She just stood her ground and cast insults at him.

In small doses, he imagined it would be rather refreshing to have a subordinate possess enough backbone to challenge him. Perhaps he would mentor Anna himself.

"It's up to you." He shrugged. "Surrender to me willingly and no harm will come to Shadowlight."

Anna's rifle remained pointed at his chest. He sighed. "Your weapons can do me harm, as you know, but they cannot kill me. I'm more powerful than that. But any attack you instigate will distract me. What do you think will happen to the youngling then?"

She swore, her eyes shifting to look at the ring of fire circling Shadowlight. Swearing a second time, she took her finger off the weapon's firing mechanism and balanced the gun on her palms to show she wouldn't attack. Bending, she placed it on the ground and then after a moment, kicked it away from her. She reached for another weapon and did the same, spending the next few minutes divesting herself of all her armaments.

When she was at last unarmed, he glanced down at the surprisingly large pile and arched an eyebrow.

"Good, now come here," Gryton instructed.

When she was close enough, he grabbed her by the throat and dragged her against his chest. Spinning her around, he locked an arm around her neck and forced her head back to expose her throat. With his other hand, he held a knife to where her pulse pounded rapidly.

She was tense but didn't fight him. Good. He called back his magic, and the ring of fire surrounding Shadowlight blinked out of existence. The boy snarled like he would if he was still in gargoyle form, but he didn't otherwise threaten Gryton.

"Good boy."

"He's not a dog you mother fucker."

Gryton arched a brow. The female had a fouler mouth than some of his men. He pulled her back tightly against him just to see if she'd loose another string of swearing. She did. His grin grew broader still. If nothing else, training this one would be fun.

Captain Vaspara came running down the path with several guards in tow. "Commander Gryton, I wasn't aware you had returned from your stay in the Mortal Realm. I would have come at once, had I known you were back."

He snorted. "Come at once with the unfortunate news of the gargoyle's escape, you mean?"

Vaspara was too professional to waste his time attempting to weasel her way out of a disaster that had happened on her watch.

"My apologies Commander, we weren't yet aware that one of his allies had come seeking to rescue him." Vaspara's eyes narrowed as she took in Corporal Mackenzie. "But this human possesses skills beyond what is normal for one of her kind."

While Vaspara spoke, he signaled the guards to capture the young gargoyle. Shadowlight didn't fight, surrendering his sword without taking his eyes off Gryton's dagger where it was pressed to Anna's throat.

"We will need to collar the gargoyle as soon as he shifts back to his true form. We can't have another of his escape attempts." He glanced down at the human trapped in his arms and gave her another squeeze. "Now can we, Anna? The cub might get seriously hurt next time."

Another stream of colorful swearing burned his ears, but she didn't struggle.

"We should begin the search for others of her kind," Captain Vaspara said and then glowered at the human.

"No need. There *are* no others of her kind. She is unique, but I know what you mean. I've been following her since shortly after her arrival. She is alone. I believe she actually went against the wishes of her superiors and the Avatars by coming here." Gryton turned and began to walk over to where Vaspara stood.

"She killed twenty-three of our men." Vaspara's lips compressed into a thin line.

He dismissed her concerns with a wave of his hand. "She was doing you a favor. The weak must be culled to strengthen the rest of the herd. Besides, your pride should be soothed knowing she isn't really a human. She's Shadowlight's Kyrsu and will one day be his Second when he leads the Battle Goddess's army.

Vaspara's eyes widened, showing a rare bit of surprise.

"Yes," Gryton said, guessing her thoughts. "The boy has already been busy."

"But he is still years away from being mature. He shouldn't even possess the ability or the drive yet." Vaspara was now studying the kid with calculation in her eyes.

Anna tensed up and Gryton applied more pressure to the knife at her throat.

"I know the youngling doesn't look like much." He looked Shadowlight up and down. "Especially now as a human boy, but he is strong in magic and quite fierce."

"As we discovered," Vaspara said warily before turning back to study Anna in more detail. "This one will be Shadowlight's second in command?"

"Yes," Gryton tapped the flat of the blade against the smooth skin of Anna's throat. "She's already completely loyal to him. And he to her. We can use that to our advantage during their training."

Vaspara looked doubtful but held her silence.

"I need to report what I've learned in the Mortal Realm. Take these two and make sure they don't escape. I don't have to tell you how displeased the Battle Goddess will be should her project get delayed again."

Captain Vaspara snapped to attention. "Be assured I will not be caught unaware again."

"Good," Gryton removed the dagger from Anna's throat. "Take them back to his cell. Keep them together for now. He'll draw strength from her and be able to shift back to his true form sooner. Send a runner to notify me when that happens."

Vaspara took hold of the human. "As you command."

With that, Gryton turned and started toward the temple in the center of the fortress city. Unfortunately, reporting to the Battle Goddess would be far less enjoyable than hunting and tracking Shadowlight's pet human had been.

CHAPTER SIX

*L*ess than a half-hour later, Anna found herself installed in her new cell. They tossed Shadowlight in with her a moment later and then slammed the door closed again. The room was dimly lit and smelled of must and mold.

Unfortunately, they'd strip-searched her and found every weapon she'd brought to the Magic Realm. Captain Vaspara was far too interested in the ward-spelled armaments and had instructed guards to bring all Anna's gear to her workroom.

Anna listened to the stomp of retreating feet. When the footfalls disappeared altogether, she turned from the door and surveyed her cell. It didn't take her gargoyle-enhanced vision long to adjust to the gloom, but it wasn't the cell her gaze landed on.

Shadowlight stood a couple of feet away, scanning their new cell. While he familiarized himself with his new home, Anna studied him. He still had long black hair held away from his face by two leather ties, and he was dressed as he had been before with the beaded loincloth his father and Gregory seem to prefer.

That's where any sense of familiarity ended.

A teen stared back at her, his expression fierce, which seemed at odds with his narrow-shouldered frame. He was still tall, about her height, but for the first time, he honestly looked like a kid.

A strangely familiar kid. He almost looked like one of her brothers when they'd been that age. Yep. She wasn't imagining it. Shadowlight had the long Mackenzie nose and the same exact skin tone.

"I touched your memories while we were linked and modeled my human body after the images I saw of your brothers."

"You can see my memories?"

"Only when we are mentally linked."

"Huh."

Shadowlight looked uncertain. "If me looking like one of your brothers bothers you, I can take on a different likeness next time." He made a face. "Though, I hope I don't have to shift to human form too many times."

"Normally I'd ask what was wrong with being human. But considering where we are, I think I'd choose a gargoyle form over a human one if I was given a choice."

Talking helped her relax, but it didn't improve their predicament much. She eyed the straw-covered floor and wondered what kind of vermin might be lurking in it.

The straw she'd seen used as bedding in the stables was undoubtedly fresher. She walked the perimeter of the cell, trailing her fingers along the wall, looking for she knew not what, certainly not a loose stone. They wouldn't be that stupid.

As it turned out, the walls were in good condition. She sighed.

Though there was a trickle of water running down the groove in the back wall. She glanced up and spotted where it trickled in from. The crevice wasn't any wider than her finger.

No escape there.

The small stream of water smelled fresh, but she wasn't tempted to taste it. She'd need to be damn desperate before drinking mystery water here.

There was also a large round hole in the floor where the water escaped.

"The latrine?" Anna muttered to herself. "Nice."

Shadowlight padded over to her. The poor kid was barefoot. At least the thugs had left her with a tank top, pants, and boots.

"The water is safe to drink. It's all we will get. The hole in the floor is for waste." Shadowlight glanced up at her with a silent question in his eyes.

"I'm truly sorry I couldn't get you out of this hellhole, kid." She switched to her mental link. *"But we're alive and in one piece. As long as we're alive, we have a chance of gaining our freedom."*

"And I'm sorry I wasn't able to shift back to gargoyle form and fly us to safety." Guilt laced his words.

"Oh, kid. It's not your fault. You were just out of resources."

Shadowlight glanced down at his bare feet and wiggled his toes in the straw, then he glanced back up at her. *"I'll make Gryton pay for this one day."*

"That's the attitude." She patted him on the shoulder and then looked around the room. Her gaze naturally settled on the trickle of water. She leaned closer and looked up at the gap in the ceiling where the water entered.

"Is there another cell above this one?"

"No. I don't think so. At least I've never heard the sound of another living creature up there."

"Small blessings. No one is going to piss in our drinking water."

Shadowlight made a face. "True."

"There is something I'm curious about," Anna said, as she leaned a hip against the stone wall and crossed her arms. "Earlier, when Gryton was talking to Vaspara he said I was your Kyrsu. What does that mean?"

"The Gargoyle Legion is led by a Rasoren, and his second in command is called his Kyrsu. They are the two highest positions in the Lord of the Underworld's army. Normally the positions are held by a gargoyle father and son." Shadowlight glanced down at his feet, looking unhappy. "But the Battle Goddess has taken that concept and twisted it, then applied those titles to us. We have not earned them."

"Yeah, well, we're already a great brother-sister team. If they want to call you a Rasoren and me a Kyrsu," Anna shrugged, "they can. I've been called much worse than a Kyrsu in the past."

Shadowlight yawned and then gave himself a little shake to force himself back to full alertness.

As Anna watched him, a rare maternal instinct kicked in. "You haven't slept in a long time, have you?"

He shook his head. "I didn't trust them."

"I know this place is no five-star, but why don't you make a bed out of the straw? I'll take first watch."

The poor kid was exhausted. He moved over to the corner of the cell closest to her and lay down. He was asleep within minutes.

Anna stood watch for a while, then started to pace and worry. She would've done just about anything to get them out of this place, but presently that was beyond her power. Her pacing didn't do anything to help either, so she settled for sitting next to him and trying to share some body heat.

When the kid wrapped an arm around her waist and pressed his face against her side and started to cry in his sleep, Anna decided only the razing of the Battle Goddess's kingdom would make up for exposing Shadowlight to what was likely to come.

CHAPTER SEVEN

It was sometime in the middle of what Anna guessed to be afternoon on this planet when Shadowlight shifted back to his gargoyle form. He didn't even wake. The poor kid must have been more exhausted than she'd realized.

She let him sleep until she heard a group approaching from farther down the hall. Anna grabbed Shadowlight's shoulder and gave it a good shake.

His eyes snapped open and in less than three seconds he'd rolled to all fours, ready for battle with his tail lashing in threat.

"Easy," Anna said as she got to her feet. She took two strides forward until she was standing at his shoulder. "There are times to fight and times to wait and see."

Shadowlight flicked an ear in her direction and grunted an unhappy questioning sound before turning toward her.

"This is one of the wait-and-see moments, isn't it?" The

words were said in a calm, very adult tone, but she could see his agitation and smell the bitter taint of his fear.

"That's right." She patted his shoulder in reassurance. "You sure they didn't hurt you before?"

Of course they'd hurt him. What she needed to know was if the succubus had touched him. Her blood surged as rage ignited in her soul. She knew what she'd do if the demoness preyed on children. It was Anna's turn to hold back a growl.

"They used magic to restrain me and pushed me around." He paused and rubbed at his side. "Two of the guards kicked me after I killed four of their number, but Vaspara punished them. I've sustained no lasting damage."

"Good. Don't fight them in the future, though, unless I say."

Shadowlight grunted again unhappily but merely nodded. "We're a team, yes?"

"Yeah. We got this." Or at least she hoped they would survive long enough to escape with their bodies, minds, and souls intact.

The noise outside the door drew nearer and then there came a rattle of the latch and a moment later the door banged open. Three bulky brutes, which would make the toughest linebackers piss themselves in fear, stormed into the small cell and forced her and Shadowlight back at spear point.

"Easy," she reminded Shadowlight as they were backed against the wall.

Commander Gryton and Captain Vaspara marched in behind the brute squad. Anna glanced behind them, to the open door. Guards stood two rows thick. No escaping this time.

Gryton stepped forward and motioned for the brute squad to get out of his way.

"Anna, it's nice to see you've talked some sense into the cub. Vaspara tells me he hasn't been the most cooperative of prisoners."

"No worries, Tin Man. I just told him to save his strength until he can inflict maximum damage."

"I see," Gryton said with a hint of humor coloring his tone. "But no matter, I have something here that will ensure Shadowlight's good behavior."

Anna had been expecting this since Vaspara and Gryton's conversation a few hours ago. And she also knew about the collar that had been used to enslave Shadowlight's father as well as the one used to bind Gregory's power for a short time.

Yeah. She'd been expecting collars. Didn't mean she wouldn't have preferred to avoid the unpleasant complication, though.

"Don't fight them, Shadowlight. There are too many," Anna said aloud and then added using their mental link, *"Alive, we still have a chance at freedom. Dead, we don't. Remember that, kid."*

"I'll remember," he whispered back along the link without any betraying expression on his face.

Commander Gryton's gaze slid sideways to meet hers. He grinned. "See, we're already starting to get along."

"I'm compliant. Don't get that confused with willing."

"Another truth," Gryton said with that infuriating tone in his voice.

His tone was already getting old. Anna glowered at Tin Man.

"Shadowlight first," Gryton said as he held up the collar.

The gargoyle snarled in warning.

"Oh. Perhaps I'll get you to do this instead." Gryton was now holding the collar out toward Anna.

"Fuck you."

"I might let you some other time; however, I need the gargoyle collared before I take you both before the Lady of Battles."

"I'm not putting a collar around a child's neck."

"Your stubbornness won't aid you here." Gryton's lips thinned. "Guards, subdue the cub by any means necessary."

When the guards moved to act, something uncontrollable and foreign rose up within her. She knocked the spear's tip away from her throat and lunged at Gryton before the guards could react.

His face was the only part visible. She took advantage of that and raked his face with her talon-tipped fingers. She'd been going for his eyes, but he'd jerked his head to the side enough to save his vision. Her talons left score marks on the side of his ornate helmet.

It wasn't enough to sate the rage uncoiling in her chest and she struck again, landing a blow to his armor-clad midsection. The impact raced up her arm and the punch likely hurt her more than it did him, but his hiss of anger was still rewarding.

Guards rushed Anna and she snarled and fought, but a blow from an unseen assailant knocked her clear off her feet and into the wall behind her. Stunned, she slid to the floor, but the rage was driving her back to her feet to meet the attackers closing in again.

A louder snarl half deafened her. Moments later her own attackers were knocked aside, and Shadowlight was blocking her view of the rest of the cell. The kid was unharmed, and reason slowly asserted itself upon the rage and drove it back, deeper inside. Anna gave herself a shake and looked around, somewhat startled to see the guards, as well as Commander Gryton and Captain Vaspara, had drawn back.

Jeez, Anna thought as she pressed her hand to her throbbing temple. *What the fuck was that?*

"Stand down, Shadowlight. We can't win this fight."

Shadowlight's expression when he looked over his shoulder was doubtful, but he didn't fight and allowed himself to be forced back against the wall.

Anna brushed straw from her uniform but didn't make any more hostile moves.

I'm a terrible role model, she admitted to herself.

"I won't fight the collar," Shadowlight announced. "Just don't hurt Anna again."

Damn it all to hell. The kid was trying to protect her. But Anna only stood with her hands fisted and watched while Gryton affixed the collar to Shadowlight's neck. Fighting would have only gotten them both killed or maimed.

Gryton's hands fell away from the collar. Then he stood back, seeming to admire his work. Anna decided that he would wear a collar one day before she killed him so he would get a taste of what his victims felt.

"Well done, youngling," Gryton said with an affectionate pat to Shadowlight's shoulder.

The kid growled in answer, but Gryton ignored him and turned his attention to Anna. He motioned her forward and that's when she noticed he held a bracelet, not a collar.

What the hell? Typically, the prisoner wore the collar and one of the hostiles wore the command bracelet.

"What? I don't get a collar?"

"No," Gryton said simply. "You aren't as dangerous as a full-blooded gargoyle, and you won't leave Shadowlight behind, so as long as he remains with us, you're not leaving us either. And this way, if you shift to gargoyle unexpectedly, we don't risk having a collar decapitate you. The bracelet is designed to be more malleable than a collar and will expand with you as you shift for the first time."

The bracelet snapped around her wrist.

"This will force the gargoyle to behave. If he acts out or displeases us," Gryton gave another of his chilling smiles, "you will be the one to take his punishment. The collar's main purpose is to prevent him from flying away the first chance he gets. However, it allows me to issue him commands, and I promise, if you act out, it will be the youngling who suffers."

"Only a short-dicked fuck, too insecure in his own manhood would think up that bullshit and inflict it on an innocent kid."

Gryton stepped forward until they were toe to toe. His gaze broke away from her to drift down her body, stopping at the usual places a pig frequently paused to admire.

When he reached her feet, he reversed course and eventually made it back to her eyes.

"I assure you, I'm most confident in my manhood, but if you require a demonstration..."

Anna grunted. "I thought I might die of old age before you finally finished your ogling."

Shadowlight growled and Gryton merely laughed. "Don't interrupt your elders, child. We are having a conversation."

"Were," Anna said.

"Were?" Gryton's one eyebrow arched up in question.

"It's done now. The next thing on your agenda was presenting us to your evil overlord, I believe."

Gryton burst out laughing. "Yes, human mutt, I was going to take you before our goddess. I would suggest you keep your tongue firmly behind your teeth or else the Lady of Battles will remove it. She is entirely without a sense of humor."

"Seems to be a rare commodity around here," Anna said as she glanced around the cell, faking indifference.

"Yes. It gets beaten out of the sensible ones." Gryton turned to the guards, and they moved aside to allow him to pass. He paused long enough to glance back at Shadowlight. "Come."

Shadowlight stumbled forward with a snarl, and Anna realized he was forced to follow.

She wove her way through the guards until she was striding shoulder to shoulder with Shadowlight.

Together they walked forward to face a demigoddess.

CHAPTER EIGHT

They were led from the dark realm of the dungeons to the upper stories of some temple complex, complete with worshiping priests and priestesses. Servants scurried out of the way of Gryton and his soldiers as they passed. Captain Vaspara had a strong hold on Anna's arm while the Commander kept Shadowlight on a short, invisible leash.

Anna didn't fight them or give them other reasons to rough up her or the kid. Besides, if she and the kid wanted to survive, they'd need to abandon their tight hold on their morals and blend in until a chance to escape presented itself.

After being led through several twisting, narrow corridors, they eventually came to a vast chamber. Pillars marched down either side and disappeared into the darkness high above her head. Somewhere up there a ceiling must exist, but the light of the torches faded long before it could dispel the gloom.

Two wide staircases at either end of the room swept down in a graceful flare until they ended at the black, glass-like floor.

"Creepy," Anna muttered. Captain Vaspara squeezed her arm in warning.

Well, it was. The whole damn fortress was some goth's wet dream.

Shadowlight glanced behind him just before they reached the first flight of stairs.

"Chin up, kid," Anna whispered along their mental link. *"We'll get through this. We're a team, right?"*

"Yes," he agreed, his ears perking up a little.

Gryton started down the stairs and Shadowlight was forced to follow. Vaspara and Anna followed close on their heels. The staircase had three landings. Two guards stood at attention on each of the landings. When Gryton's little convoy passed, the soldiers brought their fists up to their armor-covered chests in a show of respect.

When they reached the bottom of the stairs, Anna's eyes were drawn to the floor's mirror-like surface. Their reflections reminded her of bodies below the ice.

Creepy. Creepy as fuck. Check.

Vaspara took a firmer hold on Anna's arm and frog-marched her across the polished floor in pursuit of Gryton and Shadowlight. They only went part-way up the opposite set of stairs, halting at the second landing.

"Kneel," Gryton barked the order to Shadowlight. He resisted at first, his muzzle curling back from his fangs and his tail twitching, but in the end, he knelt.

"Kneel," Captain Vaspara growled in Anna's ear. "Kneel, or I break your knees."

Since she put it that way...

Anna took a step forward and knelt next to Shadowlight. Her knees had barely touched the cold stone when the tip of his tail curled around her waist. Just one coil and he seemed unaware that he was betraying his fear and insecurities to his enemies, but Anna didn't hold it against the kid.

The Battle Goddess's fortress was no place for a child, or anyone else with a moral compass, Anna amended.

A distant rattle of chains reached Anna, and she glanced sideways at Shadowlight. His deer-like ears were already swiveled in the direction the sound came. The noise of metal dragging on stone grew louder. Anna's eyes sought to see past the darkness shrouding the huge archway at the top of the stairs, but the distance was too far and the meager light of a few torches insufficient to penetrate far beyond the threshold.

With nothing else to do, she watched and waited. She was sure she'd be forgiven the small sound of surprise that escaped her when the darkness parted and a Titan wearing a long burgundy skirt and a black metal breastplate walked underneath the archway. The giantess stopped on the landing and stood gazing down at them.

Golden chains that glowed softly with power dragged at her wrists and ankles. The gargantuan woman seemed unconcerned about the chains or how they disappeared into the darkness behind her. Anna might not be up on her fantasyland mythology, but she knew enough to know the Avatars had forged those chains to hold this demigoddess trapped within her temple. But having something described and seeing it for the first time was something else altogether.

In looking upon it, Anna couldn't help but think it wasn't enough. This demigoddess needed to be neutralized once and for all. Unfortunately, unless Anna wanted to get neutralized herself, she'd have to appear to be cooperative.

Shadowlight's tail tightened around her waist. She patted it but wasn't sure if she was reassuring him or herself.

The demigoddess hiked up her long skirt and crouched down on the top landing.

"Come, my beautiful ones." The Battle Goddess called to them in a booming voice and gestured them closer.

Eh? Beautiful ones? No one had mentioned the demigoddess was unbalanced.

Shadowlight's tail tightened further. Suddenly she was lifted off the ground and was stumbling to find her footing as the kid dragged her up the stairs with him. She recovered her balance in a couple more steps and was following willingly, but if anything, Shadowlight's grip just grew tighter. She didn't blame the kid.

Seeing this Titan up close was a 'howl in terror' kind of event.

The kid stopped a dozen steps from the top of the landing. Anna halted next to the youngster and looked up at the creature that was determined to rule both magic and mortal realms.

Long skirt, bare feet, delicate features, pale creamy complexion, long glossy hair — she wasn't what Anna's imagination would have conjured up for a being known as the Battle Goddess.

Well, she supposed her actual title was the Lady of Battles. The demigoddess did hold herself in a graceful, ladylike manner and there was no rule that said evil couldn't be housed in an elegant vessel, as it indeed was in this case.

"I am both surprised and pleased how far along your powers have advanced, young one," she said, addressing Shadowlight. "By what name should I call you?"

He narrowed his eyes and then winced in pain as he fought the compulsion.

Anna came to her feet and squared off against the demigoddess. "His mother named him Shadowlight."

The goddess turned her dark-eyed gaze upon Anna. "A suitable name for a child, I suppose. I shall think upon an adult name for him, something that will suit the fierce warrior he will become under my training."

"I won't help you!" Shadowlight snarled and lunged forward only to crash into the stairs as his body wouldn't obey his mind's commands.

Anna's talons lengthened. She crouched next to the young gargoyle while glaring up at the Battle Goddess, but her thoughts were directed at him. *Don't fight unless you can win. Save your strength for later. Now is not the time to fight!*

The Lady of Battles leaned down to study them more closely. "The young one will learn in time that fighting is pointless. Bravery is nearly as useless here. You cannot fight me and win. Human are you as foolishly brave as the gargoyle?"

Anna craned her neck to look up at the demigoddess. "Bravery has its place. For example, I would give my life to save this child — though I would say it has more to do with friendship and loyalty than bravery. But if you make no move to harm the child, then I will obey your orders while I am here in this realm."

"Ah. Delightful. You speak the truth. And I shall honor you with the same. I promise no harm will come to the child by my hand as long as you both serve me."

Anna nodded but needed to make something clear. A showing of strength might be the only thing this demigoddess respected. "I'll do as I'm instructed. Serve you and your kingdom as required. However, if one of your people does something to him I cannot tolerate, I will do what I must to safeguard him. I might not yet know how to kill with magic, but I will learn and end any who mean Shadowlight harm."

"Excellent," the Battle Goddess said, sounding far too pleased with Anna's response. "It is well that you and he will protect each other. When you are both older, and your gargoyle natures are mature, you will rely on each other for survival."

Anna didn't respond but kept her head bowed.

"Tomorrow we shall begin your training," the Battle Goddess continued in a pleased tone. "Tonight, you shall eat and rest. If you behave yourselves, you will be given better quarters."

Anna would've settled for a sleeping bag.

"Your training won't be so very different than what you've been working toward for much of your young life. Gryton told me you are from a warrior bloodline. Your brothers, father, and great-grandfather are all warriors and you have inherited that spirit." The Battle Goddess shrugged. "Here you will be leading my armies instead of taking orders from lesser men playing at war. When you and the gargoyle are ready, you will lead my armies. Together, we will rule all three realms."

Yeah. That was an evil overlord speech if ever she'd heard one. If Anna hadn't figured out how to escape in a few days' time, she and the kid were likely to become a permanent part of the Battle Goddess's army.

The Lady of Battles reached out and ruffled Shadowlight's mane almost affectionately. Anna locked her jaw, so she didn't say anything to piss off the demigoddess. Eventually, the gargantuan deity straightened and stepped back.

"If you both perform well in training with your mentors, you will be given your own slaves and servants as a reward." The Battle Goddess looked beyond them to where Gryton stood. "Tomorrow their training will begin. Make sure they are well fed tonight and that they get a proper rest."

"Yes, my Lady," Gryton said.

"And make sure to spread the word that none of the troops are to play with them." The Battle Goddess laughed, the sound chilling. "Any who disobey will be executed, by my hand."

"Of course, my Goddess."

"And Gryton, make sure they are bathed before they are brought to me again."

"As you command, so shall it be," Gryton said without skipping a beat.

"Go now but have them returned here just after sunset and I will begin their journey of transformation."

Journey of transformation? Yeah, that sounded ominous whichever way you spun it. Anna was more than happy when Gryton started back down the stairs and ordered Shadowlight to follow.

hile Commander Gryton issued orders to servants to see that the Battle Goddess's wishes were carried out regarding food and baths for the prisoners, Anna was still mildly astonished to be led to a different part of the fortress. She'd honestly thought they'd end up back in the dungeons until she and the kid had proven themselves. But that wasn't the case.

This part of the city fortress was lavishly furnished with carpets and wall hangings. Polished black statues and gleaming suits of armor also decorated the stone passageways. After walking for twenty minutes, the present tunnel they traveled ended in a strange cul-de-sac with four doors spaced along the walls. There were guards here as well, but Anna's attention was focused on the first bit of natural light she'd seen in over a day. It seeped in from a dome several stories above her head.

She was standing in the base of a tower, and by a quick count, there were fourteen floors above this one. Walkways with beautifully carved stone railings guarded each of the stories. From what she could see, each level had four doors like this one.

"This tower serves as the living quarters for the Battle Goddess's captains and top-ranking soldiers," Gryton said and gestured toward a door directly ahead of them. "You and the gargoyle child will live here."

As they started forward again, the guards standing at either side of the massive wooden door opened it and bowed as Gryton led her and the kid inside. Their sudden arrival sent the servants into deep bows as well.

It wasn't lost on Anna that the servants looked distressingly human, unlike most of the captains and soldiers.

"Shadowlight," Anna projected along their mental link, *"those servants look human. Are they?"*

"Yes," he agreed. *"There are many humans in the Magic Realm. Though nowhere near as many as live back on your Earth. Some, like these servants, have been conquered. Others are allies of neighboring kingdoms, but all of them descend from humans that were brought here long ago."*

Yep. Slaves. That's what she thought.

After assessing that the servants were no threat, she took in the room and held back a low whistle. This room would put a five-star hotel to shame. Well, maybe if everything wasn't in a shade of black or burgundy, that is. But it was still a damn sight better than the dungeons. There were also five other rooms leading off this main chamber.

"Feel free to look around," Gryton said. "This is where you and the cub will stay for as long as you behave. If you do something foolish, know that your cell in the dungeons will be made available for your use."

Was that a joke? Shit, Tin Man had a teeny, shriveled bit of humor buried somewhere deep inside him. Who knew? It still doesn't make me like him any better, though.

"Yeah, thanks," she said. "We'll behave, won't we Shadowlight?"

For now, she added silently.

Shadowlight was already stalking toward the nearest of the five rooms that branched off this one. His ears were forward, his tail stiff and unmoving. He was hunting for danger. Anna joined him in scouting out the rooms for unseen perils.

The two smallest side chambers were for servants. The middle room was a bathroom. It was one of foreign design but still a bathroom, with levers that produced hot and cold water. There was also some kind of stone bench thing she was sure was a toilet complete with running water. Hallelujah, fantasyland had indoor plumbing.

She left Shadowlight playing with the levers that filled the big pool that served as a bathtub and wandered out to investigate the last two rooms. She checked out the one on the right first. It was the size of a master bedroom, decorated in the usual black and burgundy.

Was the Battle Goddess allergic to other colors, or something?

Anna wandered into the last room and found this one was designed to be a mirror image of the room on the right. Except for one oddity. There was an extra door along the west wall.

Curious and still hunting for possible dangers, she wandered over and tried the handle. It opened easily, and Anna was staring into yet another bedroom.

What the hell? Was this place designed with a rabbit's warren in mind?

Her eyes narrowed a moment later when she noticed this room had a much more lived-in feel. There were books and scrolls and even a few weapons and articles of clothing lying around.

She turned to Gryton with an eyebrow arched in question.

"The Battle Goddess made it clear that if anything happened to you or the gargoyle, she would take her rage out on my hide." Gryton gestured at the lived-in bedroom. "I like my own hide, so this door leads to my chambers. I'll be close enough should there be a problem that requires my attention."

Oh fuck.

"You sleep?" She asked just to have something to say.

"Only for short times, but yes. Don't worry, I will know if either you or Shadowlight plan to murder me in my sleep."

"I'll try to restrain myself." Even though murdering Gryton would be a considerable temptation.

"This arrangement also has the benefit of keeping you and the cub safe in case one of the soldiers happens to drink away their reason and decide to come for a visit. Gargoyle blood is potent with magic, and there are many in the Battle Goddess's army with a thirst for it. And yet others might come seeking something else since you are a beautiful female, human though you are. Males will be interested even with the Battle Goddess's warning."

Gryton took a step closer, entering Anna's bubble of personal space. This close, she noticed a ring of amber circled his irises. Humor and perhaps a touch of heat glimmered in his dark gaze.

If he came any nearer, he was going to regret it, armor or no.

The commander sidestepped her like he was merely moving past and said, "However, even the drunkest of soldiers isn't so foolish as to enter my lair uninvited."

"Congrats on instilling a thimbleful of respect into them," Anna said in a bored voice.

Gryton halted and stared down his regal nose at her. He was taller than an average human male, but still not so tall she'd let his physical presence cow her. She held her ground.

A thump and a door crashing open somewhere in the room beyond was the only warning they got before Shadowlight came bounding into the room. He jerked to a stop and growled unhappily before continuing to prowl forward. Wedging himself between them, Shadowlight sat on his haunches and leaned against Anna while his tail wrapped around her ankles, then he proceeded to glower up at Gryton with a low, continuous growl.

Subtle, gargoyles weren't.

Gryton's expression shifted into open humor as he began to laugh. "Do not fear, cub. I have no interest in forcing a female. If I should want one, there are many to choose from."

Shadowlight's huff sounded unconvinced, and he continued to stare at Gryton as if deciding which part to eat first.

Shrugging, Gryton drew back and turned to leave.

"With your loyal dog acting as guard perhaps you won't need my protection after all."

Anna returned Gryton's smile with a chilly one of her own. "Oh, don't worry about that. I've lots of experience fending off assholes with grabby hands and the occasional officer who thought a female soldier should perform some duties on her back. Funny, they never tried a second time."

Shadowlight's grumblings increased in volume, and his tail snapped against the floor every two seconds while he glowered at Gryton.

Tin Man laughed, finding Shadowlight's antics entertaining. Then he reached out to muss the young gargoyle's mane. Shadowlight was so taken by surprise Gryton had already withdrawn his hand before the kid thought to bite.

"The servants will bring you your food soon," Gryton said, leading them back out into the main room. "If you wish, bathe first, but afterward rest. I will return to collect you at dusk."

He turned and strode out into the hall. Anna heard as he paused long enough to issue orders to the guards and then he was briskly walking away.

"Tin Man's gone. I call dibs on the bathroom. I still smell like the stables."

Shadowlight wrinkled his nose. "You do. Did you roll in a puddle of horse pee?"

"No, but I might as well have." Anna sniffed at herself. Yeah, it was way past time for a shower or bath if that's all fantasyland possessed. "I'm going to go soak for a freaking long time."

"I saw clean clothes in the bathing chamber laid out for you."

While Anna knew it was a psychological trick to soften her up to their ways, she wouldn't turn down hot water, clean clothes or food.

"Stay out of trouble," she ordered.

Shadowlight nodded, his mane flying up and down with over-exaggerated motion.

"I'm serious. No exploring outside these rooms."

Shadowlight's entire being drooped, his rump hit the floor, and his front end slowly slid down to join it. With a long-suffering sigh, he dropped his head onto his forearms to rest while he waited for her to finish.

CHAPTER TEN

Her long soak was more like ten minutes. She didn't like the idea of servants, or worse, Gryton, just wandering in at any old time. Plus, she was uneasy leaving the kid to his own devices for more than a few minutes in this place.

She exited the bathroom still squeezing water out of her braids with a soft towel. Her new clothing consisted of baggy pants made of some light flowing material, a long tunic with three-quarter length sleeves, and a wide sash that circled around her waist like a belt.

If there was any particular way to tie the sash, she didn't give a crap. They could call the fashion police on her. The garments were all the same monochrome. A pale sky blue. There was a bit of embroidery stitched over the tunic's breast in a black and burgundy thread.

Anna didn't know what it represented, but she could guess: here stands a slave to the Battle Goddess.

She fingered the stitching and her lips compressed. For

now, she would wear what she was given and do what she was told, but all the while she would be seeking a way to escape.

Which her enemies likely expected, but that didn't mean she would give up.

Upon exiting the bathroom, she found Shadowlight nodding where she'd left him. He wasn't deeply asleep since his ears followed the sound of her footfalls, but he didn't bother to stir himself from his spot either.

"Go on, kid. It's your turn and you don't smell very fresh yourself. I'll keep watch and let you know when the food arrives."

At the mention of food, his eyes snapped open and he stood, sniffing to catch any scent.

When he didn't discover anything of interest, he huffed in complaint but wandered into the room she'd just exited to see to his own bath.

Anna nearly laughed at his lack of enthusiasm. Typical kid. More interested in food than getting a good scrub.

Twenty minutes later servants returned carrying several platters of food. Anna separated one servant from the group and tried to talk to the middle-aged woman, but she merely shook her head and touched her lips to indicate she couldn't speak.

Strange. Anna knew they understood her because Gryton had issued orders in the same language, so they must be under orders not to talk to them. After all the food was laid out, the servants bowed and then left.

Anna eyed the table. At least they'd been informed how much a young gargoyle could put away.

"Shadowlight, the servants brought our meal," she

called through the door. An excited huff issued from inside and she heard a great sloshing and water hitting the floor. A short time later the door was nearly ripped off its hinges as a gargoyle burst forth into the main room.

His hair was still dripping water, but he had donned a long, blue loincloth woven of the same fabric as her tunic. He hadn't bothered to wear the wrist or armbands his father had given him.

Her eyebrows drawing together, she turned and marched back into the drenched bathroom and retrieved Shadowlight's warded jewelry and then shoved them under one of the nearby chair cushions for safe keeping. She didn't trust someone not to take them.

When she made her way back over to the table, the platters had been uncovered, and Shadowlight was already sniffing at the fourth dish in line.

Bless his suspicious little heart.

"Do you detect any taint of drugs or other substances?" Anna asked along their mental link.

"No," he said, but his reply was accompanied by a little uncertain flick of his ear. *"But I'm unfamiliar with some of their scents and spices."*

He sniffed deeper at the platter he was holding.

"They won't poison us with the intent to kill. It would defeat the purpose of capturing us. That doesn't mean they're not above drugging us to make us more compliant with their wishes."

Anna scooped up a dish of what looked like stew and sniffed at it. Her stomach chose that moment to remind her that she hadn't eaten in hours.

"We're dead if we don't eat," Anna said and then shrugged and grabbed the strange, two-pronged fork that sat next to the platter with the bowls of stew. Then with stew and fantasyland spork, she retreated to the north side of the room where she'd spotted the thickly padded benches in an earlier search. Shadowlight joined her with two platters of his own food.

The thought of drugs didn't stop her and the kid from polishing off the first course and going back for seconds and thirds in Shadowlight's case. Shortly after she and the kid were finished, the servants returned like magic. They gathered up all the dishes and left as silently as they'd come.

The next hour was spent exploring the rooms in more detail. Exploring soon descended into a disagreement as to which one of them would take the room that adjoined to Gryton's quarters. Anna was dead set on taking that room because she didn't trust Gryton any farther than she could toss his heavy, metal-covered ass.

Unfortunately, Shadowlight wanted the room for the same reason.

"Fine. We'll settle this like adults," Anna said as she leaned against the door causing all the contention. "Which one of us is more likely to cross that threshold and try to kill Gryton and get both our asses tossed back in the dungeon?"

Shadowlight continued to level his death glare at the door.

"There! Hah! That look is answer enough. I sleep in this room. You get the other one. If either of us hears something we don't like, we call out using our mental link. Agreed?" Anna stated, already knowing she'd won the argument by the way Shadowlight's ears drooped.

Then he surprised her by walking over to a massive wardrobe and gave it a mighty shove. It was a floor to ceiling wooden storage unit that was a good fifteen feet long and likely weighed close to a ton. When Shadowlight shoved his shoulder against it a second time, Anna figured out what he was up to and joined him in pushing it to block the adjoining door.

"Good plan. It won't stop a raging fire elemental, but neither will it be a quiet entry." And it might be enough to give the kid some peace of mind while he slept, and that was good enough for her.

With a bit more shoving and pushing, they got the beast situated in front of the door and then sat on the edge of the bed to admire their work. Shadowlight yawned and stretched when they were finished.

"Go on," she said with an affectionate pat on his shoulder. "Get some rest. I'll be here if you need anything."

Shadowlight nodded, but still didn't leave.

"Will you read to me until I fall asleep?" He shoved his muzzle under her hand, so she gave his ears a good scratch.

During their earlier exploration, she'd found a few ancient handcrafted books. She'd marveled at their drawings and the fancy script, but while they were quite beautiful to behold, she couldn't read a word of it.

"I'm sorry. I don't have anything to read to you." Anna gave his ears another scratch.

He nodded but glanced sidelong at her with a hopeful look. "Would you tell me a story then?"

Poor kid just wanted to hear a familiar voice to reassure him. "Sure kid."

They relocated to his room where she proceeded to tell

a very sad-assed version of Snow White. She only made it halfway through the story before the kid fell asleep. If Anna survived, she'd take a parenting course or some shit, so she didn't totally ruin a perfectly good kid with her abysmal parenting skills. When she was satisfied he was deeply asleep, Anna returned to her own rooms and fell face first into her bed.

CHAPTER ELEVEN

*A*nna wasn't at all sure she wasn't already asleep and dreaming when the beautiful male voice first started whispering in her head.

"They will enslave you and the child if you remain in the Battle Goddess's domain."

"Tell me something I don't know," Anna replied to the disembodied voice. Because, really, what did one do when an otherworldly voice insisted on whispering into your mind? Why, you answered it, of course, like any good mental patient would do.

Unfortunately, she wasn't mentally ill and the voice, wherever it originated, was likely very real. It was also equally likely that it wasn't looking out for her best interests.

She wondered which of the captains this was. Gryton was familiar enough now that she was relatively confident she'd recognize his voice in her head.

"You don't have to allow that to happen," the stranger whispered.

Oddly, he didn't make her gargoyle instincts flare in warning like most of the denizens of the Battle Goddess's domain did. Anna decided to pursue this strange exchange just to see if she could later place which one of Gryton's henchmen this was.

"You have it within yourself to find freedom."

Well, that was a line of bullshit if ever she heard one.

"The Lady of Battles cannot hold ones such as you and the child."

Anna rolled her eyes. "Looks like she's doing a pretty good job."

"Only because you are too afraid to find your way to me."

She was done with mystical beings spouting bullshit. "Unless you plan on a rescue, screw off."

"Unfortunately, I am not permitted to enter the Lady of Battles domain."

"Okay then. Bye."

"However, the duality curse runs both ways. She can enter my domain no more than I can enter hers. If you come to me, you will be free of her manipulations."

"And, yet, you're in my head."

"Because as much as she seeks to bend you and the youngling to her will and lay claim to the power in your blood, you are gargoyles. And gargoyles have ever been mine to command."

Duality curse. Master of gargoyles. Anna wasn't up on all her fantasyland mythology, but she'd heard enough from the Avatars as well as Shadowlight to now have a solid idea of who, or rather, what she was talking to.

Death. The Lord of the Underworld. Master of all gargoyles.

She was so screwed.

Anna would have closed her eyes, but they already were, so she settled for fisting her hands and fought to calm her thoughts and to keep the fear from leaking through to Lord Death.

"You are gargoyle. You know me. You belong to me," he continued in that tenacious way of his.

"I belong to only myself."

"Young one, even you know that is not true. The cub already has a firm hold on you, your magic, and your soul, one that is almost greater than mine."

"That's not his fault. He didn't mean to."

"Yes, he did. He just didn't know it was wrong. You are correct. He is innocent of any willful intent to harm you." The melodious voice in her mind fell silent for a moment before continuing. "But if you stay, he will be corrupted until his intentions are no longer pure."

Anna already knew this stranger's words were true. It's what she'd feared would happen if she was unable to escape with Shadowlight. "You're not telling me anything I don't already know."

"Perhaps not, but if that is the case, you should also know deep in your soul that all gargoyles have the ability to return to me anytime they need."

Anna frowned unhappily in her waking dream. "I think the thousand or so guards between me and the gate would disagree with you."

"It doesn't matter what the guards think or do. It won't prevent you and the cub from returning to me. You simply have to will it."

"And if I was to believe you, just how do I 'will' my way to you." Anna had no intention of going. She distinctly remembered Gregory had feared that Lord Death might kill Lillian and her brother for what the Battle Goddess had done to them.

Sure, as gargoyles they might be able to somehow magically 'will' themselves to Lord Death's side, but then what? Die? No thanks. There was no way she was ready to just roll over and give up.

"All you have to do is reach for me in your mind and surrender everything."

Yep. Nope. Not going to happen. Anna strove for calm even though her heart was pounding, and a chilled sweat now coated her body.

"And just like that, we what? Magically transport ourselves to your realm?"

"My magic calls you home. It's a spell built into your very soul. No other magic can prevent it."

Wondering if he'd be truthful, she asked, "What happens to the cub and me once we reach your land?"

"I will judge you and try to cure you of my sister's taint."

"And if you can't? What will you do then?"

"What I have forever been tasked with: ridding the three realms of the taint that does not belong. You understand?"

"Yes." All too well. If she wanted to live and protect the kid, she was on her own.

"There are many fates worse than allowing me to end suffering and return a soul to the Spirit Realm."

"I actually agree with you there. But I'm not that desperate yet. I think I'll trust to my own survival skills to get the kid and me out of this mess."

"Only you can make this choice but remember I'm always here. Simply open your mind and call. Do not allow yourself to become what my sister wants."

"I'll remember that."

Now go away. I'm tired, she thought to herself.

To her surprise, the other consciousness retreated from her mind.

She blinked up into the darkness. A minute or two crawled by while she wrestled with the rush of adrenaline that was demanding she get ready for battle.

If she wasn't sleep deprived, or been startled into full, jittery wakefulness, she might have realized something sooner.

Oh my god!

"Shadowlight!" She tossed back the covers and lunged out of bed. She made it to the door, her hand on the latch when the door jerked open and Shadowlight nearly impaled her on one of his horns as he ran into the room.

"Anna, what's wrong?" He shoved her aside and paced around the room on all fours. When he didn't find a threat, he turned back to her.

She couldn't see much of his expression in the dark, even her gargoyle-enhanced eyesight wasn't helping. But she didn't need to see. She felt his presence as he searched through her thoughts.

Rushing to his side, she hugged his head and just

rocked back and forth. He was here. He was safe. The Lord of the Underworld hadn't succeeded in calling him home.

"Promise never to go to him."

"Him?" Shadowlight licked her fingers. "Anna, are you crying?"

Damn. Was she?

"No," she answered gruffly. "I just had a scare."

"What scared you? Lord Death?" He whispered into her thoughts as he glanced around the room looking for threats again.

"Yes," she said truthfully.

Shadowlight sighed a breath across her fingers as he continued to lick them. *"Silly human, Lord Death doesn't mean us harm."*

"You've talked to him?"

"Well, no. But my father's memories..."

"Don't apply to us. We are the product of the Lady of Battle's manipulations."

"Yes. But Gregory says we're not to blame for that."

God. What did she tell the kid?

"Just...if the Lord of the Underworld tries to communicate with you, promise me you will contact me. Don't do anything he says without consulting me first."

"Very well. I still think you are being silly, though." Shadowlight growled unhappily, but he soon curled his tail around her waist and leaned in for more scratches.

Slowly Anna's fears faded, and she felt foolish for panicking. And then she just felt tired. Bone weary and ready to sleep for a year.

"I'll take the first watch," Shadowlight said. "You stood watch all last night while I slept. It's my turn."

Anna would have protested but knew she needed rest if she was going to be useful at all tomorrow.

CHAPTER TWELVE

Six hours later the servants returned. Shadowlight barely had time to warn Anna, but she rolled out of bed and was standing at his shoulder by the time a servant girl pushed the door open.

"Lady Anna, Lord Shadowlight," the girl bowed, making her brown curls bounce. "I've brought clean clothes for you both."

Anna shook herself awake and then thanked the girl. Once the servant bowed and left, Anna chased Shadowlight out of her room. He stalked away to change into his own new garments, but also to see if there was any food in the main room. A deep sniff told him the disappointing truth. Sighing, he plodded into his own room.

Not long after they'd dressed in their new clothing, Gryton returned as he'd promised.

"Good, you're ready. Come," Gryton barked out the order and then exited the room as quickly as he'd come.

Shadowlight stumbled before he regained his balance. He really hated the collar's compulsion; he briefly debated fighting it.

Not because he or Anna were in immediate danger, but because he hated Tin Man.

Gran had once told him he was too young to hate, but every time Gryton appeared, something hot and ugly rose up within his soul.

Though, perhaps it was only his gargoyle nature responding to the presence of evil or simple deceit. Gryton certainly excelled at both those things. Whatever it was, he would listen. Besides, Anna hated the commander, too. The scent of her dislike rose from her skin every time she set eyes on the Battle Goddess's top soldier.

The bitter musk scented the air around him even now as Gryton and a large group of soldiers marched them back to the room with the strange mirror-like floor.

Gryton hadn't enlightened them on what to expect, so when they finally arrived at the top of the first set of stairs, Shadowlight froze. Unlike yesterday, the polished black floor was no longer empty. Two altar slabs made of inky-black stone sat in the middle of the floor. Surrounding them were four large pillars topped with shallow metal cauldrons filled with burning oil.

Then he noticed the chains hanging down from the sides of the altars.

"What the actual fuck." Anna's voice echoed his thoughts perfectly.

When he looked at her, it was to see her glancing between the altar and him and back again.

"Kid, whatever they do, don't fight. We can't escape if we're dead. Remember that."

"I won't fight," he replied along their mental link.

When Gryton ordered him forward, he wanted to resist, but the collar merely reached into his nervous system and forced him to follow.

"Get off me," Anna snarled at one of her guards. "I'm going."

She soon caught up to his longer strides, and they reached the polished floor at the same time. They walked the rest of the way to the altar slabs together. With her chin up and shoulders squared, Anna refused to be cowed by the Battle Goddess's soldiers, but she didn't do a good enough job shielding her thoughts, and her dread bled across the link to him.

It made him less ashamed of his own fear.

"Lie down," Gryton ordered and pointed at the nearest slab of stone. Shadowlight didn't resist.

Anna's movements were stiff, but she didn't fight either.

"Whatever this is, the sooner it's over, the better," Anna whispered into his thoughts.

He silently agreed.

They didn't have long to wait, which was a blessing. Shortly after the altar chains were secured to their wrists and ankles, Shadowlight heard the rattle of a different set of chains as the demigoddess walked down the second set of stairs, her chains trailing behind her. She halted a few steps from the altars and stared down at them, but she didn't say a word.

When the demigoddess raised her hands and

summoned magic, Shadowlight's heart began to pound. His growing fear was warranted. She stepped closer to him.

"Hey," Anna shouted. "Start with me. Leave the kid alone."

No emotions showed on the demigoddess's face. Anna's words went unheeded as power fell from the Battle Goddess's bare palms as if she was pouring water upon Shadowlight. Where the magic splashed against his skin, it glowed brightly for several moments before seeping into the pores.

The strange, radiating warmth came as a surprise. Gargoyle hide was impervious to most magic, but it barely slowed this demigoddess's power.

At first, it was just a strange heat beneath his skin, and then it dug deeper, burrowing through his flesh and into his bones as if it searched for something. A panicked growl escaped, and he fought the chains as the power continued to increase.

"Shadowlight, reach for me with your mind."

"Anna?"

"Yes, kid. Just do it. I think I can help."

Instinct urged him to listen to her, so he did, obeying with a mindless kind of desperation. Their link flared strongly and suddenly it was like he was no longer in his own body. He blinked in surprise. The pain was gone entirely. Even though he could still see magic flowing down onto him from the Battle Goddess's open palms, there was no more heat or oppressive power trying to squeeze past his skin and into his body.

He clung to the link Anna had helped create and just

waited for her next command. When it didn't come, he realized she was now sheltering him from something.

"Anna?"

"It's fine, kid. I've got this."

And he realized she did. Somehow, she'd figured out how to pull his pain into herself. He shouldn't have allowed her to do it, but he didn't fight to regain control, either. *"Anna, I'm sorry."*

"No worries. You can return the favor when you're older. I'll hold you to it."

Anna paused, and he sensed pain was clouding her thoughts, but she kept talking because it allowed her to distract herself. *"We're going to survive this. I promise."*

Anna might be as much a prisoner as him, but he believed her. She'd never failed him yet. He wouldn't fail her either. With that thought fortifying him, he reached and took command of their link.

"What are you doing?"

"We'll share whatever punishment they toss at us."

He sensed she wasn't happy with his statement, but she didn't fight.

Eventually, the power flowing into his body subsided, and he released her from his mental hold and his consciousness return to his own body. He was weak, shaking, and covered in sweat, but the pain was just a dull, phantom ache in his joints.

He blinked sweat out of his eyes and turned his head to find the Battle Goddess now stepping away from him.

Shakily, he fought his chains but was brought up short by a command from Gryton.

"Easy, youngling. You did well." Gryton was standing at

his shoulder, a silver bowl held in his right hand while his left gripped a knife. "Don't fight. I only need to make a small nick on your arm."

He obeyed, holding still while Gryton made a cut and positioned the bowl below it. Once he'd collected enough blood, he turned from Shadowlight and approached Anna.

Shadowlight snarled, but there was nothing he could do when Gryton reached to pry open Anna's locked jaws and pour the blood into her mouth. He was swift to slap a hand over her mouth and nose, so she couldn't spit out the blood.

Struggling against his chains, Shadowlight growled and cursed at Gryton.

After a few seconds Anna started to struggle, but Gryton just held her fast.

"Swallow and I'll let you breathe," he said in a calm voice.

Anna continued to fight and Shadowlight snarled and fought alongside her. But even as his struggles were ineffective to free him, so too were Anna's. Eventually, Anna's need for oxygen won out and she swallowed. Shadowlight could see her throat working, but she continued to glower at Gryton in a silent battle of wills.

Gryton released her and Anna choked, gasping until her lungs stopped spasming.

"Anna, are you okay?" he asked using their mental link.

"Been better, but I'll live. You?"

"Yes," he said and realized it was true. While his joints still ached and his muscles twitched and quivered, the pain was receding. He should be well enough to move in a few minutes if they unlocked his chains.

The Battle Goddess, who had retreated a few paces to allow Gryton to carry out the last ritual, now stepped forward to study them both with an assessing gaze. She seemed to like what she saw because a mesmerizing smile brightened her expression.

"Younglings, you've done well. I am most pleased with this first session." She nodded at them like a mentor pleased by a promising new apprentice. "Already, I can feel the new strength of your magic. Soon your physical bodies will grow into that power, and you will be ready to lead my armies."

Was that what this was all about? She was trying to force his body to finish maturing? He glanced down at himself, but besides the ache in his joints, everything seemed as it should. Lowering his head back to the stone, he waited to be set free.

The Battle Goddess turned and mounted the steps, swiftly striding away. Shadowlight listened until he could no longer hear her footfalls or the scrape of chains against stone.

When some of Gryton's soldiers came and unlocked Shadowlight from his shackles, he didn't fight them, more interested in getting to Anna to see what his blood had done to her.

Gryton was at her side. Once the manacles were off, he held out a hand to help her rise from the altar. She snarled and brushed away his offer of help. When Gryton moved to the side, Shadowlight saw she looked the same as she had before. At least he couldn't detect any more physical gargoyle enhancements. Then again, the changes might be internal, or his blood might still be working modifications upon her body.

Whatever the case, he was just happy she seemed mostly unharmed.

"How are you?" He asked.

"I'd be better if I could sink a knife into Gryton's smug face. Since that's not going to happen, I suppose I'm well enough, considering what just happened. You?"

"Well enough."

"Good," Anna hopped off the altar and took a couple of stumbling steps before she found her footing. *"Because we're still going to find a way to escape."*

"Yes."

Gryton surveyed them for a moment before speaking, "If you can walk without falling down, I am to take you to the hall where you will meet some of the twelve captains who lead the Battle Goddess's armies."

"Pass," Anna said with a sour look aimed at Gryton.

"This is not a request. You will meet the other captains, and I will determine which ones will be the best mentors for you."

"You're not going to beat on us yourself? I feel slighted," Anna said.

"Oh, fear not. Once the mentors deem you worthy to be tested, they will bring you before me so that I can test your newly developed skills."

"Can't wait," Anna growled and then hobbled over to Shadowlight.

He sniffed at her cheek. *"Are you sure you're okay?"*

She batted his muzzle away. *"I'm alive and plan on staying that way."*

"Come," Gryton barked.

The collar around Shadowlight's neck flared a warning, but before it could force him into motion, he padded after Gryton.

Anna stayed as close as his own shadow.

CHAPTER THIRTEEN

Still feeling like she had danced with a wrecking ball, Anna doggedly followed close at Shadowlight's heels. From what she could tell, he'd fared a bit better than she had, for which she was grateful.

If the kid had been seriously hurt...

It only hardened her resolve. She needed to find a way to escape. She had to for Shadowlight's sake.

While Anna's mind churned, Commander Gryton led them through the twisted path of corridors until they arrived at what could only be the hall he'd mentioned. The low rumble of conversation, the rattle of dishes and the scent of food confirmed it.

Shadowlight's ears perked with interest. At least he still had an appetite. Anna wasn't sure if she could eat yet. The coppery taste of the young gargoyle's blood still coated her tongue.

Gryton marched them under the tall archway, Shadowlight and Anna following close behind. The troop of guards that normally followed them around stayed outside in the hall, strangely enough.

They entered the large hall a moment later, and the reason the guards weren't needed became clear. Anna put Shadowlight between herself and Gryton.

The hall was easily the size of two football fields filled with long tables laden with various foods. Like the chamber she'd just left, this one was lit with torches mounted on the outside walls and more circling each of the enormous pillars that supported the rest of the structure above them.

Ordinary candles set out on the tables provided additional light for the diners. Only about half the spaces were occupied.

Oh, but the half that was filled was enough to make even the most well-trained Special Forces operator flee in terror. Anna thought she was getting used to all the weird. Nope. Even the strangest Clan and Coven members looked downright ordinary compared to what she was gazing upon now. A sea of horns, tusks, scales, spikes, and extra appendages met her gaze. Made all the stranger because they belonged to otherwise mostly human-shaped bodies.

It reminded her of an intergalactic bar scene in a sci-fi movie.

At Gryton's entrance, some of the monsters turned in their seats to stare. Soon others were noticing their companions' distraction and turned to watch what was so interesting. Gryton ignored the looks and walked along the wall, heading toward the front of the hall. They'd entered from a side entrance she noted.

Anna gave Shadowlight a little shove when he froze in

place, but he ignored her and pulled his lips back from his teeth in a snarl.

Great.

"Keep the aggression under wraps," Anna warned, *"you're giving too much away, again."*

Shadowlight uttered one more menacing growl before dropping to all fours to stalk after Gryton. Anna matched his pace and they reached the front of the room at the same time.

Their new location wasn't any better than the last. Now every creature in the room watched them in silence. Gryton ignored the watchers and gestured Anna and Shadowlight forward, onto the raised dais where the high table sat. They walked half-way down the length of the long table.

"We've set aside a place of honor for the two newest acquisitions to our Goddess's army."

"Flattered," Anna muttered.

Shadowlight growled softly at the creatures already sitting at the table. Anna assumed these must be the other captains since Vaspara was just a few feet farther down the bench. Gryton settled between a hulking man and an equally brawny woman of some unknown species and then gestured to indicate Anna and Shadowlight should sit.

Shrugging, Anna settled next to the mountainous male and tried not to gawk at the delicate pattern of scales covering his skin or his boney shoulder spikes. He flared his nostrils, dragging in a deep breath as he took her scent. It wasn't every day someone ran into a human-gargoyle hybrid, she supposed.

She looked away from her neighbor and studied the

dark wood of the table, but not before she'd seen the ridge of horny bone growing out of his forehead near his hairline.

While she'd been occupied staring at her bench buddy, Shadowlight had been glowering at Gryton. *"Come on, kid. We're going to be cheek by jowl with them soon, so might as well get used to this."*

"I don't like it."

"Can't say I'm fond of it either, kid."

Shadowlight took the spot to her left, but his blade-tipped tail came to land on the bench next to her right hip. His tail slapped the padded seat a few times in threat, and Anna realized the scaled male was reaching to touch her hair.

She blocked Scales and he pulled his hand back. Glancing at the kid's tail, he made a weird, hissing sound. It took her a moment to grasp it was his laughter.

"Your hair, teach your servants how it's done and then have them teach mine," he said and pointed at his own thick brown hair. A bit of leather held back the wavy mess.

Gryton leaned back on the bench so he could gaze past Shadowlight's wings. "Anna, meet Captain Sorac. He commands the fourth company. Sorac, this is Corporal Anna Mackenzie and Shadowlight."

Sorac merely nodded and looked them over. "They'll break the first time you put them in a practice ring with me."

"Shadowlight isn't yet mature but already quite formidable, and Anna has gifted me with a wound. Under-estimate them at your peril. And if you've forgotten, that human-gargoyle hybrid managed to sneak in and break him out of his cell. If I hadn't been tracking her for the better part of a day, Anna might have succeeded."

"I'd heard that. I also heard Vaspara now owes you her life. If the two had escaped on her watch, it would have gone ill for our favorite succubus." Sorac made that strange sound in his chest again. "I wouldn't mind having Vaspara in my debt for a moon cycle or two."

Gryton barked out a laugh. "She would make a necklace out of your balls."

"Probably," Sorac huffed out in humorous agreement. Then he gave Anna's tunic covered chest a lingering glance.

"I might not know Anna very well since in the past we were usually trying to kill each other," Gryton said in a pleasant tone, "but I would wager she is the type to roast a male's balls over hot coals rather than invite him into her bed. You've been warned. Besides, our Lady has said the young gargoyles are not to be touched."

Sorac chuckled. "And it's never a good idea to make an enemy of one who will grow to take command."

"A wise choice," Gryton agreed, then turning his attention back to Anna he said, "Captain Sorac is a half-breed like you. Part firedrake and part Astarte demon. His father was once worshiped as a fertility god."

Great, another sex demon.

Shadowlight's earlier antics made a little more sense.

"You knew what he was?" she asked the kid.

"Yes," Shadowlight replied in a growly mental voice. How he managed that, she didn't know.

"You could've told me."

"I did."

"With words next time. But keep up the good work. You're the best little brother ever."

Shadowlight's ears perked, and he turned to look at the female on Gryton's other side as if he was about to tell Anna what she was, but Gryton got there first.

"This is Captain Bervicta. She's harpy stock."

The female didn't show the least bit of insult, so Anna guessed either the female had heard it hundreds of times before or being called "harpy stock" wasn't an actual insult.

Bervicta looked more human than most sitting at the table. But a closer look showed that what she'd taken as spiked hair was actually a short-feathered crest. Her eyes were large and more rounded than a human's, and her face almost came to a point at her narrow chin.

When Bervicta returned to her drink without comment. Anna's gaze slid to the male on the harpy's other side. While she was studying him, she reached out for Shadowlight's thoughts.

"What about the female?" Anna asked.

"She radiates hostility, but it's not directed at us. She's annoyed with the male sitting next to her. I think she's safe enough."

"As much as any of them. Got it." Anna's gaze roamed over the male on Bervicta's far side. He was blond and had dark eyes of some shade she couldn't identify over the distance. And he had a rather too pretty face, she noted. When he looked up, his dark eyes locked on hers. He smiled and Anna, who had sworn off men after her last two disastrous relationships, became aware of him as a virile male. What the hell?

"That one is not safe." Shadowlight's said and flashed his fangs at the male in question.

"Eh?"

"He's a male version of Vaspara. An incubus."

Eyes narrowing, she leaned forward so Shadowlight wasn't blocking her view of the male. "Hey, you."

His smile grew wide.

"Yeah, you. Take that come-hither smile and shove it up your ass or I will do it for you."

Gryton choked on a mouthful of wine but managed not to spray it across the table. When he could speak, he half turned to address the other male. "Honnan, she will attempt to follow through on her threat. If she doesn't, I will." He paused and looked at Shadowlight. "Although, allowing the cub to tear you apart might be fun to watch. He's not overly fond of others playing with his pet human."

The male nodded, stood, and then with an elegant, old-world elegance, he bowed to Anna. Once he straightened, he picked up his plate and goblet and took himself off to eat with some of his officers at one of the tables near the front of the hall.

"That was Captain Honnan. And that female at the end of the table there," he pointed out a tall and ridiculously curvy female, "is Captain Ninara. She and Honnan are twins."

"More sex demons. I'm seeing a theme."

"The Lady of Battles does not judge those loyal to her."

"Whatever. Ninara can go elsewhere too. There's a new no perverts rule at the table."

"What about Vaspara?" Gryton asked in a dry tone. "You didn't seem too concerned about her."

He was wrong. At first, she'd been concerned with

Vaspara, and she still knew better than to trust anyone here, even the more reasonable seeming ones.

Anna shrugged. "You're all the enemy. But Vaspara doesn't give off the pervert vibe like the sex twins."

Gryton's amusement only grew, his teeth flashed. The rest of his face was hidden in the shadows created by his helmet.

"Vaspara has spent more time around the youngling. A succubus's power goes dormant if they spend too much time around juveniles. You need not fear for Shadowlight until he hits maturity and by then he'll be able to fend for himself if he wishes."

"Shadowlight, for the record, we're going to be long gone before then."

"Good." He agreed, but his gaze was locked on to the servants approaching the high table with platters of food.

Anna was somewhat surprised when her own stomach gave a rumble at the first waft of food. The servants laid out their trays and then retreated to stand against the wall behind the table. It was weird having someone standing at her back watching, but Anna just shrugged it off and picked a bowl of what looked like hot porridge and fruit from one of the trays. The grain probably wasn't oats, but the food was a hell of a lot more familiar than she thought it would be.

She was just about to dive into hers like the others at the table when Gryton's head jerked up. A moment later Shadowlight issued one of his 'I mean business' snarls. Beside her, Captain Sorac made a low hiss. It sounded more threatening than welcoming.

"Ah, Captain Taryin, nice to see you've returned."

Gryton stood to make introductions, which just hammered home that this female was one of the major powers if Tin Man was stirring himself to make proper introductions.

"There's still much to do before the armies are ready to wake, but word reached me of the newest additions to the Battle Goddess's court." The speaker was a woman of average height, pale skin, and dark brown hair. She could have been human if not for the power Anna felt rolling off her. "I was curious after hearing some of what the human-gargoyle hybrid managed."

"Anna. This one is very dangerous," Shadowlight whispered in her mind. *"I know her from my father's memories. She was the one who captured him and was also the one to help trap the female half of the Avatar's soul in the body of a dryad."*

Shit. That made her almost as dangerous as Gryton and the demigoddess, maybe even completing some unholy Trinity. Anna mentally added this newcomer to her list of must eradicate.

"Corporal Anna Mackenzie and Shadowlight, meet Blood Witch Taryin."

Blood witch? Well, that certainly didn't inspire warm and fuzzy feelings.

"A pleasure," Taryin said as she made her way around the end of the table. Captain Ninara shifted out of the way for her and then left the table altogether a moment later, going to join her twin.

"That's really fucking telling," Anna said to Shadowlight.

He nodded his agreement.

But there wasn't anything either of them could do. Taryin settled on the bench next to Gryton, and soon servants were bringing a trencher for the blood witch.

The meal continued in silence. It was the most uncomfortable meal of Anna's life. It put the Mackenzie family reunions to shame.

When it was over, at last, Gryton urged them up and away.

As it turned out, he had a tour of the fortress planned. He showed them gardens, stables, practice rings and even a big, three-story library.

But no matter how far away they walked, it still felt like the blood witch's magic was crawling over Anna's skin.

CHAPTER FOURTEEN

After the tour, he and Anna were escorted by Captain Vaspara and Commander Gryton to a sub-level storeroom filled with every item one could possibly want. Shadowlight inhaled deeply and sorted through the odors. Fabrics, leathers, the metallic tang of metals and armor. It didn't come as a surprise when Gryton led them to a wall of shelves filled with various pieces of armor.

"Once you've earned your swords, our metalsmiths will forge you both armor befitting your new rank in the army," Gryton informed Shadowlight, and then he suddenly turned to Anna, "and if you try to take what I have not given you, I'll see that Shadowlight is punished in your place."

Anna cursed and replaced a dagger back on the shelf.

"I was only looking," she said with a growl.

"Look with your eyes next time," Gryton said, though he didn't sound that angry.

Shadowlight studied him with narrowed eyes, but before he could pinpoint what bothered him about the older male, he ushered them thirty feet further down the aisle then stopped and dug through a few pieces of armor until he pulled out a cloth wrapped bundle.

"This should fit you," Gryton said to Anna as he passed her the large bundle.

Turning to Shadowlight, Gryton looked him up and down. "You are almost fully grown. Your father's armor should fit you with just a few adjustments."

Shadowlight held his breath and then let it out on a burst of sound. "I can have my father's armor? Can I see it now?"

"Easy, kid," Anna's thoughts were suddenly in his mind. *"I know you want something that was your father's but remember no gift here is truly free. They seek to win us over by any means necessary."*

Some of Shadowlight's pleasure drained away.

"Kid, I'm not saying you shouldn't take this gift, but remember everything we're given or 'win the right' to own will have strings attached."

Of course Anna was right. Shadowlight clamped down on his excitement and just stood watching and waiting.

Gryton stared at Anna. "Now, whatever did you say to the poor kid to make him practically wilt?"

Anna made a face, only now realizing they'd just exposed their secret ability to Gryton, and then said, "The truth."

"The youngling will take his father's armor whether you want him to have it or not."

But this time Anna smiled. "I didn't tell him not to take the armor."

Gryton muttered something under his breath that was too low even for gargoyle ears. Then he turned sharply on his heels and commanded Shadowlight to follow. Not given a choice, he stumbled after the armor-covered figure. Anna jogged along beside him, her bundle rattling and clanking with every stride.

Gryton eventually halted halfway down a side aisle where he took a bundle from a shelf and handed it to Shadowlight.

It was bigger than the one he'd given to Anna.

"Keep moving," Gryton barked. "We still have several stops to make before I deliver you to your weapons instructor to assess your abilities."

Shadowlight hurried to follow before the collar took the choice from him. Anna grumbled something under her breath which sounded like 'hard-ass drill sergeant.'

Commander Gryton hadn't been exaggerating. They made many stops. Weapon belts, buckles, clothing to wear during practice, even more formal attire for special occasions. They gathered all that and more. Gryton explained that the colors of the uniforms marked what rank they held in the army. Pale blue meant innocent and not to be killed before they'd had a chance to prove themselves.

By the fourth stop, they were so loaded down with supplies that Shadowlight was starting to feel like a beast of burden. Gryton eventually took pity and bellowed for servants to carry the supplies back to their quarters.

"You won't need the armor today anyway," Gryton

explained after the servants came and took everything. "Tomorrow will be soon enough for that."

So that's how Shadowlight came to be standing inside the training area empty-handed. Now that he was outside, he very much wanted to go for a run or a hunt. But the practice ring also held his attention. Anna's, too, if her ramrod posture was anything to go by.

The practice yard was a vast sand-covered area with at least a hundred individual rings where opponents were testing their skills while mentors and other students looked on.

Scraps of conversation and shouted orders drifted to him over the clash of steel on steel. While a good half of the combatants were fighting with swords or other bladed weapons, there were also others that were engaged in different forms of hand-to-hand combat.

Watching the various styles, Shadowlight was a bit surprised to find he wanted to try his hand at some of them. He'd been trapped inside walls for days and hadn't seen the sky in longer than he liked.

He glanced sideways at Anna and then reached out to her thoughts. *"Is it bad that I want to take part?"*

Anna turned to meet his eyes. *"No, because we need to do this. Just be careful and watch yourself. Somehow I doubt our new instructors will be as patient as Gregory was with us."*

"I understand," and he did. If they didn't rise swiftly to become the best, they were likely to suffer. The Battle

Goddess did not seem the type to forgive weakness or failure.

And he also knew from some of what Anna had told him that the sooner they gained the trust of their instructors, the sooner they might earn liberties that could lead to opportunities for escape.

PART TWO

*N*othing had gone well in the last week, which shouldn't have surprised Lillian. Since nothing ever went her way. But over the previous three weeks, she'd really, truly won the shitstorm sweepstakes.

Her doppelgänger had arrived. Shadowlight had been kidnapped. Their father had been wounded—perhaps mortally. Their mother was in a coma, which Lillian thought a little guiltily, might have been a blessing. Then Anna had gone off to rescue Shadowlight, but there was no way of knowing how she fared.

To top it all off, Daryna had revealed that Gryton was the child of the Avatars and she'd acted to protect her child from Gregory.

Yep. Shitstorm sweepstakes.

And the cherry on top: she was hormonal and emotional from the pregnancy.

All in all, Lillian was proud she was keeping her shit together for the most part. Gregory needed her support, and she'd damn well be there for him even if it meant being civil with her doppelganger.

The one upside to this grand mess was that she now knew where the Sorceress's allegiance lay. With her son, Gryton.

Lillian still had trouble digesting the fact she and Gregory had broken their vows and had a child in a past life. Gryton! What trickster god was behind this? But Gregory had repeatedly confirmed that Daryna was telling the truth about that catastrophe.

At least Gregory was wise enough not to trust the woman who was temporary host to the other half of his soul. He'd hypothesized that the rapid growth of her temporary body had somehow damaged Daryna's mind. Lillian agreed wholeheartedly.

Now Daryna was under continuous watch by members of the Clan and Coven. No one had told the human military about Daryna's actions. The council agreed that particular bit of knowledge needed to remain hidden for now or they might find themselves at war with both the humans and the Battle Goddess's army. While that might be true, Lillian still didn't think keeping this secret from the humans was a good idea. But she and Gregory had been outvoted.

Which was why Gregory was taking a 'hunting break' from training the humans to answer a summons from Daryna. He'd been less than pleased to be summoned, but his other half had claimed there was something important they needed to discuss.

Lillian hadn't been about to let Gregory go alone. Now they traveled together, running side-by-side through the forest. Had they not been going to meet her evil doppelgänger, Lillian would have enjoyed the run with Gregory. But things were what they were.

They soon reached the small game trail that led to the cabin where Gregory had stowed Daryna. It was hell and gone from the nearest road or military patrol. They'd passed several of the fae guards on their run, and more walked the perimeter of the meadow surrounding the small cabin. There was a third line of defense inside, watching for any hint of Daryna's spell work.

If the Sorceress had wanted to escape, she could have easily overpowered her fae guards, but she had remained because she didn't want to drive a bigger wedge between herself and Gregory. Or, at least, that was Lillian's theory.

The peak of the cabin soon came into view, and they sprinted across the meadow, parting the long, buttery-colored autumn grasses as they ran. They'd only just reached the door when Daryna opened it and ushered them inside.

Lillian noted Greenborrow, the pooka, and the banshee were Daryna's guards today.

"Why did you summon me?" Gregory growled as he reared up to stand on two feet.

Lillian arched a brow at his sharp tone but merely folded her wings against her back and crossed her arms to watch. Gregory had never been one for niceties, but he'd been downright cranky since he learned of Daryna's deceit.

The sorceress merely nodded at Gregory's snarled tone. "Durnathyne, I fear I must tell you that Anna Mackenzie failed to rescue Shadowlight."

Lillian's lips curled back from her teeth and it was her turn to growl. "How do you know that?"

"Is Anna still alive?" Gregory added.

Daryna smiled at them both. "Gryton spoke to me at great risk to himself to share what news he was able to procure."

"Good for him," Lillian snapped, pretending the news of Gryton's aid didn't come as a surprise. *Though it wouldn't astonish her if he was playing both sides.* "Answer Gregory's question now."

"The human is alive and well according to my son."

"Right. So that means she's lucky not to be dead." Lillian's tail flicked in agitation.

"You need not be so hostile, Lillian."

I'll be hostile if I damn well wish it, Lillian thought to herself.

"Go on," Gregory urged.

"Anna and Shadowlight are both alive, and at present are not in immediate danger, but we mustn't leave them there given what Gryton has shared with me."

"That's what I've been saying this whole time." *Not that anyone ever listens to me,* Lillian thought sourly.

"I am aware," the sorceress said in a dry tone. "Unfortunately, now that Anna is there with him, the danger is greater. Soon, the Battle Goddess will be able to use his blood to start converting other species and those new gargoyles will be under Shadowlight's command."

"Not for a couple of years at least. It will take that long for him to mature enough to serve the Battle Goddess's needs. I plan to bring the fight to the demigoddess long before that," Gregory said, a growl thickening his voice.

"The Battle Goddess has ways to get what she wants much sooner than that. She's been experimenting on gargoyles using blood magic for a few hundred years now and has learned things. The Lady of Battles will use that knowledge and force Shadowlight to share power with Anna. As the human grows stronger, so too will the cub. In a mere turning of the seasons, she'll be in possession of a mature Rasoren and Kyrsu to lead her armies."

"What?" Gregory snarled. "You sent Anna there knowing our enemy has resurrected blood magic?"

"I did not know that when I first sent Anna back," Daryna said, her eyes tight with a worry she tried to hide. "I only just learned about this from Gryton."

"We must spearhead a rescue," Gregory said, now looking more thoughtful than pissed. "The military has been hounding me to put the newly trained human soldiers to a test for days now. This might just be the time to test their skills in a trial run before we wage open war."

Lillian didn't really care about testing the newly trained soldiers in the field, but she was entirely on board with saving Anna and Shadowlight from a terrible fate.

"When can we leave?"

Gregory turned to look her up and down and then paused at her belly where the new life they'd created was already starting to show as a large bulge.

"You aren't going," Gregory said with a menacing growl.

"Try and stop me."

"Actually, he can," Daryna injected. "However, Lillian will be needed should something happen to this body. The female half of the Avatar soul must have a direct path back to Lillian should something unplanned occur while we're in the Magic Realm."

Gregory's gaze snapped toward Daryna. For the first time, he looked uncertain. "How long before your body fails."

As angry as he was at Daryna for keeping what she'd learned about Gryton to herself, deep-down he must still love the other half of his soul. He couldn't help it. And even Lillian knew that while Daryna had made the choices she had to protect her child, she hadn't wanted to harm Gregory. Lillian knew that in her heart. Gregory likely did too.

Watching Daryna's body fail would be like witnessing his beloved dying all over again. Poor Gregory.

Sometimes the Divine Ones seemed exceptionally cruel to their Avatars. Lillian curled a wing around Gregory's shoulders, startling him. But he soon leaned into her warmth and dipped his muzzle to sniff along her skin before bestowing a couple of gargoyle kisses to her cheek.

After a moment he straightened to his full height. "Thank you, Daryna, for speaking the truth to me this night, but now I must go seek out Resnick again and secure the military's aid."

Gregory turned and left before Daryna could respond, then once he was bounding away across the meadow, Lillian's doppelgänger turned to her. "I never meant to hurt my beloved gargoyle, but I had to help my son."

Lillian felt a stirring of unease. Her hand dropped to rest against the slight bulge that was now visible even in gargoyle form. To have to choose between her mate and her child was unthinkable, and yet Daryna had been forced to do just that. Lillian only hoped fate never required her to make the same horrible choice. Then looking upon Daryna with pity, she said, "For what it's worth, I am sorry you had to make that decision."

"As am I."

"Lillian. We must go!" Gregory shouted from across the meadow.

"He's still hurting," Daryna said. "Comfort him in whatever way he'll allow."

Lillian sent Daryna another pitying glance and then dropped to all fours and ran after Gregory. In time, he would heal from the shock and betrayal he'd suffered, and if Shadowlight and Anna weren't in mortal danger, she'd focus solely upon Gregory's emotional healing, but for now, they had other priorities.

When she reached his side, he glanced sidelong at her and playfully swatted his tail along her rump, saying, "Keep up."

"I'm not the slow one!" She put on a burst of speed and bolted ahead.

Gregory growled out a challenge and pursued. Even as she playfully raced him through the forest, Lillian's mind was turned toward her younger brother and his predicament.

Hold on, little brother. We're coming for you.

CHAPTER SIXTEEN

Anna kept an eye on Shadowlight even while she listened to her new mentor demonstrate various forms of combat. Over the last three days, she'd started to grow accustomed to the routine set by her new mentors.

Today, she'd been assigned Captains Sorac and Bervicta as her instructors and Shadowlight had been ordered to follow Captain Honnan and Vaspara. Gryton had left to attend to other duties and Anna was happy enough to see his back.

While she might not be familiar with the mating habits of fire elementals, she was pretty damn sure that was interest she'd seen in Gryton's gaze a few times over the last three days.

That complication could be a curse but also a possible blessing. If she played him right, it might make Shadowlight's stay here a little less dangerous. Gryton's protection couldn't harm the kid.

She'd seen enough of this world to know she and Shadowlight were walking a metaphysical tightrope over a pit with no safety net and monsters waiting below to eat them. They needed allies, but pickings were slim.

Her mental list was broken down into parts: List A contained the names of mentors who were somewhat more personable. List B included the names of those most likely to pick the meat from her bones.

Captain Sorac and Vaspara had already made Anna's short list of potential allies. Sour-faced Bervicta, too, might get added, but Shadowlight's other instructor, the incubus named Honnan, nope, not making the list.

If she had to take one for the team with Gryton — that was one thing, but she wasn't going to get passed around if she could help it.

There might be others from the captains she could cultivate, but thus far, they were otherwise busy dealing with preparations for waking the army. Whatever that meant.

"You and the gargoyle will report back here same time tomorrow," Captain Sorac informed her. "Bring your armor. We'll be using honed weapons."

Anna nodded at Sorac, keeping her gaze on him, but she could sense Shadowlight approaching on her six. He'd been released by his instructors. Good.

"Captain Vaspara will see you to your next training session." Sorac dismissed them and turned to his next students. They wore green tunics, which she'd learned was the next level up from blue.

Anna might have watched them fight to see how they measured up to her training, but Captain Honnan arrived to transfer his command of Shadowlight's collar to Vaspara.

When she'd first witnessed the transferring of control, she'd been a bit surprised. She'd assumed that any of the mentors could command Shadowlight, but that wasn't the case. Only one captain at a time could hold command over Shadowlight besides Gryton.

At the time, Anna had stored that bit of news away for later. She still wasn't quite sure how she would use it, but there was always the possibility that once she and Shadowlight were farther along in their training, their enemies might let their guard down. If she was later able to get the upper hand and overpower one of the captains, she might be able to force them to surrender control of the command collar. If it came to dying by her hand or releasing Shadowlight, her target might surrender. She'd just have to pick a captain who loved their own ass more than their goddess.

Patience was key. Once she'd familiarized herself with the fortress and the captains, she'd learn their every weakness.

Once Honnan finished transferring control of the collar to Captain Vaspara, she started away with a barked command to follow.

Shadowlight hurried to catch up but glanced back at Anna to be sure she was following. She nodded to the kid in reassurance and lengthened her stride to catch up.

CHAPTER SEVENTEEN

Captain Vaspara led them back inside the city-like fortress. Anna would have preferred to remain outside, and by the way Shadowlight's ears drooped, she knew he would as well.

They walked for another twenty minutes and made their way down deeper and darker stone passageways until Anna feared they were headed back to the dungeon. If that happened, it would be disastrous for their chance at escape.

They turned down another side corridor, entering an unfamiliar area. Not even Gryton's second tour had led them here. The floor was still covered with thick rugs and the walls had fine tapestries to insulate against the chill of the stone, so, at least, this wasn't another wing of the dungeons. Anna's fists slowly relaxed.

The hallway forked ahead and Captain Vaspara turned down the left branch. Torches still lined the walls and these carpets and tapestries were just as pristine as the ones in the hall they'd just left, but something here made sweat trickle down her spine and stood the hair on the back of her neck on end.

An unclean presence pushed against her skin and scraped along her mental shields, and more telling, her gargoyle senses flared a warning.

Shadowlight's lips curled back from his teeth. Although, he hadn't loosed a growl yet.

"You're doing better," she told him. *"The less of an open book you are, the harder it will make you to read."*

"I need to be better in every way if we want to survive."

Anna couldn't fault the kid for his logic. It also applied to her now, too.

Especially since her gargoyle nature would only grow with each blood exchange.

So far, Anna hadn't seen much difference in herself, but eventually, that would change as her new nature exerted more control. She pushed that worry away for later. They'd reached their destination, which was a stout, old wooden door.

It opened a moment later and a guard emerged. Recognition lit his face at seeing Vaspara, but he didn't speak, merely coming to attention and holding the door for them.

Ah. Anna knew him now. He was the male she'd seen with Vaspara in the stable the first night Anna had ventured into this city in her ill-fated attempt to rescue Shadowlight. She mulled over the guard's expression. It wasn't sexual in nature. Something else then, almost like he wanted to tell Vaspara something but thought better of it.

The mystery would have to wait. Anna followed Vaspara and Shadowlight into the chamber. It was lined with shelves full of various-sized pots. Unfortunately, all of them were labeled in a language she couldn't read. The spell the Sorceress had woven over Anna to allow her to understand the spoken languages didn't extend to their corresponding written forms.

Anna studied the room. Drying herbs and tables filled with pots suggested this was a workroom. Possibly a healer's or surgeon's area. That might account for the coppery smell of blood.

Captain Vaspara swore and then led them to an old ironbound door at the back of the room. She raised her gauntleted hand and rapped hard twice. A moment later a female voice called for them to enter.

Vaspara glanced over her shoulder at them. "Don't ever open this door without first gaining permission. If the blood witch is working on an active spell, breaching the door will break the ward spell sealing the room. The backlash of power such an event could unleash would have unfortunate effects for all."

Anna filed that bit of news away for later. As soon as Captain Vaspara pushed open the heavy door, the stink of blood intensified. Cursing again, the succubus pushed further into the room.

Anna slid past Shadowlight, wanting to be the first to face whatever was inside.

The room was barren except for another large stone table with a body laid out. She'd just found the source of the blood scent. The deep cuts at wrist and groin were all too easy to see. The cause of this unfortunate bastard's death was no mystery.

"Kid, I'm sorry I couldn't shield you from this."

"I've seen death before."

"You shouldn't have." Anna's hand clutched into a fist, and she wished they could've kept their training weapons with them, but Captain Sorac always made sure the servants took them back to Anna and Shadowlight's quarters after practice.

Captain Vaspara scowled at the dead body but didn't comment on it. "Gryton wants you to teach them battle magic, but you'll need to assess their level of development to gauge how soon you'll be able to start."

Taryin looked them over with a critical eye. "I look forward to the testing."

Vaspara snorted. "And that's why Gryton also ordered me to watch over them, so you don't forget yourself and overstep your authority. They are not to be harmed."

"Of course," Captain Taryin replied with a chilling smile directed at Shadowlight.

Anna's dread inched up another degree. Even Gryton didn't trust this blood witch if he was making another of his captains stay and watch.

"If you'll turn over command of Shadowlight's collar to me, I'll begin now," Taryin said.

This time Vaspara barked out a short, humorless laugh. "No. I will see that he complies well enough for you to do your tests on them."

Taryin nodded placidly as if the other captain's words did not insult her in the least. "Very well."

When she reached for Shadowlight, Anna stepped between them.

"You can start with me."

"As you wish." Captain Taryin pulled a small blade from

a tether around her neck. At first, Anna had thought it was a pendant, but now she saw it was a ceremonial knife. The blade was no longer than Anna's palm.

Still, despite its diminutive size, it wasn't very reassuring when Taryin brought it up close to her neck. There was a tug and a sawing motion and suddenly the captain was holding the end of one of Anna's braids.

Better hair than a body part, Anna supposed, but adrenaline still coursed through her blood.

Taryin set the hair aside in a bowl and then brought the tip of the blade down in a shallow cut along Anna's left bicep. Then the blood witch held the bowl under Anna's dripping arm. Once a few drops of blood had covered the braid, Taryin looked around. "Let's go to the other room where my herbs are stored."

Yeah. Totally fine with that. Anna shoved Shadowlight through the open door to get him moving. He'd been staring between Anna and the dead body of the male. It didn't take a rocket scientist to figure out the kid was concerned that the same thing might happen to her.

Taryin went to the shelves and sorted through a half-dozen pots before she found the ones she wanted. Placing three pots on the nearest worktable, she pried off their lids and sprinkled fragments of dried herbs onto the hair and blood. Next, she reached for a pitcher of some dark, fermented liquid. Anna thought it was wine by its fruity and yeasty scent.

Once the hair, herbs, and blood were covered in liquid, Taryin raised the bowl, closed her eyes, and began a chant.

Fire flared and raced along the surface of the liquid, igniting like an extremely reactive accelerant. After ten seconds, Taryin's chant changed in pitch, and a ball of fire and magic rose up out of the bowl. Five seconds later the flames burned entirely away, leaving a ball of tightly woven magic floating in the air.

"Very nice," the blood witch purred. "Oh, the spells I could create using your blood."

"The Battle Goddess will never let that happen. These two are more important than fuel for your spells," Captain Vaspara said in a droll voice. "But if you still plan to test Shadowlight, get on with it. I need to find permanent slaves to serve as body servants for them and then acquire appropriate clothing for the feast."

That was the first time Anna was hearing about a feast.

"Very well," Taryin said, her expression unreadable. "I wouldn't want to waste your valuable time."

Vaspara snorted disdainfully but didn't vocalize her thoughts.

Anna decided Vaspara had just taken top spot on the potential list of allies even though she was a succubus.

The blood witch stepped closer to Shadowlight. She used her knife to cut a lock of his hair and then nicked him in the bicep. Anna didn't like seeing the blade used on the kid any more than she liked having it used on herself.

Oblivious to Anna's glowers or merely uncaring, the blood witch continued with her task, and soon there was another flash of fire and magic, this one much larger than when Anna's sample had ignited.

"Unsurprising, but excellent all the same." Taryin nodded to Vaspara. "I can start training the youngling in battle and blood magic tomorrow; the human will need at least two more blood exchanges before we start any mean-ingful training. But at least she won't be hopeless."

"I'll have them returned here tomorrow after their time in the practice ring." Vaspara agreed.

"Actually, keep them at the practice ring. There's always plenty of blood spilled on the sands there, and if we exhaust that supply, then I'll just take what is needed from some of the trainees."

Vaspara nodded as if bleeding random victims was everyday news. The succubus was just turning to leave when there was a sharp knock and the guard from earlier entered from the hall outside. He glanced at them and muttered an apology for the interruption but ushered in a man and woman. Two steps behind them, a girl and boy followed. All four had their hands tied and Anna's stomach plummeted in horrified realization.

"Captain Taryin, I've brought the slaves as you asked."

"I told you to wait until after I was finished with the Rasoren and his Kyrsu."

The guard apologized again and then swept into another deep bow. The move was both graceful and fast, but not so fast that Anna missed the moment when the guard's gaze slid to her for a brief moment. But she had caught the look and recognized it for what it was, a glimmer of rebellion.

Since this was the same guard who'd been leaving when they first entered, his arrival now, with the four slaves, wasn't an accident. Anna was certain of that. He'd wanted to arrive with his prisoners while she and Shadowlight were still within the blood witch's grim workshop.

"Who are these people?" Anna asked. "And what does

the blood witch want with them?" Oh, but she already knew, and Anna didn't care what she had to barter, she was going to save the kids, at least.

It was Captain Vaspara who answered. "They are all traitors to the Battle Goddess."

"The children, too? Surely they weren't plotting against the demigoddess."

"They didn't," Vaspara said with a bored shrug. "Nor did their parents, not directly, but they tried to flee this city."

"And that's enough to warrant death?" It likely was in this place, and if the parents were that desperate, it must have meant they thought their children were as good as dead if they stayed.

"The male and his brother," Vaspara pointed to the father and then jerked her thumb over her shoulder to indicate the dead guy back on the stone slab. "Both served Shadowlight's parents as free servants. After Stalks the Darkness and River made their escape with Shadowlight, we later learned that Darkness had warned the brother about his escape plan. The human traitor then sought out his brother and family and convinced them to flee."

Beside her, Shadowlight stiffened and looked at the family. "You knew my parents?"

None of them answered Shadowlight's question, but Vaspara confirmed it. "Yes. They served them but are now traitors stripped of all rank and soon the blood witch will strip them of their lives."

Vaspara sounded bored, but she locked gazes with Anna like she was trying to convey something important that she didn't want to say out loud. Anna's mind whirled and then understanding struck.

"Gryton said he'd return all the possessions belonging to Shadowlight's parents to him in the coming days if we were biddable." Anna paused to spear the blood witch with a challenging look. "We have held up our end of the bargain. These slaves now belong to Shadowlight, and this even saves Vaspara the need to hunt up servants for us."

Vaspara nodded, still pretending boredom. "That is true."

"They are traitors," the blood witch snarled. "They deserve death."

"Hmm," Anna said, looking around the room slowly before returning to the terrified prisoners. "I disagree. Sounds like the instigator is already dead in that room back there. These four merely had their hands forced."

"They still must be made an example of. I only follow the edicts set down by our Lady."

"Time for the bluff of all bluffs," Anna sent to Shadowlight and then drew herself up and faced down Taryin. "I was there when the demigoddess told Gryton to treat us with the honor our rank grants us. I order that the slaves be delivered to our quarters immediately."

The blood witch recoiled.

"Ah, you didn't think I'd figure that out so fast, did you? Or you thought I wouldn't have the ambition to take what is rightfully ours." Anna smiled coldly. "I've always been driven to rise up and conquer every challenge tossed at me. Shortly after I was attacked by the Riven, Shadowlight found me and gave me a choice, a quick, clean death or I could take his blood and fight to overcome the taint and if I survived, I would be tied to him for life."

Anna circled around the blood witch. Sensing her surprise, she latched onto it like a weakness. It might not be fear, but she could work with surprise.

"I agreed to Shadowlight's offer because I will always fight to win. I do not know how to surrender. Die or adapt. I've always adapted. I might not yet know a lot about magic, but that will change."

She reached out and grasped the still glowing ball of magic that floated above the table. Her talons lengthened, and she flexed her fingers, crushing the ball of magic and absorbing it into herself.

Shadowlight prowled closer to Taryin now, too. "Gargoyles don't surrender."

Anna nodded. "So, you see? We've looked around and studied how things work around here and we will now adapt. We will become what the Battle Goddess demands. But we won't be the victims you expect."

"You are both children," Taryin said, a hundred thoughts flashing behind her eyes.

Anna laughed. "Then you are about to get your petite ass handed to you by a pair of the most ambitious and determined children you've ever met."

"I will not be spoken to in such a manner by a mere human!"

"You are a fool, Taryin," Captain Vaspara said. "There is nothing mere about the humans of her world. Gryton told me about their world. They have perfected the art of death. In a little over a hundred years, their wars claimed millions of lives. They are capable of breathtaking violence;

their atrocities rival anything that we have ever done here in our realm."

Anna was familiar with some of humanity's darkest hours, but when it was put that way...she winced.

"That is—" Taryin was cut off by Vaspara.

"Gryton let me look directly into his mind. The humans of the Mortal Realm have created weapons that can destroy millions of lives in a blink of an eye. Our Lady knows this. It honors her. That is why she will one day rule both realms. The humans have earned that honor. Anna and Shadowlight will lead the way."

The blood witch glanced at Anna, her surprise melting away to be replaced by a glimmer of respect.

Anna's stomach churned a little.

"That's why," Vaspara continued, her bored expression back in place, "if Shadowlight and Anna want the slaves, it is their right to claim them."

"Very well," Taryin agreed slowly.

Anna didn't wait around for the powerful blood witch to change her mind and she planted her hand against Shadowlight's back and applied enough pressure to get him moving. They were almost through the door when Vaspara glanced back at the soldier who had brought the family. "You will escort the slaves."

"Yes, my lady."

Once they turned the first corner, Vaspara relaxed enough to slow her stride. She cast another glance over her shoulder at the guard and then looked to Shadowlight. "That guard and many more like him used to serve your mother. It is within your right to reclaim them."

Shadowlight's answer was swift and short. "I claim them all."

Vaspara nodded, "As the Rasoren wishes, so will it be done."

"We're going to become tyrants," Anna told him without a hint of guilt or self-loathing.

"We make a good team," he said, sounding so very proud.

CHAPTER EIGHTEEN

Feeling more than a little proud of himself, Shadowlight dropped to all fours and paced a circle around Anna and the family they'd rescued. These new people, even the guard, were now part of his tribe, his to protect.

His magic stirred as his thoughts focused on what Vaspara had said. There were others, guards and servants alike, who rightfully fell within his ever-increasing sphere of protection. He would find them, claim them, and then one day free them once he and Anna found a way to escape. Until then, they needed allies.

With a new sense of purpose driving him, he continued to circle his new charges but now approached the two children.

"Hello," he said, giving each a good lick. "I'm Shadowlight."

Both children started in surprise. The girl squealed and laughed. The boy recoiled.

He was hurt by the boy's rejection. Everyone liked him. Why didn't this boy?

"I won't hurt you," he offered. "You're safe with Anna and me. Vaspara said your family served my parents."

"We did." The boy replied but kept looking to his parents who were talking with Anna and Vaspara.

Anna was busy interrogating their new servants, so the boy was on his own.

Now was as good of time as any to try to win over the boy and girl.

Before Shadowlight could vocalize his thoughts, the boy spoke. "We served River and Stalks the Darkness, but they abandoned us." The boy glowered at Shadowlight. "Why should we trust you?"

Shadowlight was taken off-guard by the anger in the boy's tone, but his gargoyle nature also told him it was deserved. His parents had abandoned these people when they'd fled to Earth to help Lillian and to keep him from becoming the Battle Goddess's tool.

In the end, it hadn't helped. He was among the enemy. But there were other victims here as well.

For the first time, he felt shame for what his parents had done to save him. They'd abandoned those loyal to them to face the Battle Goddess's rage alone.

Anna was suddenly at his side, her fingers giving a reassuring scratch.

"What are your names?" She asked the two children.

It was the boy who answered. "I'm Brannan and my sister is Fayon."

"Well, Brannan," Anna said, her expression fierce. "I don't leave friends behind. Shadowlight doesn't either. I can't promise to keep you safe from all dangers and I can't promise you your freedom either, but I can promise we won't willingly betray you or your family."

The boy was surprised by Anna's blunt words. Shadowlight could smell it.

"I thank you for the truth," the boy said at last. "One doesn't often hear it in this place."

Anna nodded sharply, though her lips compressed in that way he'd come to understand was her expression for some dark emotion that she couldn't vent, but he did catch her muttering about evil bitch goddesses enslaving children.

"Kid," she said along the private link. *"I know this makes our escape more difficult, but I'm still going to try to get us and these poor souls free of this place. Don't ever allow the blood witch or her 'lady' to crush your hopes."*

"I won't," he promised.

Together they returned to their quarters where their new servants went to work stowing away all the supplies Gryton ordered for them. They hadn't had much time in the last three days to sort it all, but that didn't faze the servants.

While the two children attended to the fireplaces, stacking wood and kindling, their parents saw to the clothing and armor. The mother, Lanya, laid out clothing for the feast they'd only learned about a few hours earlier. It was supposed to take place in a little over an hour, just before dawn. Shadowlight was still adjusting to the nocturnal routine here, but he was hungry again, so didn't really care if supper and breakfast had been reversed.

Anna grumbled something about shift workers that he

didn't understand. While Lanya was seeing to their attire, her mate, Barrick was helping Anna understand all the leather straps and buckles of the armor she'd be expected to wear tomorrow, at least until Lanya overruled her husband and said she needed to get Anna and Shadowlight ready for tonight's feast.

Shadowlight was the first to be chased into the bath by the domineering older woman, but he didn't complain. She reminded him of his mother. Once Shadowlight was finished his bath, she soon cowed Anna into following orders as well.

While Anna was busy with her bath, he stood in his own room, looking over his clothing for the celebratory dinner. His new knee-length loincloth was black velvet, its edges lined with rubies and silver embroidery. Sighing, he picked it up and donned the clothing without complaint, although he didn't like how the added weight of the jewels made the long skirt of the loincloth slap against his legs as he walked.

Fashion was foolish.

When he padded out of his room, Lanya was lying in wait, a large torc held in her hands. She explained that it would fit over his control collar, effectively hiding it. Next came wrist and armbands made of the same silver and rubies as his torc and loincloth.

She wasn't done yet, though. There was a matching set of bands that clipped around his ankles and then she pulled out two silver cones and attached them to the tips of his horns. Every time he moved, the suspended ruby attached to each tip clicked against his horn.

He wrinkled his nose and stomped into Anna's room to

see what she would be forced to wear. A body-size mirror suspended from a hook in the wall caught his attention. He paced over to it and then sneered at his reflection in its silver surface.

Foolish vanity. He looked like an idiot.

Lanya followed him into Anna's room, more grooming tools carried in her hands. "Perfect. Stay right there, I'll finish up with you and move on to Anna as soon as she's done with her bath."

Lanya stood behind him and then started to work his hair into braided sections.

Fifteen minutes later, Anna stuck her head in her room, and the servant was still working to tame his wild mane while he glowered at himself in the mirror.

Anna looked him over, a merry light in her eyes and then she started to laugh. At least until she'd dried her tears of mirth and got a good look at what she was to wear. All merriment vanished, and she sighed unhappily.

Shadowlight glanced at his reflection again. "I look stupid."

"Think of it as a different type of armor," Anna declared, "We're the Battle Goddess's new favorites and will one day be expected to rule over everyone else in that hall. This finery is to remind them of that."

Shadowlight huffed. She might be right, but it didn't mean he liked it.

"I still look foolish," he complained.

"It will just be for an hour or so."

Anna stepped out from behind the dressing screen and stomped over to the mirror where she glowered at her formal dress in the reflection.

"Of all the fucked up—"

"I told you it was stupid."

She glowered at the kid where he was napping at the foot of her bed. His tone dripped with an "I told you so" to Anna's ear.

"It looks like something a villainess in a comic book would wear," she growled as she twisted and turned to view it from different angles.

"You look lovely, my lady," Lanya said in a soothing voice as she affixed a large, ruby encrusted silver pin into Anna's hair to hold the braids in place. At least the servant hadn't unbraided her cornrows. The woman had had that "I want to play with your hair" look on her face the entire time she helped Anna dress. If time wasn't a factor, she was sure the servant would have been sculpting her hair into some outlandish style.

Glowering at her reflection, Anna looked away from her hair to scan the full outfit. A second appraisal didn't improve it.

The top wasn't too hideous. The dress's bodice was rather plain and sleeveless. There was a black metal breastplate that went over it that had enough rubies encrusted on it to satisfy even the most jewel-hungry person.

The wide leather harness that had been dyed black to match the breastplate was more her style. At least its presence meant she would be wearing a sword. Any weapon was a good weapon.

The bottom of the outfit was where the evil comic

book villainous vibe came in. The skirt was ankle-length burgundy velvet, a red so dark to be almost black, which was okay. However, she could have done without the slits up the sides that bared her legs when she walked.

Anna outright refused to wear the pile of leather straps that were supposed to be shoes. She still wore her boots. When she'd asked Lanya where the dress had come from, the servant informed her Commander Gryton had had it sent over with the other items.

Muttering unhappily, Anna went over to the chest at the end of the bed and dug out her daggers and sword. Once she strapped the leg sheaths in place, Anna decided the blades were her favorite part of the costume.

With Lanya's help, she adjusted the sword's harness to allow her skirt's fabric to lay naturally.

"You look lovely," Lanya said again. She took in Anna's entire outfit, looking pleased with what she saw until she got to the boots. "Are you sure I can't—"

"Yep. And if Gryton really wants the sandals worn, he can wear them himself."

Anna tugged at the dress, but nothing made the slits go away.

"Can't believe I let you dress me up like a dominatrix."

"You look powerful, beautiful, and deadly. The others will think twice before challenging you and the young gargoyle."

"What's a dominatrix?" Shadowlight asked. Anna's eyes cut across the room to where he was curled in a ball eavesdropping. His eyes were closed again, but he'd just proved he wasn't sleeping.

"I'll explain when you're older," Anna said with a roll of her eyes heavenward.

"Well, if you won't surrender the boots, I think we are done." Lanya folded her hands.

Shadowlight climbed to his feet, made a show of stretching, and then leaped down to pace across the floor in a stiff-legged gait that spoke of his annoyance.

"If you'd taken any longer to get ready, I would have perished from hunger," he complained.

"Fine," Anna huffed at the kid as she followed him out of the room. "We'll go so you can eat your weight in food, but afterward I'm going to burn this dress."

He turned and rolled his eyes at her. "It will just be for a couple of hours."

Had the kid just tossed her own words back at her? Yes. Yes, he had.

She was pretty sure Shadowlight was transitioning from cute kid to obnoxious teenager in gargoyle years.

CHAPTER NINETEEN

Anna had only just exited her chambers when Commander Gryton called her. Her mood darkened further, and her annoyance grew as she turned toward his familiar voice. Upon seeing him, she drew in a surprised breath.

If not for his voice and general height, she might not have recognized Tin Man without his armor. She frowned as she studied him.

Of course the fucker would have to be handsome. And it wasn't just 'oh he's cute' Nope. He was the type of man that females between the ages of thirteen and one hundred and three halted whatever they were doing to admire the superb specimen of pure masculine beauty.

His long, sleek black hair spilled over his shoulder and drew her eyes down to his powerful chest which narrowed to a trim waist. Years of combat and sword training had given him a toned body with lean muscle and tight abs. Tight and trim everything.

His formalwear didn't include a shirt, just wide bronze armbands, a matching belt, loose pants and body paint. At least she thought the symbol on his chest was painted with some metallic bronze paint, but then again, it could be a magic tattoo. Whatever it was, it drew the eye.

The fabric of his pants was lightweight. Perhaps a silk or linen mix of some sort. When he moved, the material shifted with him, giving glimpses of his muscular thighs and powerful calves.

Fortunately, Anna wasn't about to be led around by her hormones or let them trick her into doing something foolish. She knew Gryton only looked out for his own ass, spectacular though it might be.

Still, it didn't change her earlier determination to use any kind of weakness against him if it would further her goals to protect the kid from the evil of this place.

Gryton's long strides brought him to her quickly. He wore sensible boots, Anna noted, not the stupid strappy sandals Lanya had kept shoving at her.

After a moment, her gaze left his boots and sought out his face. His amber-ringed brown eyes sparkled with humor as his gaze fixed on her feet. Soon a smile tilted the firm line of his lips into a curve.

The prick had a dimple. A. Freaking. Dimple.

Anna was proud she didn't try to punch the smug look off his face.

When he halted before her, light rippled along the strange symbol stamped on his chest. Okay, so much for body paint, magic tattoo it was. It glowed bright, like embers from a campfire. Before she could stop herself, she shifted her weight and stepped back, only to realize what she was doing and then retook the lost ground.

Tin Man's grin grew broader. Anna ignored the smugness and studied the strange, impossible-to-miss, glowing mark on his chest.

"What's with the technicolor tat?"

Gryton arched his brow but must have understood her question, for he tapped a finger against it, making it glow brighter each time his finger struck skin.

"It's a birthmark."

"Birth? You have parents?" Anna said as she curled her fingers around her sword's hilt. Not that she knew how to use one, but it was a handy place to rest her hand.

"Most living creatures do have them. Parents, I mean."

"Until now I wasn't entirely certain you *were* a living creature. My working theory was a disembodied spirit had taken up residence in an old armor suit."

"Ah," Gryton's fangs flashed in a grin. "As you can see, I'm very much a flesh and blood male. You are welcome to explore if you'd like to put your doubts to rest."

Lame pickup line, dude. Aloud Anna asked, "You mean like with my dagger to see if you bleed like a real flesh and blood person?"

His smile never faltered. "That's not quite what I had in mind..."

No, Anna didn't suppose it was.

Shadowlight growled, the sound more menacing than usual. "I'm hungry, and if we don't go to dinner now, I'm going to take a bite out of Gryton."

The commander burst out laughing, surprising both Anna and Shadowlight.

"Come then, young ones. I'd rather not have a gargoyle take a chunk out of my hide."

Gryton led them back to the hall. It looked much like it always had. The only difference she could see was an increased number of candles and more of the seats were filled than usual. Plus, like Gryton, many of the diners had forgone armor. That didn't mean they were weaponless. Anna still saw lots of daggers, maces, swords and whips.

As they made their way to the high table, she also promised to stop bitching about her outfit. What some of the other diners wore made her attire look positively modest and concealing.

When they reached the high table, there were a few familiar faces.

Commander Gryton took his customary seat and Shadowlight flopped down next to him without being asked. Good kid.

As much as she hated Tin Man, he was still the most known commodity in the room. She'd rather Shadowlight not be exposed to the others any more than necessary. Case in point, Anna's eyes sought out the woman sitting three seats down on Gryton's other side.

The more bodies between Shadowlight and Captain Taryin, the happier it made Anna.

Gryton leaned back in his chair so he could see her past Shadowlight's massive wings. "Now that you've had a chance to meet and be tested by all your mentors, your training will begin in earnest tomorrow. From this point on, you will be expected to complete the tests and tasks set by your teachers and show daily improvement." Gryton paused to sip at his goblet of wine and then continued, "Rest assured that the instructors have orders not to cripple you or the cub. They will practice restraint until you both reach your full magical potential."

Well, isn't that thoughtful of them, Anna muttered silently in her own mind.

"I know you don't trust me—" Anna's snort made him pause, but he merely arched an eyebrow and continued, "but I am much more trustworthy than some."

His gaze cut away toward the blood witch before returning to her.

"No worries. I don't trust anyone here."

"It's likely for the best," Gryton agreed with a shrug and returned to his wine.

The servants placed food in front of Shadowlight and Anna at the same time. The young gargoyle dug into his food with more appetite than usual, his manners completely forgotten.

Anna wasn't particularly hungry but soon cleared her own plate.

Shadowlight glanced back at the large platter of the cooked fowl, looking hopeful and sheepish at the same time. Anna dragged the platter closer. That was all the encouragement the gargoyle needed to refill his plate.

"I see he has a healthy appetite," Gryton said in an offhanded manner.

Anna shrugged. "He's a gargoyle."

"A young and growing one at that. I will make sure that he's given a chance to have another quick meal between some of his classes."

Anna didn't thank him. There was something he wasn't

saying. She could sense it, almost like a smell rising off his skin. Not a lie, no. An omission.

"Your appetites will increase," Gryton said as he nibbled on the leg. "As your metabolisms require more food for your growing bodies. Since Shadowlight isn't yet mature, he'll need more to fuel his growth, but as your own changes occur and your gargoyle nature begins to assert itself, you'll find yourself developing a greater appetite as well."

Anna was already aware of what the Battle Goddess's sessions were doing to them, but she didn't have a solid timeline yet for how quickly they would change.

She needed details if she was going to form a plan that culminated in a successful escape.

"How often will we need to go before the Battle Goddess?" Anna asked between bites of her meal, hoping that it came across as small talk and not an eager inquiry.

This is just polite table talk, nothing more, she projected and hoped Gryton believed the lie.

"Once your training starts in earnest, the Lady of Battles thinks two days between each of her sessions will be optimal for Shadowlight's development. Any closer and it would be too stressful for his body. As he matures, so too will your gargoyle nature."

Okay. So, they had a couple of days before their next visit with the Battle Goddess.

"The blood witch mentioned I'd need a few more sessions before I could start training under her, but Shadowlight has a firmer grasp on his magic, and she thinks he can start tomorrow. Do you agree?"

Gryton chewed thoughtfully at his food. "Yes but stay

close to Shadowlight during his times with Taryin and don't run any errands for her while he is in her company."

Shadowlight had stopped eating to listen to Gryton's words, but he only huffed softly in agreement and then returned to his meal.

She already knew Gryton didn't trust the blood witch from the earlier verbal exchanges between Vaspara and Taryin, yet she hadn't expected him to so openly warn her.

"How long will this process take? I mean until Shadow-light is mature and I'm a full-blooded gargoyle?"

"If you think you'll be able to escape then, I must disappoint you. Our Lady's power will also instill a new sense of loyalty in you both."

"Figured as much. Guess I'm just curious how long it will take until I no longer care about things like escape."

"Three moon cycles, or months as you call it, and then Shadowlight will be mature and you'll have full command of your gargoyle nature." Gryton picked up a warm roll and buttered it. Taking a bite, he chewed as he watched her thoughtfully. "You'll both be well into your training by then. If you exceed our expectations, the Lady of Battles may even send you back to the Mortal Realm at the head of her army."

Anna stared into the mirror-like surface of her drink. That was not how she and the kid were returning to Earth.

It couldn't, no, it wouldn't, come to that. She'd just have to come up with a plan, put it into play, and then success-fully escape before they no longer *wished* to leave.

The meal continued and Gryton chatted about various aspects of their training. On her right side, Captain Sorac added a few other suggestions on how to get Anna up to speed in various martial arts.

"I'll make a sword master out of you, human," Sorac said with a soft hiss. No doubt it was his version of a friendly conversational tone. "I'll beat you into shape over the next moon cycle, you'll see."

Gryton and Sorac leaned back in their seats and broke into a seemingly friendly banter over some of the other captains. They talked about mundane things like Anna and Shadowlight weren't sitting between them, sucking up every little piece of information they let drop.

After a few minutes of nursing her drink, Anna glanced sidelong at Shadowlight. He'd finished another plate and was now glowering down the table toward where the blood witch sat talking with Honnan. Anna didn't blame him. They were her two least-liked and least-trusted acquaintances since she'd come to this place.

Much later, tables were pushed aside, and musicians came out and began to play. The music, played on a variety of foreign stringed instruments and woodwinds, was slow and surprisingly beautiful, not something she'd expect from such a violent and warmongering society.

The first few hauntingly beautiful pieces flowed into more upbeat songs and some of the diners got up and danced while others clapped their hands or stomped their feet in time to the music.

None of the music touched Anna, her heart and mind too full of worry over what this place was going to do to one innocent, young gargoyle.

swordmaster Anna wasn't. She knew that before she'd even set foot in the outdoor practice ring. But she and Shadowlight reported to Captain Sorac for testing as ordered, so here they were. Anna was fully expecting to get her ass beat but compared to some of the other things they'd already endured, it wasn't so strange that she was looking forward to training sessions.

"Draw your sword," Captain Sorac barked as soon as he walked into the sand ring.

Shadowlight complied gracefully, his sword coming free of its scabbard in one smooth motion. Anna copied the kid but already knew her movements were jerkier than his.

Sorac speared her with a look, his expression a blank mask for a heartbeat or two and then he roared with laughter. Between big whoops, he summoned over another of his students. This girl was human-looking, and if Anna was to guess her age, she'd go with seven.

The captain then shooed them into the next ring and

turned his attention back to Shadowlight. Anna went. She wasn't happy to be even that far away from Shadowlight here in this place, but she went.

While Sorac tested the young gargoyle's skills, the girl showed Anna some of the most basic forms of swordsmanship. Distantly, Anna tried to follow the instructions, but her attention was divided. Sorac wasn't holding back in his bout with Shadowlight.

The kid's skills with the sword were much farther along than hers and he was able to block Sorac at first. At least until their mentor upped his game. The strikes came fast and furious, their blades a blur. Shadowlight stumbled and Sorac came far too close to decapitating him. Only the gargoyle's quick reflexes allowed him to recover his balance and block the strike.

She'd expected Sorac to stop at that point. He didn't. The strikes became more brutal.

Anna wasn't even aware she'd burst into motion. Yet she was just suddenly running, that protective magic sleeping inside her roaring awake. Her strength and skills in hand-to-hand combat caught Sorac by surprise and she slapped his sword arm aside and flexed her talons, aiming for the narrow strip of throat just above where his armor ended.

Unfortunately, Sorac's surprise lasted all of two seconds. Grinning at her, he slammed his hand against her breastplate. At the instant of contact, magic rippled in the air, expanding outward. A tremendous wave of force sent her flying backward violently. She didn't stop until she crashed into the crowd of watching students.

Gasping, she looked up into the night sky and stared at

the stars. With shaking hands, she felt up the breastplate covering her chest, expecting to find it and her chest caved inward. Marvel of marvels, it wasn't even dented, and no part of her body was screaming at her about broken bones.

I think that was the mother of all spankings, Anna thought to herself.

"Dafuq?" Anna huffed out as she rolled off the other unfortunate students. "Why didn't you warn me you were into bowling?"

Laughing, Sorac walked over and helped her to her feet.

"Just testing your berserker response. Gryton warned me about it, but I honestly thought he was over exaggerating. So far, you've seemed calm under pressure, but the young gargoyle is a trigger."

Captain Sorac gave her a companionable pat. "I'll guide and hone that into something breathtaking to behold on the battlefield. The Battle Goddess will be impressed."

Faster than she could react, Sorac switched from patting her shoulder to clamping her throat in a vice-like hold. "If you ever attack me again, make sure you can win, or I'll beat you until you cry tears of blood."

Shadowlight snarled in warning. Sorac released Anna and spun to face the gargoyle. "And snarling only warns your opponent of an incoming attack. If you wish to survive, you need to be the master of your instincts."

The growling stopped, but he still flashed a good bit of fang, which Sorac ignored. "The blood witch will start your training in battle magic next. She'll meet you at the stone ring at the south end of the practice fields. There was blood spilled there recently." He pointed off to the left of where they stood. "Captain Vaspara still has command of your control collar. I wanted you and Shadowlight to be able to act freely for this test. But now off you go."

Damn it. How had Anna not noticed Vaspara hadn't transferred control of Shadowlight's collar to Sorac when she'd escorted them to the practice field? She needed to be more observant, not less, if they had any hope of escape.

Mentally kicking herself, she followed as Shadowlight headed off in the direction Sorac had indicated. When they reached the outer edge of the practice field and left its many torches behind, Anna squinted out into the darkness. Downslope of their position, she could just make out a large ring of standing stones backlit by one of the rising moons.

"That looks ominous," Shadowlight said, his tail twitching ever so gently.

"Yep," Anna agreed and doggedly started forward, Shadowlight close on her heels.

With each limping step, her armor grew heavier. She swore it found every last bruise with pinpoint accuracy. If she already hurt this much now, tomorrow was going to be so much more fun.

"Someone needs to remind that sadistic prick that he's not supposed to kill us," Anna muttered as she allowed herself to hobble now that they were out of Sorac's sight.

"At least you didn't break anything," Shadowlight added helpfully.

"Fine, you get to be the bowling ball next time Sorac feels like playing tenpin."

Besides a few bruises that would heal in a day or two thanks to her new gargoyle genetics, she wasn't hurt. At least not physically. Starting now, she really needed to step up her game.

Anna studied the night-shrouded landscape as they approached the standing stones. The blood witch could even now be studying them.

CHAPTER TWENTY-ONE

Shadowlight scented Anna's rising alertness, a scent akin to nervousness, but not quite. His own scent likely betrayed his weariness and the hint of fear. As far as he was concerned, fear was a natural, healthy response when one was walking to meet one such as the blood witch.

Though Anna wasn't a fan of Captain Sorac, he wasn't so bad, and even Gryton didn't make Shadowlight's gargoyle nature scream warnings the way the blood witch did.

He debated attempting to kill her. He'd gladly accept the repercussions if not for two things. First, they'd surely harm Anna instead of him as Gryton had threatened. And second, he wasn't sure if he could match one as powerful as Taryin in battle, even if he caught her unaware.

"I heard that," Anna said along their mental link. *"Don't do anything foolish, kid. We need to learn more about her abilities before we get into a duel with her."*

As usual, Anna's words were wise. He'd heed them. He just didn't like having to work with a creature with such a blackened soul.

They approached the ring of stones. Now that they were closer, the murky red glow cast off by the symbols etched into the stone was easier to see. The breeze shifted, and he caught the scent of old blood and a hint of sugary-tinged rot.

"What's that stench?" Anna used the back of her wrist to cover her nostrils. She had a dagger gripped in each hand. After a moment, she lowered her hand and breathed through her mouth before he could warn her not to. "Gawd. I can taste the vile crap now, too."

"It's the beginnings of a blood magic weaving," he told her.

"How do you know that? It's worse than what we smelled yesterday at Taryin's dungeon abode," Anna made a face. "And we're outside for fuck's sakes. I would've noticed if it was this bad yesterday."

"My father's memories show me some things I'd rather not know. This is one of them." Shadowlight paced up to the outer edge of the standing stones and sneezed violently.

It didn't improve the scent.

He circled the stone ring, scanning for any signs of Vaspara or the blood witch. "I don't see either of the captains," Shadowlight said as he gazed at Anna and then toward the sky. He switched to their mental link, *"Sorac didn't order me to wait for Taryin. Only said that she'd meet us here. I wasn't ordered to stay."*

Excitement made his heart race. His wings unfurled as blood pumped into the membranes.

Anna's hand landed on his shoulder. *"Hold up, kid. This is either a test, a trick, or a trap. All of the above will likely land us back in a dungeon before we can say 'oh shit.'"*

Her words extinguished childish exuberance and his earlier excitement turned to embarrassment. His ears drooped.

"Don't punish yourself for looking for weaknesses in their guard. It might provide our only chance at freedom. This one was just too early and too easy. They won't let their guard down anytime soon. Or, at least, not until we prove our willingness to be good little demonic soldiers." Anna's thoughts felt like a physical hug, so he didn't feel quite so bad about practically leaping into such an obvious trap.

"Well, we might as well get this over with," Anna said aloud and then stepped between two of the standing stones. They flared, the power trapped deep in the stone reacting to her passage.

Shadowlight followed a moment later. As soon as he was inside, a wall of energy expanded between each of the stones until they were surrounded by a solid looking dome.

Twisting, he slapped his blade-tipped tail against the barrier. As he'd expected, the barrier just flared brighter where he struck. Narrowing his eyes and pinning his ears, he edged closer to Anna and waited for an attack.

Anna slowly walked around the stone in the center of the ring, her attention locked on it. Drawing closer, he inhaled. Ah. That's what had caught her attention.

"That's not just a big ass chunk of rock, is it?" She halted before the stone that wasn't a stone.

"No," he agreed.

The magic emanating from the stone fluctuated and then drew in upon itself. The powerful illusion shifted and rippled like living darkness and then vanished in a blink. Captain Taryin stood before them where the rock had been.

"You did well to see past my little spell so quickly. I've fooled more than one of the other captains with it before. What gave me away?"

"Your scent," Shadowlight answered honestly. "We would have picked it up sooner had the other blood magic not overpowered everything else."

The blood witch motioned them over to another flat stone. She settled upon it like she would a bench, but an old reddish stain told any onlooker precisely what it was. He shifted, herding Anna farther from it.

If the blood witch thought to use them to increase her power...

"Fear not, young one. I have no intention of harming you or your Kyrsu. I'm here to instruct you in the ways of battle magic. There are various forms based on what lineage one hails from. But if a person is truly strong in magic, they can learn all the forms."

Anna cut off the blood witch. "What you did there looks like shadow magic but wasn't. The scent was different, so was the feel."

Taryin nodded. "I had an opportunity to study a gargoyle and his shadow magic for many years."

Anna's expression, which had been hostile earlier, shifted to something darker and colder. "You might have enjoyed years of experimenting on Shadowlight's father, but you will not treat the kid in such a way. I won't let you. Understand?"

To Shadowlight's surprise, the blood witch only laughed. "I like my immortal existence. If I did permanent harm to the gargoyle, the Battle Goddess would burn me alive. However, if I killed you, she might let me live."

Shadowlight growled.

"Silence, youngling. I have no wish to destroy your Kyrsu." Taryin smiled, but it was chilling and didn't reach her eyes. "Now, let us begin. I will show you the foundation spells for the most common forms of blood, death, and battle magics."

In the next two hours, the blood witch explained the history of the various magic forms. Then she demonstrated them and asked him to copy what she'd shown him.

Reluctantly, he did as he was told. Some of the spells were familiar from his father's memories, while others were completely foreign. During the uncomfortable training session, Anna sat and glowered. Sometimes she asked questions, even things he was uncertain about, and that's how he knew she was learning alongside him even if she wasn't yet strong enough in magic to work the difficult spells.

By the end of the second hour, he was feeling weary and unclean, as if he were coated with a fine dusting of grime.

Taryin snapped her fingers closed on a bit of blood magic she'd been spinning; the rusty colored flash was now a familiar sight, and he'd long since gone nose-dead to the odor.

"We're almost out of time, since you need to report to Captain Honnan for your lessons in our history," Taryin said, looking altogether too pleased with herself. "But before you go, I would like to do one more spell showing you how to tap into the potency of fresh blood."

"And I'm sure you'll just happen to need blood that isn't your own," said a feminine voice from out in the darkness.

Shadowlight looked over his shoulder. Captain Vaspara stood on the other side of the magic barrier, her arms crossed over her chest.

"Ah, Vaspara," Taryin said with a hint of disdain in her voice. "We were just finishing up, but you're correct, I didn't bring fresh blood for the spell. I've run out since the Rasoren and his Kyrsu deprived me of the fresh bodies I was having delivered yesterday. I'll have to procure a new source soon."

"You do that. Now lower the shield or I'll do it for you," Captain Vaspara warned. "I need to get these two to their next lesson."

The shield surrounding the stones crackled and then vanished from sight. He breathed a sigh of relief as the night breeze blew cool across his skin. Vaspara didn't need to tell him to come, he was more than happy to escape the blood witch.

Anna was right there beside him. When they were out of earshot, she said with a somewhat sickly laugh, "I never thought I'd look forward to history lessons taught by an incubus. But I totally am. Anything is better than where we just were."

"I want a bath," Shadowlight whispered back to her.

"Just one more lesson and then we will be allowed to escape until last meal."

At the mention of food, he perked up a touch.

CHAPTER TWENTY-TWO

Their first week of training turned out to be routine, no better or worse than the first full day of lessons, Anna supposed. As Gryton had promised, every third night they went before the Battle Goddess to undergo the same ritual ordeal they'd survived the first day where Shadowlight was required to absorb a portion of the demigoddess's power, and Anna was force-fed a few drops of the gargoyle's blood.

It was never good. Each time they had to go before the Lady of Battles marked yet another three days where Anna had failed to find an escape.

Weapons practice with Sorac was a favorite session, followed by Honnan's lessons in history. So far, the male demon hadn't tried anything, and Anna was certain that was because Gryton threatened to have the blood witch geld the sex demon if he so much as looked at Anna with a lustful gaze. So, all in all, it could have been much worse.

One week turned into two.

Before long two weeks of training slid into three.

Anna could see the gradual changes in Shadowlight. He was an inch or two taller and she thought he'd bulked up a little more. It was hard to judge with no other gargoyles around to compare him to.

And he wasn't the only one changing. She was growing stronger and faster. It wasn't her imagination either. Captain Sorac had commented on her quicker reflexes.

The Battle Goddess's captains weren't the only ones to notice Anna's new abilities. At the end of every third night, when Anna was just drifting off to sleep after a long night of training and lessons, another terrifying being came to visit her.

Lord Death haunted her dreams, whispering promises of escape if she and the young gargoyle would simply surrender themselves to him.

If she was absolutely certain Shadowlight wouldn't be harmed, Anna would have agreed to go with this other demigod. But he never promised to save anything more than their souls.

He was honest at least. If he found them incurable, he would free their souls before what his sister put into motion could taint their spirits.

Which, hey, was important and all, but Anna would have liked something with better odds than Russian roulette. If what the Battle Goddess had done to Shadowlight was not something Lord Death could fix, then seeking his aid would be tantamount to suicide.

"Simply find the most peaceful darkness within your mind and pass through it to come to me." Lord Death repeated those words at the end of each of his dream visits.

Anna just wasn't that desperate yet.

Though, she might be in the coming weeks if she hadn't found a way to escape with the kid.

"Is it possible for gargoyles to reach Lord Death from anywhere?" Anna asked Shadowlight as she stirred her steaming cup of tea. She was sitting in a chair by the hearth in what Anna had come to think of as the living room. Shadowlight was drowsing in front of the fire.

He blinked open his eyes. "Hmmm, my father's memories say it is possible. It is an offshoot of gargoyle shadow magic."

That actually made sense, in a twisted kind of 'magic' logic.

"I still don't like it," Anna muttered.

"It might be better than staying here." Shadowlight fingered the collar around his throat. "This prevents me from calling shadow magic unless I'm given permission during a training session."

Secretly, that was a relief. She didn't want the kid running back to Lord Death with only a fifty-fifty chance that he'd survive the encounter.

"I've been thinking about the collar. Some of our instructors trust us now more than when we first got here. They're starting to relax. If I can catch one of them off-guard, I might be able to force them into surrendering control of the collar to me," Anna said.

A loud rap sounded at the door and one of the servants quickly opened it.

"Lord Gryton," Lanya said in a voice that was a touch louder than normal. "Shadowlight and Anna are almost ready."

She hadn't said out loud that it was still early, but the question was clear.

Anna wondered why Gryton was here. It wasn't one of the Battle Goddess's ritual days, and Gryton didn't typically seek them out on the days when it was just lessons as usual.

"We'll talk more later," Anna said to Shadowlight. He bobbed his head in agreement.

Together they walked over to greet Gryton.

"You're both to go before the Battle Goddess," he said in a cold, clipped tone.

No niceties or even a bit of flirtation, which she was starting to come to expect.

That couldn't be good. All business was *never* good.

After issuing the order, he turned sharply and marched back out the door and down the hall.

She and Shadowlight scrambled to catch up before he reinforced his statement with a verbal command.

Anna glanced sidelong at Shadowlight and then whispered along their mental link. *"Someone's in a pissy mood."*

Shadowlight huffed in agreement.

When they reached what she'd come to think of as the altar room, she gave it a quick scan. It looked the same as it had yesterday, the two altars made of gray stone with manacles just waiting for them.

Was the Battle Goddess planning to do this daily now? Or had something gone wrong with yesterday's ritual?

Or had the blood witch gone to the Battle Goddess complaining that Anna wasn't progressing fast enough?

Guards came forward to secure them to their altars. They didn't fight. She wanted to though; her gargoyle instincts picked up some hint of danger or new deception, more than usual at least.

They'd just finished chaining Shadowlight down when she heard the Battle Goddess approach. Involuntarily, Anna's muscles tensed. A few seconds later the demigoddess was in her customary place at the top of the stairs.

"My children, I am most proud of your progress." A smile brightened the Battle Goddess's features. "However, Captain Taryin informs me the female half is falling behind in her magic studies because her gargoyle nature isn't developing as it should."

Anna was almost used to the way the demigoddess labeled them, like they were two halves of the same creature, instead of two separate persons. She wondered if that was the plan, to train them to work as such a tightknit unit that she and the kid eventually lost their individuality and just became killing machines ready to carry out all the demigoddess's orders.

It wasn't the most reassuring thought, but it made sense. Gryton had commented more than once that she wanted to create her own version of the Avatars to lead her armies.

On the surface, Anna obeyed and allowed herself to be labeled like an inanimate object, but it didn't mean she was just going to roll over and become whatever the Battle Goddess wished.

With that in mind, a week and a half ago she'd attempted to exert her will over her gargoyle heritage, controlling it, instead of being controlled by it. So far Anna thought she had some success going by how annoyed Captain Taryin had become.

"Tell me, little hybrid," the demigoddess said, "Have you been holding back?"

Anna kept her lips sealed. If she lied, they'd know and punish the kid. If she told the truth, they'd probably punish her disobedience by punishing the kid.

"Are you defying your goddess?" Gryton snapped.

"No," Anna answered when Gryton drew a knife and stepped toward Shadowlight. "At least not with malicious intent. I don't want to lose who I am. But I can feel it happening."

The Lady of Battles settled cross-legged on the top landing. "Your concerns are understandable. However, they are unfounded. You will not become less than you are, nor will you lose your sense of self. You will still be Anna Mackenzie, born to human parents, but you will become more - an immortal, a powerful creature of magic. Whether you wish it or not."

"I'll do better," Anna said a little desperately, sensing her plan was about to go sideways.

"I'm sorry." The deity waved at Gryton and then Shadowlight. Gryton nodded. "I can't allow your fear to hold you back."

"I can overcome this." Anna tugged at her chains.

"Yes. You will, with some help." She looked toward Gryton a second time. "I've changed my mind. Have Captain Ninara summoned here. I'm sure Honnan's twin can help us with this problem."

Commander Gryton relayed the order to have Ninara come to the altar room. Anna hadn't worked with Ninara much, but she hadn't liked what she'd seen either. Worse,

Captain Vaspara had a mildly horrified look on her face before she'd mastered her expression.

Not reassuring. Not in the least.

Anna stared up at the dark ceiling high above, forcing herself to calm as she summoned tendrils of shadow magic. In the first week, she'd learned that the others were unable to sense shadow magic unless she drew on a large outpouring of power. This was just a tiny bit sent to study and infiltrate the links of the chain and the locking mechanism spell on each cuff. Hopefully, it wasn't enough to draw their attention.

All too soon Captain Ninara came striding down the stairs and joined Gryton, Vaspara, Honnan and the other guards circling the altars.

"My Goddess, how may I serve you?"

"The human has reached a plateau in her development, but I think we can force her past it if the young gargoyle's blood becomes more potent. I want you to see if your power can trigger him into the next level of his development."

"I can only try. He may not be old enough for my power to affect him."

"Do not fear, Captain, I will not punish you for something even my magic hasn't yet managed to accomplish."

Ninara nodded and then moved forward to where Shadowlight was chained to the altar.

"Hey!" Anna shouted and pulled at her chains. "Let's all leave the kid out of this. I'll embrace my inner gargoyle or whatever the fuck you want from me. Just leave the kid alone."

"You should've thought of that before trying to resist

the transformation." Gryton laid a finger on her lips and then stroked it over her chin and along the vulnerable skin of her throat. "This will teach you to swallow your stubborn pride and do as you're told."

Anna stared into Gryton's brown, amber-ringed eyes and promised herself she'd see him dead one day for his part in this.

Shadowlight snarled a warning. Anna looked at him and rage rose within her. Ninara was leaning over him, magic rising from her skin and cascading down upon him. He twisted, trying to prevent the foreign power from touching him, but his chains only allowed for a minimal amount of movement.

He snarled louder and lashed out with his tail. The blade-tipped end came within a few inches of impaling the succubus. Only her twin brother's swift reflexes deflected the blow.

A louder, fiercer growl echoed through the vast chamber, and Ninara jerked her head up and glanced over at Anna. There was a look of surprise and a hint of fear in the Captain's eyes.

It fed the wild, chaotic ball of magic and rage in Anna's chest. The power reached some kind of flashpoint, expanding outward beyond her ability to control. Icy power raced down her every limb, covering her skin with gooseflesh and a dusting of frost.

Seeking out the weakness she'd already hunted out in the metal of her chains, she unleashed a savage wave of shadow magic upon that point. Even as she shattered the chains holding her down, the power within continued to rise.

Snarling in victory, Anna rolled off the altar and lunged toward her prey. Talons lengthened from her fingertips and wings shredded her tunic as they burst from her back. She snapped her new wings open to their maximum expanse, instinctively blocking her prey from breaking either left or right.

Kicking out at the succubus with the intent to gut her, Anna was somewhat dumbfounded to see her feet encased in boots instead of ending in long clawed toes. The kick still landed with enough force to lift the other woman off her feet and toss her back from Shadowlight.

Anna leaped to follow. Beating her wings powerfully, she caught the other female and then wrapped her talons around the other's throat. She tried to drag her struggling prey up into the air with her, but she couldn't get lift.

Guards were hauling on the trailing ends of her chains. She snarled at them, then leaped into the air a second time and beat her wings harder. This time she dragged them across the polished floor and smashed them against the altar stone she'd been chained down to only moments ago.

All the while, Ninara twisted and fought, trying to break Anna's hold. Snarling, she buffeted the other woman with shards of shadow magic propelled forward by powerful slaps of her wings. She didn't stop until the succubus was bleeding from her ears, mouth and nose.

Other guards were rushing forward, but they wouldn't be in time to save her.

"Stop," Gryton shouted. "It was a test. Stop now."

Anna snarled at him. He could shout all he wanted. It wouldn't do any good. She didn't have a control collar around her neck.

Her fingers tightened farther around Ninara's slender throat, her talons digging into the soft flesh drawing a flood of rich copper scent and warm blood. The succubus twisted and fought, but her blows bounced off an impregnable shield of Anna's shadow magic.

Gryton and the Battle Goddess both bellowed for order.

Even Captain Honnan was shouting Anna's name. Growling, she tracked his voice, sensing some new danger. She found him poised over Shadowlight with the deadly tip of his sword pressed against Shadowlight's neck. The young gargoyle snarled and broke his chains, deflecting Hannon's sword.

Seeing her opening, Anna tossed the smaller succubus higher up into the air and then kicked out with all the force in her lower body. Ninara flipped through the air and then crashed into her twin brother, and both demons slid across the floor ten feet away. Honnan's sword spun through the air before landing on the floor and skidding until Captain Sorac's foot slammed down upon it.

Sorac wasn't fighting. He was laughing, deep body-shaking chuckles.

"Anna, stop." There was a command there, one so deep and pure she couldn't fight it.

Anna's muscles tensed. She wanted to finish off her prey, but with a soft snarl, she landed and dropped to all fours. Stalking over to the one who'd issued the order, she inhaled deeply of Shadowlight's comforting scent. She shoved her muzzle against his side and on up to his shoulders and face, where she gave him a quick lick. She tasted no taint and found no injuries.

The most powerful scent wafting from his skin was nothing more concerning than his surprise, so she relaxed marginally and dropped back down to crouch at his side. Though her tail still flicked in a slow warning to the others in the room, telling them if anyone attempted to harm her Rasoren, she'd tear them apart.

"Easy, Anna," Shadowlight said with another reassuring pat to her head.

"It was a test," Gryton added, "Shadowlight was never in danger."

Anna growled at Gryton. He stood unmoving with his sword out, blade bare.

"Don't be foolish," he warned.

The other guards she'd used to mop the floor had fallen back. Only Captains Vaspara and Sorac were still within striking distance, but they weren't presently threatening Shadowlight, so she ignored them and leaned into Shadowlight's fingers while he gave her a good head scratch. Her tail still lashed back and forth in warning.

Sorac held his hands out, showing them empty of weapons. "I'm not a threat." He said with another laugh, "but I'd pay dearly to see that again."

Anna growled when he took a step forward, but he ignored her. "Told you, you'd be breathtaking in battle if you learned to tame that berserker rage into something more constructive. Though, this wasn't what I had in mind."

"Spectacular!" Loud clapping accompanied the words. The Lady of Battles was standing on her customary landing. "You sliced through Ninara's protective magic like it wasn't even there. What a breathtaking show of raw, untrained power. And Shadowlight has begun to master his control over you. Once you're both fully trained, you will bring great honor to my kingdom."

Anna growled softly, but the Lady of Battles didn't seem concerned. She merely turned and vanished through the darkened archway behind the landing.

The sound of the Battle Goddess's chains hadn't even faded entirely before more guards arrived, hauling ass down the opposite set of stairs.

Eyes narrowing, Anna decided if anyone threatened her Rasoren again, she would kill them, test or no.

She was so focused on the squad of approaching enemy, she wasn't expecting the weight of Shadowlight's restraining hand on her shoulder. *"Anna, you need to calm yourself."*

The touch of his mind startled her out of her murderous, predatory state.

Blinking, she shook her head. *"What the fuck just happened?"*

Shadowlight rubbed at his muzzle, looking somewhat guilty. *"You shifted to gargoyle form and lost your mind for a little while. Gryton told me to order you to stop before someone got killed."*

"Eh?"

"I commanded you." He glanced sidelong at her. *"I'm sorry."*

Anna huffed. *"Well, don't be. It's better than us both landing back in the dungeon. Shit, I can't believe I'm a gargoyle."*

Events were still a little blurry, but the weight of wings dragging on her back was solid proof of her new gargoyle body. She touched her face and nearly went cross-eyed staring at her muzzle.

Wings? Check. Muzzle? Check.

She half turned to get a look at her wings. As she did, something dragged on the floor and bumped against her legs.

She spun in a circle to get a better look at it. "Holy fuck, I've got a tail." But of course she did.

Tail? Check.

Horns?

Reaching up she slammed her hand into one and then was more careful at exploring the other. Yep. Horns.

"You have gargoyle ears, too," Shadowlight said and touched one. She flicked them back and forth trying to evade the kid's ticklish touch.

"Hey, stop that." He did and then moved to her two horns. All the while his expression said he was delighted by the changes.

"You're nearly full-grown." He moved to her wings next, stretching them out and comparing them to his. His were bigger, but overall, so was he, so it made sense his wings would be larger. Anna tried not to feel competitive about it.

"It was as I expected," Captain Taryin said, having returned from wherever she'd vanished to when Anna had first taken on gargoyle form.

Had the blood witch been present when Anna was going berserk, she would have been her primary target.

"Your own insecurities were holding you back from your new potential," Taryin continued, not knowing she was in danger of still becoming a target. "All you needed was the proper incentive."

Gryton stepped between them and looked Anna up and down. She realized she'd shredded her tunic and pants. Plus, there was a draft on her hind end where she now had a brand-new tail. At least the tunic's long top covered the necessary bits. Anna would look into getting the magic, shapeshifting clothing the gargoyles wore as soon as she could talk with Lanya.

Unconcerned by Anna's wardrobe malfunction, Gryton continued his conversation with the blood witch. "You are correct. I'll remember this while planning her future training."

Gryton's squirrely little mind was already proposing ways to use Anna's new gargoyle strength and subsequent instincts against her.

Great.

Shadowlight sat and leaned against her. Anna was reminded of another time she'd seen the kid do this to another gargoyle. That time it had been Gregory.

The kid might not even realize it, but he was looking for a protector. She just wished Gregory was here because Anna knew she was nowhere near good enough to protect the kid from all the enemies here.

"Anna needs rest," Shadowlight barked out.

"No doubt she does," Gryton agreed. "Shifting for the first time is wearying. Go. Take the rest of the night off. I'll adjust Anna's future training to include her new form. In the meantime, I'll have a meal sent to your chambers."

Anna barely listened, too distracted by the feel of her new wings being tugged on. She would've slapped the hands away except it was Shadowlight examining them again.

He seemed to be exercising them. Physiotherapy for wings?

"You don't want your wings to get a chill. You worked up a sweat and the muscles aren't used to work yet. If you don't cool them down slowly, they'll cramp." He released his hold on her wing and stepped back.

Well, he'd know what he was talking about. She gave them a few experimental stretches and could feel what he was referring too, so she beat her wings slowly every minute or so. Now that the show was over, the other captains were leaving.

Dismissed, she and Shadowlight started away but didn't get more than twenty feet before the blood witch called out. "The hybrid might need rest, but the gargoyle is perfectly capable of attending his lessons."

"Nope." Anna spun around. Facing Commander Gryton, she stared him down.

She didn't know which way the silent battle of wills would go until he opened his mouth and broke the silence with a profoundly male chuckle.

"As the Kyrsu commands."

The blood witch appeared furious but swallowed her complaints and stormed away.

Anna and Shadowlight continued up the steps, eager to escape under the archway and into the hall before Gryton changed his mind.

CHAPTER TWENTY-THREE

By the time they made it halfway back to their chambers, Anna was shaking from the effects of adrenaline and her shift to gargoyle form. She walked on two legs because that was still more natural and presently, she wasn't sure if she could coordinate four limbs at once.

Shadowlight paced alongside her on all fours, his tail flicking with concern. Every few steps he would gaze up at her. The small wrinkles around his eyes also confirmed his worry.

"I'll be fine once I get back to my room and sit for a bit," Anna told him, nearly tripping over the words. Speaking now that she had a muzzle was freaking strange, but she could still talk, so that was a plus. Her voice even sounded similar. Maybe a touch deeper.

"I'll share power with you once we're there," he said, sounding far too adult and decisive.

Anna knew gargoyles could strengthen and heal each other by sharing power, but a part of her didn't want his help. Obviously, he was growing stronger and his power was changing, Anna thought sourly as she looked down at her new gargoyle body. It wasn't just his power that was changing.

In the last few days, she had noted he was more forthright and prone to making decisions for them. He still sought her opinion, but he was forming his own now too. Which would be fine under normal circumstances, but she was now worried something darker was going on. He'd ordered her to stop during the fight and she'd been forced to obey. No, not forced. She'd wanted to obey with every fiber of her being.

They were changing faster than even Gryton had thought they would.

That was bad. So, very fucking bad.

Yep, drawing on more of his power wasn't going to be beneficial.

"I'll be fine," Anna told him. "Promise. I just need time to get used to the new me."

He made a grumpy little sound but didn't contradict her. "I'll send a servant to fetch you something to eat and drink if the news of your change hasn't already reached them."

"Fine." She wasn't going to refuse food because she was already starting to feel hungry.

They reached their assigned chambers and Anna made straight for a large chair. Shadowlight grabbed her arm before she could throw herself down. "Careful of your wings."

Crap. The last thing she needed was a trip to the doctors, or menders as they called them here. Anna unfurled her wings and fought for balance as their weight screwed up her center of gravity. With an annoyed huff, she eyed the chair again. "I've seen you and Gregory rest on your wings from time to time without coming to harm."

"Yours are new, and though large enough to carry your weight in the air, aren't fully grown yet. The bones, joints, and tissues will be soft and prone to damage." Shadowlight poked and prodded at her joints as he spoke.

"Hey, that hurts!" Anna twisted out of his reach.

"Don't be a baby. Just sit on benches and sleep belly down for a few days," he advised with a shrug. Then he continued their conversation using their mental link. *"We'll have a much better chance at escaping now that you are fully gargoyle."*

Anna didn't disagree. *"I'll have to learn to fly first. Something better than that drunken sailor flopping."*

"I'm sure Sorac will add that to our lessons tomorrow. He's been talking about starting aerial combat in the last two lessons."

That surprised Anna. She never got a chance to hear everything Sorac discussed with Shadowlight because she was too busy fighting her own opponent and not getting impaled by the business end of a sword.

"Flight lessons. Can't wait." Anna settled on a bench facing away from the fire. The heat felt good on her aching wing joints. When Shadowlight turned away to find a servant and see about food, Anna took the time to gaze at her body, a strange new landscape of rippling muscles and onyx skin.

At first, she'd been too full of adrenaline and the compulsion to protect and hadn't noticed the signals her body was sending. Her wings weren't the only thing bitching. Her feet hurt like hell. Glancing down, she saw the busted laces and the split seams. So much for her favorite boots. Prying them off, she stared at her feet and wiggled her talon-tipped toes.

"Ouch."

"What's wrong?" Shadowlight raced over to her side.

"I now know what an elephant would feel like wearing stilettos."

Shadowlight gave her his best 'humans are strange' look. But before he could say anything, Lanya entered the chamber carrying a basket of fresh linens. Her gaze landed on Shadowlight and showed surprise at seeing him during the time when he was normally training. Then her eyes slid past him and spotted Anna.

"Oh! My lady, you must be exhausted. Let me just put these down." Her voice increased in volume as she hurried into the other room. "I'll have the children fetch food and drink for you while I draw you a bath. The heat will help relax your muscles."

"Thank you," Anna said and slumped down on the bench, using her arms as a pillow. The older woman was already bustling away.

Anna must have dozed for a bit because next she knew, Lanya had returned with her son and daughter in tow. They carried large trays of food.

While her children were moving a small table closer to the bench, their mother eyed Anna's shredded tunic. "I see I will have to adjust your wardrobe as well. Hmmm...Give me an hour. By the time you've eaten and soaked, I'll have something new for you to wear."

Anna just nodded. Presently she was happy to lay on the bench and absorb the fire's heat. Shadowlight settled on the floor between her and the fireplace.

"I promise I won't fall off the bench and roll into the coals."

"You should eat before you fall asleep."

"Nah. Chewing is too much work. I'll just nap for a bit first."

Shadowlight snorted with humor and lavished her with several sloppy gargoyle kisses. He refused to stop.

"Ugh. Gross! Stop." But it worked. She was now sitting up and Lanya shoved a bowl of what smelled like home-made soup into her hands. Anna didn't used to be a soup fan — but she found herself happy to eat whatever was put in front of her these days.

She perked up more when she smelled the warm, buttery breadsticks.

"I'm not even going to ask what magic you performed to pull this together this time of night."

"I told my son to tell Cook that if she didn't have something to feed a hungry new gargoyle, said gargoyle might come and eat her."

Anna's muzzle twisted into a gargoyle smirk. "Whatever works."

Shadowlight, always ready to eat, sat next to her and took another of the bowls.

After the first bowl of soup and three breadsticks, she started to feel human again. Well, maybe not human. She flexed her wings and craned her neck to behold the full effect.

"So freaking weird." And they were, but the more she

shifted and flexed them, the more a part of her they became. The wings and tail really drove home the fact she wasn't human anymore.

She reached up to touch the horns. "Things have ventured into the land of the bizarre."

"I imagine you will grow accustomed to all the changes in a few days. When I emerged from my mother's hamadryad, I was uncoordinated for the first hour but was soon able to fly with my father. Your instincts will guide you."

"Not sure if I'll ever grow accustomed to this." Anna thumped her tail against the bench a few times. "But if these changes will help us escape, I'll gladly embrace my new gargoyle nature."

After they finished their meal, Anna went for a long soak. Eventually, Lanya returned with towels and ordered her off to bed.

Anna dragged her ass off to bed and then tossed herself face first onto the covers and arranged her wings over herself.

"At least they're good for something," Anna muttered to the servant before drifting off to sleep.

CHAPTER TWENTY-FOUR

Her own stomach growling woke Anna. *What the hell, didn't I just feed the beast?* Grunting she tossed back her blanket and looked around. *Wait?*

Anna touched her back and then glanced down her body. *Oh, thank God.* The entire 'turning into a gargoyle' episode was just a dream. Sighing, she dropped her head back against her pillow, only then realizing she was naked under the blanket. She never slept naked.

The hell?

But a knock at her door heralded Lanya's entrance. Her arms were full of another black and burgundy garment. Formal dinner wear, then, not comfortable training tunics. Ugh.

"Did you sleep well?"

"Er…" Anna lifted the blanket and arched an eyebrow.

"When I came in to check on you, I found you'd returned to your human form sometime while you were sleeping," the servant explained. "You didn't wake when I covered you with a blanket, so I left you to sleep off yesterday's trauma."

Anna frowned, realizing how out of it she must have been. Normally she slept lightly. Her frown deepened as she reached for Shadowlight's mind. She calmed a moment later when she got a sleepy mental grunt from him.

Good. He wasn't presently in danger.

"No need to worry," Lanya said, "The gargoyle child is fine. I told him and Commander Gryton you needed to be left alone to rest."

Anna gave herself a little shake and a mental command to wake up. "Gryton visited while I was asleep?"

"Yes, but Shadowlight wouldn't let him take more than three steps in from the hall, and I told the Commander that I would be glad to relay any message."

And that's why Anna never slept in the nude. It was tempting fate. "What did Tin Man want?"

The servant winced at the nickname. "Commander Gryton will be having last meal with you and Shadowlight here in your chambers."

"Lucky us."

"Here's a dress you can wear tonight since you shifted back to human form." The servant laid the clothing out on the end of the bed. "While you were sleeping, I also spoke with the seamstresses and the metalsmiths. By tomorrow, the seamstresses will have some ward-spelled clothing that will shapeshift with you, and within a few days, the metalsmiths will have new armor made to fit your gargoyle form."

Anna hadn't even thought about the next time she'd

have to shift to gargoyle. Hopefully, it wouldn't require further dramatics. "Thanks."

"Of course," Lanya said and started to brush invisible dust from the dress.

The whole idea of having a body servant was just down-right weird, so Anna shooed her away and dressed. This was a simple, elegant dress. No slits up to the thigh with matching daggers.

When she emerged from her room, it was to see Brannon being scolded by his mother. "Why isn't Shadowlight ready yet? Commander Gryton will be here any moment."

The gargoyle in question was just emerging from his own room, stretching and loosening muscles like he'd fallen back asleep after Anna had woke him earlier with her mental touch.

"Hey," she said. He dropped to all fours and padded over to her. When he bumped his muzzle under her hand looking for a scratch, she obliged. "Sounds like we are getting an unwanted visitor."

Shadowlight growled under his breath and Anna tapped the side of his muzzle.

"Behave. We don't need trouble with Gryton."

A flash of fang expressed what Shadowlight thought of that.

"I'm serious. Go let Brannon get you ready for dinner." *Or breakfast or whatever damn meal of the day it is,* she thought to herself. *Stupid nocturnal cycle.*

Shortly after Shadowlight disappeared into the bath-room, a small army of servants arrived carrying covered dishes. Lanya oversaw the placement of everything and then ordered the servants away again. Then she roamed around the room, lighting more candles as she went.

When she was done, the room had a romantic candle-light dinner vibe going for it. Fuck. There was even a spray of flowers for a centerpiece. Double fuck.

She was probably reading more into it than there was, though. After all, there were three table settings, so it wasn't like it was a romantic dinner with just her and Tin Man.

The door opened again. This time Lanya's husband entered. He held the door open and Gryton swept in.

He wasn't dressed in his customary armor. This time he was bare-chested, his glowing tattoo on full display, drawing the eye to his battle-hardened form. Dark leather pants molded to his powerful thighs and calves.

Such a waste that he was also an evil prick in service to an equally monstrous demigoddess who wanted to rule all three realms.

Gryton marched over to the table without so much as a hello, then waving off the servants without even looking at them, he poured two goblets of wine. He held one out to her with an eyebrow raised as if challenging her.

Anna grunted, walked over to the table, sidestepped him, and then poured her own goblet.

Gryton watched her as he set down his spare goblet, unflustered by the brush off.

"You look lovely," Gryton said between sips of his wine, his gaze never straying from her.

"Just rolled out of bed, actually. Feel kinda like I was run over by a LAV. Probably look like it too." Anna grunted and parked her ass against the table and glowered at Tin Man. "But I guess there's no accounting for taste."

Gryton's expression turned merry. "If I understand your reference, you're referring to one of those big, ugly, metal, wheeled monstrosities," his hands drew a pretty good approximation of the boxy shape of a Light Armored Vehicle, "that roar and belch fumes, yes?"

"Ugly? Have you actually looked at some of your minions lately?"

"But surely your kind could have created something more pleasing to the eye? And quieter."

Anna didn't respond and Gryton returned to his drink.

Lanya exited Shadowlight's room and approached them. When she reached them, she bowed deeply. "Shadowlight will be along shortly. Is there anything else you would like?"

"No. Leave us," Gryton's tone left no room for question. Lanya bowed and departed.

Once they were alone, Gryton turned to look at the door leading to the bathroom. Anna heard the sounds of splashing and the servant boy's wry complaint about how bathwater was supposed to remain in the tub.

"I didn't know you were coming over for dinner or Shadowlight and I would have been ready sooner," Anna said.

"Actually, I came early hoping to catch you alone. There is something we should discuss that could be mutually beneficial." Gryton stood and walked around the end of the table. He leaned a hip against the dark wood and continued to sip at his drink, but he now watched her with something other than humor.

Yep. Here it comes. Anna had been expecting Tin Man to make some kind of play for days now.

He reached out and caressed her cheek. "You truly are a stunning female."

"I'm supposed to be flattered, I assume."

Gryton chuckled. "You don't sound the least bit flattered, but I am telling the truth, which is rare. And I don't often express interest in women, which is also a rare truth."

"You prefer men," Anna drank from her goblet to cover her surprise since she hadn't seen that coming, "but you'll swing on over to the other side of the fence if it suits your ambitions?"

Gryton's thumb played along her lower lip. "You misunderstand. I don't often find a partner I consider worth the effort to pursue."

You're still totally an evil prick. Move along now.

"My choosiness doesn't mean I am unskilled. I am far older than you; with age comes experience."

Again, that smile; the one that didn't reach his eyes. *Nope, so not interested.*

"My life is complicated enough as it is. I don't need a man to fuck it up more." Anna brushed his hand away. "Thanks for the offer though."

Something other than humor and lust glimmered in his eyes. "You could at least wait to hear me out before turning me down."

"Your offer would have to be damn good to be worth the aggravation of going to your bed." Anna pretended boredom. "Go on, let's hear what you have to offer."

Gryton looked startled. "You're offering sex as payment

for some favor I might bestow?" His brows arched up. "I didn't think you are that kind of female."

"No. Not for money or jewelry or some silly privileges." Anna said, narrowing her eyes. "It would have to be something much bigger."

Gryton snorted. "Like control of a certain slave collar?"

"The removal of Shadowlight's collar," Anna clarified, "But we both know that isn't going to happen."

"No," Gryton agreed.

Anna stood up and met his gaze. "Then you have nothing I'm interested in trading for."

Gryton stepped closer. "I like your ruthlessness. It will serve you well here."

Anna held her ground, not allowing him to back her against the table. When he stepped closer, she cupped the front of his pants and flexed her fingers. Claws sprang from the tips, digging into Tin Man's junk.

His eyes widened a touch, but he merely laughed. "No woman has ever been brave or foolish enough to venture there uninvited."

Anna just shrugged and held her ground, flexing her claws ever so slightly. Gryton neither pushed into nor pulled away from what had to be a very unpleasant prickle. Talk about having balls of steel.

"I could make yours and the child's stay here more pleasant."

"I doubt that."

He arched an eyebrow. "What if I reassigned Captain Taryin to the outer lands? The stone armies always need tending and feeding by ones strong in magic."

Hmmm. Getting the blood witch reassigned farther away from Shadowlight would be a bonus.

A moment later the bathroom door opened and Shadowlight stepped out, his ears perked forward, no doubt with eagerness at the smell of food. At least until he saw Gryton and her having their battle of wills. Shadowlight loosed a roar and lunged across the room.

"Halt," Gryton bellowed.

The young gargoyle leaped forward like he didn't even feel the bite of the slave collar as it blazed bright as day. One moment, she was ready to remove Gryton's balls, the next he was gone. Two seconds after that, he crashed into the wall at the opposite end of the room.

Gryton recovered quickly and was already on his feet, summoning a raging wall of fire magic. Anna darted forward, putting herself between Tin Man and Shadowlight.

"Enough," she yelled, magic rising up inside her. She fought back the gargoyle nature that wanted to come out and play. Nope. Not going to happen.

Drawing a deep breath, she placed a restraining hand on Shadowlight's shoulder when he moved to sidestep around her and go after Gryton. The firm pressure of her grip was enough to catch his attention and he glanced back at her. Though a low growl still issued from his throat, he obeyed her command.

"Gryton, you brought that on yourself," Anna said to him and was relieved to see he wasn't advancing on the young gargoyle. Next, she looked to Shadowlight. "And what you saw was Gryton and me having a disagreement.

Thank you for your aid, but it wasn't required. I had Gryton well in...hand."

Tin Man snorted. "Anna *was* doing just fine protecting her own virtue."

Shadowlight growled softly again, but when he didn't further threaten Gryton, the commander swallowed back his fire magic and gave them both a chilling smile. "Now that we got that out of the way, I believe we should eat this meal before it gets cold."

After much glowering and a bit of posturing, all three of them took a seat and started to eat. Though it was more to get it over with than out of actual hunger.

But Anna's mind was on other things. Like the way Shadowlight had been able to resist Gryton's command. That was very interesting. And more interesting, Gryton didn't strengthen the spell or call the guards. It was like he was expecting the response he'd gotten.

What game was Gryton playing at here?

Then it clicked. This was just the second part of Gryton's earlier test. It wasn't anything like she had expected, but the longer they sat and ate without saying a word to each other, the more confident she became.

At last, they finished the meal and Gryton stood and started for the door.

"Did we pass or fail your test?" Anna asked as she watched Gryton stride across the floor.

He halted but didn't look back at them. "This was Shadowlight's test. He surpassed even my expectations. That collar would have inflicted enough damage to force any normal gargoyle to shift to his stone form to heal. The Battle Goddess will be pleased."

She might not be the only one. Anna didn't miss how the kid stood a little taller at Tin Man's words.

Damn it.

They needed to escape sooner rather than later if Shadowlight was actually preening at a few words of praise from Gryton.

Tin Man would not be Shadowlight's new father figure.

Hell to the no.

Gryton continued to the door but paused before opening it. "Shadowlight will get a new, more powerful collar tomorrow. Don't bother attempting escape. I will be tripling the guards and will have the blood witch create a few nasty surprises along the perimeter for the unwary. And, Anna, nothing I said to you was a lie. My offer still stands."

The door closed with a thud and Gryton was gone. Shadowlight growled softly and Anna was tempted to join him.

"He's going to be a thorn in our side," Anna muttered as she scratched Shadowlight between the ears.

CHAPTER TWENTY-FIVE

The next night Anna and Shadowlight reported to the practice ring as usual only to find Captain Sorac missing and Vaspara there in his place, instructing his regular students. Folding her arms against her chest, Anna glowered and flicked her wings in annoyance.

She wouldn't admit it to anyone, but she'd been a touch anxious about tonight's session. It was supposed to be her first flight lesson. Earlier, she'd managed to shapeshift into full gargoyle form without any kind of help. She hadn't even needed a rest afterward, for which she was glad. It meant she was getting stronger. Hopefully, luck would be with her and she wouldn't humiliate herself too badly, or crash and break something.

She'd hyped herself up and was ready to begin, or at least, get this first flight behind her and improve from there. However, apparently, Sorac wasn't as hyped.

Which annoyed her greatly. The brute was never late. "Where's Sorac?"

Vaspara glanced over her shoulder. "Ah. You're early. Good."

The captain finished going over one of the sword forms with a young girl with a mop of brown curly hair. When Vaspara was done, she turned back to Anna and Shadowlight.

"Captain Sorac will meet us along the southern cliffs. Come, I'll show you the way." Vaspara gestured for them to follow.

Anna and Shadowlight dropped to all fours and paced after her retreating form.

Leading them out of the practice field, she guided them along the fortress's southern curtain wall. Here the wind howled, buffeting them with sudden shifts in the air currents. The ground grew steeper and rockier as the green grass gave way to a drop-off, leaving only a narrow trail with the towering wall on the left and empty sky on the right.

The succubus seemed unconcerned by the sheer drop just feet away. She even stooped to pick up the occasional fist-sized rock to toss down the side of the cliff so she could listen as it bounced and smashed its way down the cliff face.

Anna grit her teeth. The evil bitch had to be doing it on purpose just to rattle her.

"Here we are," Vaspara said, as they, at last, eased around a sharp bend in the trail.

Anna and Shadowlight followed close on her heels.

Glancing around, Anna didn't see what made 'here' special enough to warrant being a destination. The path was only slightly less narrow than the part they'd just left.

Though, they were somewhat more protected from the wind, since this section was shielded from the prevailing winds by a large outcropping of rock jutting from the cliff side.

There was enough room for her and Shadowlight to crouch shoulder to shoulder and look out over the dark valley below them. The two moons were sufficiently bright for her gargoyle vision to pick out small details far below. A small herd of wild goat-like creatures were picking their way up the rocky lower slopes, grazing on what sparse clumps of grass they could find.

"Captain Sorac will be here shortly," Vaspara said and patted them both on the shoulder. "Good luck."

With that she left, leaving Anna and Shadowlight to gawk after her.

"She's just leaving us here?" Shadowlight said in disbelief.

"Seems that way." Anna scanned the sky, and then the rockface around them. "This totally feels like a test."

"I hate tests," Shadowlight said with a little growl at the end.

She was about to agree when a massive black shadow sailed over a ridge and into the valley below.

"Holy fuck, what is that? And is it hungry?" Anna switched to their mental link so she wouldn't give away their location to the flying, transport truck-sized shadow. It climbed higher with breathtaking speed, and soon its massive wingspan was blocking out the stars. Silhouetted against the night sky, its sinewy body and long serpentine neck were displayed to full advantage.

"I'm not sure. It's too far away and it's downwind of us," Shad-

owlight said and leaned out into the air to try and get a better look.

"Don't dislodge any loose rocks. It's probably got super hearing since it's hunting at night."

Shadowlight didn't disagree.

The beast, dragon was the name that came to Anna's mind, loosed a roar and twisted in the air, diving down toward the herd of wild goats. Its maw gaped open again, but this time instead of a roar, a gout of flame burst forth.

It was an honest-to-God fire-breathing dragon.

A hungry fire-breathing dragon by the way it snatched up the cooked goats and gobbled them down. It made quick work of its meal while still on the wing before climbing back into the sky where it circled lazily.

Anna thought it was leaving until one of its diamond-bright eyes zeroed in on their perch and it rolled in the air, streaking back toward them. Its jaws parted in a predatory smile and the amber glow of fire became visible through the rows of deadly teeth.

Oh. Crap.

"Anna, it's—"

"Going to barbecue us! Move!" She slammed her shoulder into Shadowlight's back and shoved for all she was worth. A second later Shadowlight was falling. She only had time to note his wings snap open as he began a swift descent.

Praying to whatever god might be listening, Anna launched herself off the narrow ledge just before a stream of fire hit the cliff somewhere above her head.

She'd lost Shadowlight in the seconds after she'd launched herself from the cliff. Where the hell was he?

Anna desperately tried to find him, but the wind buffeted her now that she was out in the open and her wings flailed, her tail instinctively lashing back and forth to level out her flight. Cartwheeling out of control, she was about to smash into a fast approaching ridge but then Shadowlight was suddenly directly in front of her and his voice whispered in her mind.

"Anna, follow my lead. The wind is your friend. Let it fill your wing membranes."

"Friend my ass!"

Shadowlight stayed directly ahead of her, blocking out her view of impending doom, but even though she was only moments away from wrecking on the rocks, she somehow managed to listen to his continued instructions. The kid was calm in the face of death, she'd give him that.

Slowly, her flight leveled out, and he guided her away from the razor-sharp rocks that would shred her wings and break her bones. When they were halfway to the valley floor, and the dubious safety it represented, Anna chanced a glance behind, wondering why the winged transport truck hadn't flamed her good.

The beast was on her ass. Literally on her ass! The tip of his nose almost touching her tail. Shadowlight must have known, for he banked hard to the left, circling back toward the cliffs. Anna followed suit, knowing they weren't going to make it, not both of them.

Summoning shadow magic, she readied herself to send it stabbing into the creature's eyes. She didn't know if it would be effective, but it might slow the beast down, distract it, or piss it off enough to get it to follow her instead of the kid.

"Anna, it is Sorac," Shadowlight said, his voice penetrating her spinning thoughts.

No.

It couldn't be.

She chanced another look behind. The beast was grinning at her.

"You've got to be freaking kidding me! I hate you so much right now," Anna shouted behind her as she continued to follow Shadowlight. She was tempted to bite the kid in the tail for his part in this, too. He knew and didn't say anything.

"Why didn't you tell me it was Sorac!"

"I tried."

"Not hard enough!"

"You shoved me off a cliff!"

"Now, now, children. Stop fighting and follow me," Sorac the dragon said in a booming voice behind her. He swiftly outpaced them in the air and came to a graceful landing on a large flat section of cliff that looked like it had been carved for that purpose.

Shadowlight landed next. Anna followed him in, where she managed a sort of controlled crash. She gave herself a shake and then went and sat off by her self.

Seated, she craned her neck to look up at Sorac. "So, you're a dragon. Guess I should have put two and two together. Shadowlight said you were a fire elemental and you have scales."

"I," he puffed out his chest and stretched his neck proudly, "am a firedrake, not a dragon. One of those fat lizards would never be able to keep up with me."

Okay. Note to self. Firedrakes were elitist and touchy.

Sorac bent his neck to bring his large head in close to her. She couldn't tell his color in the darkness, but his plate-sized scales gleamed. If she was to speculate, she'd guess his coloring to be black or some other dark color. Maybe a deep green or a wine tone.

It was too bad they never trained in daylight. She'd bet he was stunning. Though it didn't matter how pretty he was, she was still pissed off at him.

"I didn't think you could possibly be worse at anything than you were with the sword," Sorac said. "I've just been proven wrong.

Was the prick actually bitching about her poor showing after he tried to fry her? "Hey! You tried to barbecue me. I didn't have time to get ready."

"Barbecue?" He huffed softly, steam curling from between his lips. "I don't know what that is, but I didn't try to harm you. That was only a bit of fun. In the future don't run from a firedrake, we can't help but give chase. It's in our nature."

"Jeez, thanks for the warning." Anna rolled her eyes heavenward.

"You're welcome," Sorac said with a snort of humor. "Now, let's try to improve on that shameful first flight."

PART THREE

CHAPTER TWENTY-SIX

A year ago, if anyone told Lillian she would be spending her days watching an elite military team track down and 'kill' fae hidden by powerful magic, she wouldn't have believed them. Mind you, her everyday life was on a sliding scale of the mildly odd to breathtakingly bizarre.

Hence, she was standing in the headquarters for the joint task force watching the mission unfold on a monitor streaming a live feed from the soldiers' body cams. So far, the soldiers were winning, having managed to track, locate, target and 'kill' each of the fae hiding from the patrol.

They weren't using live rounds, of course, and the fae weren't hunting the humans, but Lillian was still impressed with what the humans had accomplished. And it wasn't all thanks to Gregory and Daryna's training, either. In the past few weeks, the military teams had surpassed even Gregory's hopes, not that her closed-mouthed mate would praise a human.

Soon, she promised herself, *soon we'll be ready to launch a mission to rescue Shadowlight and Anna.*

She didn't fear they'd fail in their mission. Gregory never failed her, but she feared Shadowlight and Anna's condition after all this time.

Yesterday when she'd shared her fears with Gregory, he'd assured her that as long as they were still alive, he and Daryna could heal anything that had been done to them. And the Battle Goddess would not kill Shadowlight or Anna. She needed them.

That still hadn't been all that comforting, but then he'd explained that since time flowed differently here than in the Magic Realm, only about five weeks had passed there compared to the eight weeks here.

Five weeks was still plenty of time to do horrible things to her little brother. And Lillian didn't fool herself; as much as Anna would try to protect the young gargoyle, there was nothing she could do as a fellow prisoner.

Having to wait until the human-fae teams were adequately trained to attempt a rescue mission was horrible enough on its own, but there were other stresses in Lillian's life. Her hands strayed to her belly. Having Gregory's child made her happier than she could ever express, but it also added another layer to her fears. If she could not protect her brother, how was she going to safeguard her child in the coming months?

"They have done very well in recent sessions," Daryna said, drawing Lillian back to the training session and the others all standing around watching.

"Yes," Gregory agreed. "They are almost ready to venture into the Magic Realm."

"I would like to drill them in the layout of the fortress city and the lands around it first," Daryna added, but nodded, "though, I agree."

"I told you they were ready," Major Resnick said, and then came to stand at Lillian's shoulder, where he frowned down at the screen showing a soldier targeting the pooka.

Lillian knew the waiting hadn't been easy on Resnick either. Anna was like a daughter to him.

And then there was Anna's real father, Brigadier General Mackenzie. The day after Daryna had received word from Gryton of Anna's capture, the general had stormed into the workroom where Major Resnick was overseeing Lillian and Gran as they created ward spells for the human weapons.

The general had bellowed about Resnick's incompetence for a full minute. Lillian knew it was a father's worried reaction. When she'd seen him a second time, he'd been cool and composed as one would expect of a highly decorated general.

But even after they rescued Anna and Shadowlight, Lillian still thought there might be trouble.

The general didn't strike her as the type to meekly accept that his daughter was now magically bound in servitude to another being. And Gregory and Daryna weren't so sure they could sever the link between Anna and Shadowlight without killing them both.

"My superiors are meeting again in three hours," Resnick told Gregory and Daryna. "Once we get the go-ahead, both teams can be ready to move within a few hours."

"There is still something Lillian, Gregory, and I must

do before we venture into the Magic Realm. Spells that must be performed." Daryna said and then looked pointedly at Lillian.

Resnick nodded and turned to go speak with his superiors.

Gregory huffed softly and then urged Lillian and Daryna out of the military headquarters.

He didn't speak again until a half hour later when they were once again surrounded by trees, well away from the humans and their technology.

Gregory was still uncomfortable surrounded by things from the modern world. Lillian might have found it humorous under other circumstances, but the last two months hadn't been easy.

"Lillian, if you truly plan to come to the Magic Realm with me, you'll need to give our child into your hamadryad's keeping," he said with steel in his voice. "Or you and Daryna can both remain here together."

There was no way Lillian was letting Gregory risk himself alone. "No, I'll have to give up my child soon any—"

Daryna cut Lillian off. "I will not sit by safe in the Mortal Realm while my other half ventures into the heart of enemy territory."

Lillian folded her arms as she and Daryna both leveled a 'we'll kick your ass if you try' look at Gregory.

"You've been outvoted," Lillian said. "Whatever we find in the Magic Realm, we'll face together."

Gregory huffed out a disgruntled sound as his tail flicked back and forth. "I only want to keep you both safe, our child too."

"I know. But the best way to keep our baby safe is to rescue Shadowlight and Anna, thereby depriving the Battle Goddess of another weapon in her arsenal."

"Yes, but Lillian, being separated from your child..."

"Will suck. But it would happen soon anyway. All hamadryads gestate their dryad's child. Even I know that."

"There's more to it than that," he said softly. "When you journey to the Magic Realm, you will feel the separation far more acutely."

"He is correct," Daryna said. "Even though dryads must give over their children to their trees, the dryad doesn't usually venture far from her hamadryad during those years."

Lillian cradled her stomach, even now feeling the pulse of life within, a tiny fluttering heart. Her gargoyle magic could sense the child now. Not the gender, not yet, but Gregory said they would be able to scent the sex of their child in another few days.

"But me being away from the tree won't weaken the hamadryad or harm the child, right?"

"No," Gregory reassured her. "Your tree is strong. Our child will be safe with the Clan and the Coven guarding her glade."

"Then I'm going with you. I'll transfer the child to my hamadryad now."

"My beautiful, brave mate," Gregory said as he stepped forward to embrace her. "Tomorrow will be soon enough."

Gregory's hand caressed her belly, and she smiled at his expression of absolute wonderment. Lillian would raze an evil demigoddess's temple to the ground if that's what it took to protect this tiny new miracle.

CHAPTER TWENTY-SEVEN

Gregory nuzzled Lillian's cheek and at that moment he wanted to be away from everything so he could spend some time alone with his mate. Daryna must have sensed his mood because she bestowed him with a mischievous grin.

"Go. Take Lillian hunting." Daryna gestured at the darkening forest all around them. "You both deserve some time alone. It's likely the last chance you'll get for a while. I can find my own way back to the cabin."

It was true. Once Lillian went into her hamadryad, she'd remain there for two days, but when she emerged, she would be in peak form, ready for the mission to the Magic Realm. After today, they'd be accompanied by the humans and fae until the mission's end.

"Come," he whispered to Lillian, "hunt with me. Daryna and Gran will inform us later what the humans decide, but I already know they will 'green light' a mission to the Magic Realm as soon as possible. They have no more choice than we do. The Battle Goddess has set her sights on this world."

His words might not have comforted Lillian, but she nodded.

"I'll hunt with you and then tomorrow I'll surrender our child to my hamadryad." She paused, her expression turning fierce. "And then after that, we start a hunt of a different type. The Battle Goddess might not know it yet, but she will feel the rage of the Avatars for her interference."

"That she will," Daryna agreed darkly. "If she has harmed the young gargoyle or his Kyrsu, I will show her what true rage is."

Gregory reached out and hugged Daryna, surprising both women. "I love you and forgive you for attempting to protect Gryton, but if you do anything so foolish again while we are in the Magic Realm, I will see that you can't attempt such a thing again."

While Daryna and Lillian were both put off balance by his words, he turned and dropped to all fours. As he ran past, he slapped Lillian in the backside with his tail. "Come slow one, if you can catch me perhaps I will reward you."

As he darted off into the forest, Lillian's curses and Daryna's delighted laughter reached him. He didn't run fast or particularly far before he heard Lillian giving chase. She was catching up to him, so he knew she'd shifted to gargoyle form.

Lillian was fast and enjoyed stealing the lead from him, but this game trail was too narrow and thick underbrush hugging close to the path would prevent her from passing him. He grinned and set a slower pace that he knew would bother her.

She approached swiftly and wasn't slowing down.

"What are you—"

She leaped upon his rump, stampeded over his back, and then was springing forward to land on the path ahead.

"You're too slow and I'm hungry. Go hunt by yourself," she shouted back at him as her tail-tip vanished around a bend in the game trail.

He did so love a good challenge. Lengthening his stride, he surged forward, thundering down the trail in pursuit of Lillian.

She led him on a merry chase before eventually slowing enough for him to run at her heels. When the underbrush finally thinned, he ran alongside her and used the proximity to lick at her shoulder and dragged in a great lungful of her scent.

"Food before sex! Stop being so very male."

Her tone lacked bite, so he nuzzled her the next chance he got.

"I'm not joking. I could eat an entire deer by myself." She smacked him with her tail hard enough to make him stumble. That was no loving, playful swat. Right. Hormones. Feed the pregnant female or else.

When he regained his stride, he surged ahead. "Then I had better bring down the biggest buck I can find if I want even a small bite or two."

"My mate is wise," Lillian agreed.

He soon found a promising scent trail and followed it to a small herd of five deer. He picked his target and swiftly separated him from the others.

Lillian followed close behind, but not so close she'd catch a stray kick from a panicked deer. They'd agreed that while she was carrying their child, she'd allow him to make the kills.

Gregory soon ran down the deer and gave the buck a merciful death.

Many hours later the cool night breeze blew along Gregory's back, but he was content, his mate slept snuggled in his arms. A thick blanket woven of shadow magic cushioned them from the roots and stones of the forest floor and their wings were enough to banish the chill.

Both his mate and their unborn child rested peacefully. He tucked his wings tighter around Lillian and snuggled closer, simply enjoying the moment even though sleep eluded him. Besides, he was happy for that. These few wakeful hours gave him more time to simply revel in the new sensations.

He'd sired a child with his beloved for the first time. Well, second time, since Gryton was undeniably his offspring. While he would do what he could to save the fire elemental and attempt to instill some sense of morality in him, Gregory wanted this second child to never know the pain and horror Gryton must have faced.

Gregory only hoped he would be given a chance to be a parent to this one.

Lillian stirred in his arms and blinked open her eyes a moment later.

"Have you not slept?" she asked as she stretched.

"No," he said, not bothering with a lie. He never wanted to lie to her. "I couldn't sleep, but it pleases me to just hold you and watch you while you sleep."

"Mmm." Lillian yawned and stretched. "Way to rock that stalker talk."

She bumped her muzzle against his and predictably forgot about her horns, clinking them against his.

"Damn it. Horns. Sorry," she said as she rolled over and reclined facing him. "Now what's the real cause for those little worry lines between your eyes?"

"I was just thinking how much I wanted to be able to give this child the love he deserves."

"He? You got insider info you're not sharing with me?" Lillian drew in a deep breath, trying to catch the scent of their child on her skin.

"No," he laughed. "Son or daughter, I'll love this child. And I haven't used magic to discern the gender, I promise."

"You better not."

"I was just thinking that this little miracle might be the only one we are ever granted."

Lillian laughed, surprising him. "Once we win the war and give the Battle Goddess a really good spanking, I'm planning on retiring from being an Avatar."

"Retiring?"

"Yep, just for the rest of this life. I'm planning on growing a crapload of hamadryad cuttings from my tree until I have an entire grove. Then I'm shoving my soul and Avatar power into one of them."

"Ah," he said in a noncommittal way. Though he

thought he knew where she was going with her 'grove' of hamadryads. He fought to hold back a silly grin.

"Once they are old enough, I'm going to use the hamadryad grove to carry all our children. It might take a decade or two, but I plan on having one of those crazy, big-ass families with ten plus kids."

Gregory grinned at her, but as much as his heart liked the future she painted, his mind knew if there was open war, demigods and Avatars might all find themselves once again within the Spirit Realm. "I hope we are given a chance."

Lillian's merriment vanished. "You think we're not going to survive?"

"I cannot see the future and I cannot promise you that we will both survive this."

"God, Gregory," Lillian reached out to him. "Don't think like that. We're the Avatars, we've lived thousands of lifetimes together."

"And we've died at the end of each of those many thousands of lifetimes too. Some by choice. Some unexpectedly. There are no guarantees except everyone returns to the Spirit Realm, eventually."

"That's a terrible way to view life."

"It is the truth."

"I know, but I will go forward with the belief that there is always hope. And I will hope enough for the both of us."

Within Gregory, his hope warred with despair. "I do not know what the future will bring, but this child is a miracle, and I hope we are blessed with many more such miracles over the years."

Lillian cupped his cheek and would have said something more, but he placed his fingers on her lips.

"I don't know if we will survive this war, and for the first time in my existence, I fear death. We have failed the Divine Ones twice now. First with Gryton and now with this child. I do not regret creating life with you. I should, but I don't. However, I think our creators might see things differently than I do. After Gryton, they wiped one entire lifetime's worth of memories. I don't know if that was intended as a punishment or as a kindness so we wouldn't have to exist knowing we'd broken our most sacred vows." Gregory tilted his head back to the canopy above and wished he could see the stars through the leaves. "I fear this might be the last time we are reborn as the Avatars, like we are being given a second chance. I simply do not know."

Lillian's eyes widened, and her large deer-like ears flattened into her mane.

"You really think that the Divine Ones would punish us so severely for having a child?" Her one hand came to rest on her belly.

"No, not for that tiny innocent life." Gregory shook his head. "I speak of Gryton. I think he is the mistake we are intended to rectify in this life. Though, I haven't a clue if I'm supposed to save or destroy him. Though I would attempt to save my son—the Divine Ones would know that about my character."

"What happens if we fail? They'd just strip us of our purpose as punishment?"

"Yes, but they wouldn't see it as a punishment, my beloved. They would be granting us a reprieve from having our soul sundered each time they would have called upon their Avatars."

Lillian's eyes widened. "Then we must defeat the Battle Goddess once and for all. If we don't, there might not be anyone powerful enough to stop her the next time. I will not leave my child to fight that battle."

"I do not plan to," Gregory said, "I just don't want there to be any lies between us and Daryna has had the same fears as I."

Lillian gripped his jaw and forced him to look directly at her. "Well, it's good that I have enough passion for life to sustain you, me, and Daryna, then, isn't it?"

A wave of magic rolled over her body and suddenly he was holding a dryad in his arms instead of a gargoyle. Drawing him forward, she pressed little kisses to his muzzle. Urgency swiftly rose within him, flooding his body, mind, and soul with the need for his mate. Lillian's responses told him she felt the same. It fired his need to greater heights, but there was more to it than just physical release. This might be the last time they could enjoy each other's bodies fully.

There was no telling how long Daryna would survive after they completed their rescue mission. When her body failed, Lillian would become the Sorceress, as was right. The survival of all three realms depended upon that merging. Why then did the thought of regaining his true Sorceress at the cost of losing his mate hurt so damn much? Sex was the only part of their relationship they'd lose.

And it wasn't like they hadn't abstained before. It was just sex.

"Gregory, when we come together it is never *just* sex. It is an accumulation of a hundred thousand lifetimes of our love."

She was right, of course. Their soul always yearned to rejoin and heal itself, to be made whole. The act of physical love was as close as they could come while still caged in flesh, blood, and bone.

His eyes drifted shut as Lillian nipped her way down his neck, her lips and tongue caressing him in a way that melted his heart and fired his blood. By the great God and Goddess, he would miss this.

A deep rumbling purr escaped him, and Lillian chuckled.

If this were their last time, he would embrace his fierce joy and sorrow, wrapping Lillian in so much pleasure that she would remember this always. He sat up and grasped her around the waist, hoisting her into his lap.

"My beloved dryad, how do you want me, human or natural?"

Lillian continued to stroke him, her quick fingers making short work of his loincloth. "I don't care. I just want you. Fierce, brave, beautiful you."

Hmmm, fierce suited his mood this night. He pushed her onto her back and followed her down. Lillian yelped once in surprise, but she wasn't harmed, the blanketing shadow magic cushioned her. Smiling, she wrapped her arms around his waist. He'd retained enough wherewithal to know that in his present mood, if he kept his gargoyle form, she'd likely be sore tomorrow.

He closed his eyes and called on power, maintaining the image of his human form in his mind's eye.

"I'm fond of wings," Lillian whispered as she reached to stroke the sensitive membranes.

Gregory's concentration shattered, the image of his human form melting away. Damn it.

"My emotions are too chaotic, I'm not sure if I'll be as gentle as I should," he admitted.

"How about a compromise?" Lillian grinned up at him, her thumbs stroking his jaw. "Half and half because kissing is fun, too."

Ah. His human-gargoyle hybrid form. Somehow it seemed poetic to wear the shape he'd worn when they first kissed. He shifted to his half-human form and pounced. Lillian giggled, but he silenced the sound with his mouth.

She eagerly returned his rising passion, matching it and driving his own higher. Snatching her hands in one of his, he guided them above her head and pinned them there. Knowing Lillian's giving nature in bed, if he didn't restrain her, this would be over far sooner than he wanted.

"Not fair," she said with a little pout.

He kissed her until she was breathless and the pout long forgotten. Using lips and teeth, he uncovered her breasts and lavished attention on each until she was purring his name. In time, she found other ways to distract him and freed her hands. Soon he lost the fight to hold back his rising passion and urged Lillian's knees apart. Looking down at her, he met her gaze. Heat and desire reflected back at him.

Draping himself over her, he folded his wings around them both. With her held in the protective cage of his arms, he nuzzled her jaw, kissing and nipping his way to her ear. "You mean everything to me."

"You're the only one I've ever loved." Lillian nuzzled him in return.

Alone far out in the dark forest, their passions rose, peaked, and began rising anew. Hours passed before they finally collapsed and curled up together, deeply sated.

"Gregory. That felt too much like goodbye," Lillian whispered afterward, sadness in her voice.

"Not goodbye. Never that. A memory to carry us through more difficult times." Gregory reached out and brushed a lock of hair off Lillian's sweaty cheek. "You have my promise that I will do all in my power to live for both you and our child. There is nothing I'd like more than to fulfill that future dream of yours. I, too, would like a big family."

"Good, I'm going to bind you with that promise." Sighing happily, Lillian lowered her head to his chest and allowed her fingers to slowly caress him. After a few minutes, her hand stilled in sleep. At last, he let sleep to claim him, too.

CHAPTER TWENTY-EIGHT

*L*ast night in the forest, just before Lillian had fallen asleep in her mate's arms, she'd concocted a plan. She wanted to give Gregory something that represented both their eternal love and their future dream of having a family, even if it was only for this one lifetime.

Unfortunately, there was no way Gregory wouldn't notice if she just sneaked off to go shopping and it wasn't like she had the magic skills needed to make what she wanted. But Daryna was the Mother's Sorceress. She shouldn't have a problem providing what Lillian needed. She just had to explain everything to Daryna without Gregory being the wiser.

She'd thought that part was going to be the problem. At least until the solution just let herself into their bedroom while Gregory was still in the shower.

"Daryna," Lillian called softly and gestured her over to the far end of the room, putting as much space between them and the bathroom as possible. Though even a gargoyle's exceptional hearing was at a disadvantage with the spray from the water drowning out most other noise. "Perfect timing. I have something I want to ask you while Gregory is occupied."

Daryna's eyebrow arched with unconcealed interest. "Why, I didn't take you for the secret conspiracy type."

Lillian rolled her eyes. "It's nothing nefarious, just something I want to give to Gregory. You might even think it's silly."

"I will gladly help you make something for our beloved." A smile spread across the Sorceress's face. "Tell me more."

Feeling somewhat awkward, Lillian explained what she wanted to do. "What do you think? Will Gregory think it's a silly human custom?"

"I think it's something that we Avatars would never think about doing, but I love the idea. Gregory will love it too."

"I'll love what?" Gregory asked as he stepped out of the bathroom, a towel wrapped around his waist and another around his wet mane.

"It's nothing much," Lillian hedged, scrambling for something to say that wasn't a lie or end up triggering his need to ferret out the truth.

"Then why don't you tell me what it is." A wicked grin flashed across his face.

"Lillian wants to give you a present if you must know," Daryna snapped. "And she asked me to help."

"A present?" Gregory prowled closer.

Daryna crossed her arms and glowered at him. "It's a secret. We're not telling you what it is, so stop pushing, you great lug."

Gregory's expression shifted to a pout and it was on the tip of Lillian's tongue to tell him her plan when a loud knock sounded at the bedroom door.

"Lillian? Gregory?" Jason called through the door. "You better get out here."

Daryna was closest and opened the door for Lillian's older brother.

He stepped in and nodded to the Sorceress but was able to pick out Lillian with ease. "Your mother just awoke from her coma. Gran thinks it's best she learn the news about Shadowlight from you or Daryna."

"I'll do it," Daryna said before Lillian could respond. "It was my plan that Gryton deliver Shadowlight to Lord Death as proof of what his sister was doing and when that plan went awry, it was my fault that he ended up the Battle Goddess's prisoner instead."

"I'll come, too," Lillian said.

Gregory walked over to the bed where he'd left his beaded loincloth. He dropped his towels and began to dress.

"Oh, gawd, I'll be in the car. I was supposed to give you a lift to HQ, but I might now be blind." Jason said as he fled the room with a lot of dramatic groaning and bitching about naked gargoyle junk.

Gregory ignored the human and continued to dress. Daryna just rolled her eyes and then looked at Lillian. "You know, our gargoyle has never been modest, but I think he does this intentionally because the humans are so very silly about nudity."

"I'll be waiting in the car," Lillian said and shook her head. She followed the sound of her brother's muttering.

Lillian stood in one of the lower levels of what used to be a community building but was now just called HQ. The office had been converted into a hospital room and she now leaned against the wall with Gregory while Daryna explained to River that her youngest child was now a prisoner of the Battle Goddess.

Her mother was on crutches, and while her hair had started to grow back, her body was still covered in terrible burns. Gregory had been working some healing magic, but even so, anyone with two eyes could see it was pure determination on the dryad's part that she was on her feet at all.

"She has my Shadowlight?" River whispered in horror, her already pale complexion from being bedridden for over two months washed out farther. "Darkness and I gave up everything to see that he wouldn't grow up there."

"I know," Daryna whispered. "And I am sorry. You have my word that we'll get him back."

Lillian wasn't sure if her mother could be trusted, but she did feel sympathy for the poor woman. To learn her mate was dead, or the next thing to it, would be a great enough blow after waking from a coma. Then to learn that her youngest child had been stolen away? Those two losses would cripple those with lesser fortitude. River was tough, though, and Lillian could see the rage rising within her now. Her weakened body did not lessen the fire of her spirit.

"Your word? Your word means nothing!" River slapped Daryna's consoling hands away. "This is all your fault!"

Gregory stepped between them and gently pushed Daryna behind him while he spoke to the dryad in soft tones. "We will get him back. I promise you that."

Stepping forward, Lillian joined them. "At least my little brother isn't alone. Anna is there with him. She refused to stand down and went against orders to attempt a rescue."

Lillian sat down on the edge of the bed and urged the surprised River to sit next to her.

"The human was the only one who went?"

"Yes," Lillian answered. "She loves Shadowlight like a little brother. And while she knew the odds were bad, she chose to go anyway."

"A human?" River whispered. "Only the human was brave enough to go."

"Yes."

River's expression hardened. "Then Shadowlight picked well. She is a worthy Kyrsu. When we get them back, I will tell her as much."

Lillian hugged the stranger who was her mother. "We will get them back."

"Yes, we will," River's nostrils flared. "Just don't expect either of them to still be the same."

Her mother had just given voice to one of Lillian's greatest fears. At the words, even the age-old Avatars looked a touch more worried than they had before.

Drawing in a deep shaking breath, Lillian vowed that

no matter what had happened to Anna and Shadowlight, or what they had become, she would still stand by them. Surely, they couldn't be worse than Gryton, not after only a few weeks' exposure to the Battle Goddess.

Lillian prayed that was true.

CHAPTER TWENTY-NINE

*T*hick autumn dew sparkled brightly on the hamadryad's soft needles. The sun hadn't been up long enough to burn it away yet, and the glade had that damp, earthy smell that always reminded Lillian of home. Later in the day, as the sun warmed the fallen leaves, the scent would change to a sweeter, richer essence.

But she wouldn't see that today. Shortly, she would step inside the hamadryad and feel its bark close in around her. Well, she wouldn't actually feel the bark closing, since she'd already be drifting to sleep, but it would still happen.

And then her tree would take something precious from her.

Touching the round curve of her belly, she told herself she would have had to do this in the next few days anyway. A dryad only carried the fetus for three months before giving it to her tree to gestate for the remaining years.

Giving the fetus to the tree a few days early wouldn't harm her baby, but it would allow Lillian to go with

Gregory. There was no way she would let Gregory venture into the Magic Realm by himself.

She took a step closer to her tree, her chin high and shoulders square.

"Once you're inside the tree, you will sleep. You won't feel anything until the tree releases you and you wake fully recovered." Daryna said.

Recovered? Since when was being pregnant an illness? But she knew what Daryna meant. Lillian would emerge fit and ready for battle.

"The Sorceress is correct," River agreed, surprising Lillian. River and Daryna had only just met an hour ago but had already developed a strong dislike to each other.

Gregory's hands settled on her shoulders. "Take as much time to prepare as you need."

"I'm ready." Lillian untied the belt of her robe and Gregory mantled his wings around her.

Stepping forward, she raised her arms away from her body, caressing the hamadryad's branches as she called on the earthy power of a dryad.

Her senses expanded out in all directions and even into the ground. Below her feet, magic pulsed with a steady slow rhythm, a slow, barely heard pulse. It was the heart song of the planet. Humans might not realize it, or even stop to think about it, but Earth was a living entity as much as she or Gregory, or any one of the fae and military personnel she sensed nearby. When she called on her dryad magic, she felt a true connection with the Earth.

She reveled in the power of the vast forest all around, until she felt calm and as unmoving as the land. Stable. Firm. Fixed in place.

When she brushed at the hamadryad's branches a second time, they shifted, moving out of the way so that she could reach the thick trunk.

Sensing what she needed, or perhaps feeling the life inside Lillian, the tree shifted and shook as a fissure formed a foot above her head. The crack continued all the way down the trunk until it hit the root base. Widening farther, red, fibrous tissue pulled back exposing a dark cavern inside. Lillian drew in a deep breath and stepped inside.

Already the tree sang to her. A deep, slow melody wrapped around her and her consciousness started to recede. As the tree cradled her, she sang of ancient times and the slow turning of the seasons, telling how everything unfolded for a reason and that all would be well with her child.

The last thing she remembered was Gregory's thoughts in her mind. *"Sleep well, my beloved mate. Know that I will stand guard and never leave your side."*

The earth turned, the sun journeyed across the sky, and the forest whispered its knowledge into her mind. She was aware, and yet she wasn't Lillian. She was hamadryad and all the worries and cares that haunted her dryad form did not concern her in the least.

All would be well. Even now her gargoyle mate stood guard and fed her magic-laced blood as was right and proper.

The earth turned.

Day gave way to night.

Turning, always slowly turning, night once again surrendered to the day.

Hamadryad thought about sleeping and keeping her dryad, too. The cold season was coming and surely her dryad would much prefer to wake again when the warm rains returned.

"No," her gargoyle mate scolded her, though his emotions were more amused than alarmed. *"Return my dryad mate to me. She and I have much to do before this realm is safe."*

He was an old and wise one.

Very well, Hamadryad agreed.

She pulled back her enfolding bark and allowed cold air to wake her dryad. Once her dryad began to stir, Hamadryad turned her attention back to their child, singing to her so that she would not miss the sound of her mother's heartbeat. She crooned of love and magic and the slow turning of the seasons.

Lillian gasped as she came awake. Like the first time she emerged from the hamadryad, gravity threatened to drag her uncoordinated body from the tree before she was ready.

Unlike last time, Gregory was there, lifting her into his arms.

Though this time he wasn't the focus of her attention, not entirely. A hand came to rest against her now flat belly. She'd known the child would be gone when she awoke, but it wasn't anything like she'd expected. There was no sense of abandonment. She was still with her child. Her child was still with her.

She didn't know what was different this time, but she'd never felt the connection with her hamadryad as strongly as she did now. It must be because of the child. All she had to do was close her eyes and reach for the hamadryad and she could feel her baby sleeping deep and safe within.

"It's done," she told Gregory.

"I know. You did well."

"Now we need to go find Shadowlight and Anna."

"Yes," Gregory agreed, and he started to lick the sticky, sweet sap from her skin.

Lillian batted his muzzle away. "Hmm. Maybe a shower first before we go save the world."

CHAPTER THIRTY

Gregory stood off to one side of the clearing and summoned power from both Magic and Spirit Realms. Daryna took what he provided and wove it into an intricate, knotted tapestry that, once finished, would form a portal to their destination.

While the spell that had carried Anna to the Magic Realm was similar, this one's power requirements were greater. They were transporting a much larger group, but this one also needed to remain open. Once they found and freed Anna and Shadowlight, they'd need a swift exit.

During the two hours they'd worked on the spell, Lillian was never further from him than an outstretched wing. Her concern for him, while not warranted, still warmed his heart. Which was about the only thing on or in his body that was warm.

A fine coating of frost now covered his body as power continued to roll off him in waves. Even though Lillian couldn't manipulate the magic that went into a higher level spell like this one, her body had been created to house the soul of the Mother's Sorceress and could withstand the river of power rushing from him. That same power would vaporize an ordinary mortal.

Significantly further away, Major Resnick waited with his two teams. Even further back, the rest of the human herd, which seemed to follow him wherever he went, waited and watched and measured and recorded. Gregory huffed in annoyance. Why did he allow these gnats to hover around him again?

Oh yes, because he'd agreed to an alliance and these scientists were part of the deal.

"Gregory, pleasant thoughts," Lillian said with a touch of humor. "Even I can see that stray bit of magic snaking its way toward the good doctors."

He huffed in acknowledgment and gathered the stray power back in line.

"Thank you, Gregory," Daryna said, dragging his attention to the spell work. "That will be sufficient for now."

She was correct. The spell was almost complete. Certainly, further along than he'd realized. It was foolish to allow himself to become distracted by the presence of a few human scientists.

As he swallowed back the flow of unneeded power, he watched Daryna put the final touches on the transparent walls of shimmering energy. This portal spell looked more like a maze or a labyrinth than the usual smaller, flat disc.

The level of control and strength it took to form such a spell here in the Mortal Realm impressed even him. "Your spell work is magnificent."

Daryna laughed. "It better be. Our lives may count on

this spell for a swift return if things go ill once we're in the Magic Realm."

Nodding agreement, he stepped into the powerful circle and gestured Lillian forward. Once the three of them wove their way to the center of the spell, Gregory called out to Resnick.

The human had proven brave in the past and he showed his inner strength again by walking into the spell without hesitation. Daryna indicated where Resnick should stand, and he swiftly followed orders. The rest of the two teams were just as efficient.

Though perhaps he shouldn't be surprised. The humans had been briefed at length on what to expect.

Once everyone was in place, Daryna nodded and Gregory gave the warning. "Brace yourselves. Breaching the Veil between the Realms is never pleasant."

"We're ready," Resnick said.

Daryna needed no other prompting. The translucent walls of the labyrinth-like spell solidified, snapping around each of the travelers to hold them in place. The network of lines and the interconnecting knots holding it all together glowed brighter, taking on the brilliance of a miniature sun at circle's center.

With a stomach-jolting tug, the spell activated, sending them hurtling toward the Magic Realm. A great pressure compressed his lungs, stealing his breath. It only lasted seconds as he knew it would, and then the weight shifted. Powerful currents of power drove him forward. The rushing continued and suddenly it was like he'd been tossed off a cliff to freefall through space.

Beside him, Lillian let out a whoop of surprise and she

wasn't the only one. Major Resnick was laughing as if this was the most fun he'd had in years. The human truly liked this? There was something seriously wrong with the man.

Slowly, the pressure and madly rushing power slowed. The world righted itself. Gregory looked up at the surrounding mountains where no mountains had been before.

"Welcome to the Magic Realm," he told Resnick and his teams while he waited for his stomach to sort itself out of the knot it had put itself in.

Now the truly difficult part would begin.

Major Resnick and his men fanned out, searching for unseen dangers. Gregory sent his magic hunting for the same thing.

After several minutes, Resnick and Gregory both concluded their arrival hadn't been noticed.

"We're lucky," Resnick noted.

"Luck has nothing to do with it," Daryna said. "The spell was designed so no one would sense our arrival by magical means and I dumped us far enough away from the city that we wouldn't be seen by random patrols either."

"Two suns," Resnick muttered with a shake of his head. "You told me, and I didn't believe you.... but two suns! That's going to take some getting used to."

Daryna glanced at Lillian. "Welcome home."

"I hope we don't stay long. I don't fancy becoming a slave," Lillian shot back.

"Nor I," Gregory agreed and then glanced upslope to the mountains high above. Long shadows were already reaching down from the slopes to cover the valley floor in shadow. In another hour it would be dark.

They'd planned their arrival to correspond with the setting of the first sun. Once the second sun vanished behind the horizon, they'd begin their travel, and if all went according to plan, they'd arrive at the fortress-city just before dawn when many of its protectors would be sleeping or have their senses dulled by the day.

Once the second sun made its descent, Gregory nodded to Resnick and the major gave the order to move out. Several team members fanned out around the still glowing portal spell—they would remain behind to guard it—while the rest of the humans moved away into the trees. Silent and swift, Gregory, Daryna, and Lillian kept pace.

All in all, Gregory admitted a little grudgingly that the humans were handling their foray into the Magic Realm well. Perhaps he'd have to rethink his opinion of humans. At least these humans.

Once they were away from the dampening spells built into the portal, Gregory's magic picked up the essence of two gargoyles to the north and west, deep in the Battle Goddess's domain. Not that he'd doubted Daryna's message from Gryton, but this just confirmed that Anna and Shadowlight were very much alive.

Alive, but changed. The two were much more powerful than they'd been last he'd felt their essence back in the Mortal Realm. It was not unexpected, but it was still shocking.

Lillian was looking off to the north and west as well. "That's them I feel, isn't it?"

"Yes," he said quietly.

"Gods, Gregory. They feel so much stronger, so different."

"Yes, but it doesn't matter. We will fix whatever the Battle Goddess has done to them. Now we just have to get them out of there without getting a lot of our friends here killed."

Lillian nodded in agreement.

If all went well, by this time tomorrow, they should be home with Anna and Shadowlight.

CHAPTER THIRTY-ONE

Captain Sorac didn't believe in fear, weakness, or hesitation as Anna's first flight lessons highlighted. They were very much learn or die.

Maybe not die, she admitted as she sat squeezed between Shadowlight and Captain Sorac on the bench and ate her dinner. If she died, it would have enraged the Lady of Battles, but even so, Captain Sorac wasn't above shoving her off a cliff when she took too long reading the wind currents.

After her first couple of ugly flight lessons, it did become easier. As Shadowlight promised, her wings, tail and horns began to feel like a part of her. Now, in the fifth week of her unwilling stay, Anna could shift to her gargoyle form and back to human the same day without falling into a dead sleep for hours afterward.

Shadowlight was also growing more powerful, both physically and magically. Worse, Commander Gryton no longer needed to chain him down when they were taken before the Battle Goddess for her special sessions.

He wasn't the only one growing complacent. If Anna was honest with herself, she'd grown to like Vaspara and Sorac. Captain Vaspara had been teaching Anna and Shadowlight how to protect themselves from mental attacks by building impenetrable shields around their minds. It had been working, not even Gryton was able to sneak in and look around without her knowing.

As promised, Sorac was turning them into, if not masters, then at least proficient students of the sword.

Both mentors were fair, never unduly harsh—even if one was a succubus and the other a dragon. Well, actually, Sorac was something called a firedrake. Though, a fire-breathing, flying lizard was still a dragon in Anna's books.

Oh, on a fundamental level, Anna knew Vaspara and Sorac were the enemy. She hadn't forgotten that. Just compared to the blood witch, it was hard to get worked up about them.

Besides, she had bigger problems. One of them visited her dreams nightly now, able to slide right past her new powerful mental shields like they weren't there.

Lord Death was a persistent sort. In the dream, the bodiless voice asked the same questions every night.

Did she wish to be a slave?

Or did she wish to be free?

The answers were no-brainers on the surface. Of course she didn't want to be a slave. And, yes, she wanted to be free. And with each passing dream, she was even more certain Death's version of 'free' was more along the lines of 'free the soul from the body' than freed from slavery.

Yep. Nope. No thanks.

So, each night she ignored the darkly seductive voice and each day she did what she needed to keep herself and Shadowlight alive. Though, not once had she stopped seeking a way free of this mess.

Every time she thought of escape, her mind circled back to that night over three weeks ago when Shadowlight had attacked Gryton, completely overwhelming his collar's control for a short time.

While that entire episode had been a test concocted by Gryton to see if Shadowlight had leveled up in power, Anna was more interested in how the kid had overcome the collar and how soon he could do it again.

Each day, when the city slept while the sun was high in the sky, Shadowlight practiced calling his shadow magic without permission. At first, when Gryton had fitted him with his second collar, he hadn't been able to accomplish much, but the stronger Shadowlight grew, the more he could resist and overcome even this new, stronger control collar's influence.

They weren't ready to make their escape just yet, but Anna was working on a plan. Each day they saved back foods that wouldn't spoil and hid it in the base of their wardrobes. Soon they'd have enough supplies for the journey.

When they finally were ready to make their escape, they'd need to include the human family. After three weeks, Anna was sure the humans were trustworthy and wouldn't willingly betray hers and Shadowlight's escape plan, but that didn't mean one of the captains wouldn't be able to read their minds, so Anna was keeping them in the dark for now.

Once they were ready to make their escape, they'd inform the family and then flee with them. But that was at least a few days off. So, in the meantime, Shadowlight practiced his magic in the daytime and Anna embraced her flight lessons.

Staring down at her food, Anna continued to eat. It was another of the thick stews. Someone really needed to teach Cook a few new recipes.

As usual, Gryton sat to Shadowlight's right. She still trusted Gryton only a touch more than she did the others, but so far, he'd earned her grudging trust since he'd never laid a hand on the kid in anger. Not even during the test when Shadowlight had tried to toss Tin Man's ass through a wall.

"Vaspara, I'm not part of your meal," Gryton said in a low voice, one not intended to carry beyond the high table. Though Anna's gargoyle hearing had no trouble picking out the words even over the steady hum of conversation.

Vaspara sat up straighter and cursed softly.

"You may have the evening off to attend to your needs," Gryton said between bites of food.

She apologized and quickly excused herself.

"Do I want to know what that was all about?" Anna asked. She didn't want to seem too eager, but anything that changed routine was worthy of note.

"Vaspara has been spending much of her time tutoring or guarding you and the young gargoyle." Gryton leaned forward so he could see her past Shadowlight's larger mass. "It has suppressed her need to feed, dulling her hunger so to speak. But her succubus nature still needs to be fed, or she risks having her nature overwhelm her at inopportune times and attempt to drain power from another."

Ah. Vaspara had tried to feed on Gryton and he'd gotten his knickers in a knot. As long as no one was preying on the kid, she didn't care who ate whom.

Anna dismissed Gryton with a grunt and returned to her own meal.

"I'll assign another to guard you tonight since the Lady of Battles requires me to report on your progress."

Anna pretended she was more interested in her food than what Gryton had to say. It wasn't the first time she and Shadowlight had been babysat by one of the non-mentor captains. In truth, Gryton, Sorac, and Vaspara were more focused and alert.

Oh, sometimes Sorac pretended sleepy boredom, but he missed nothing. Anna would bet her favorite dagger the blood witch was another who missed no detail. Thankfully, Gryton never left them alone with her.

Of her usual babysitters, Ninara and her twin brother, Honnan, were the most likely to let their guards down. A reaction Anna and Shadowlight had been cultivating by never giving their babysitters reasons to remain on guard.

Being willing and biddable went a long way to gaining trust.

Unfortunately, there were some new players Anna hadn't interacted with enough yet to get a good read on their personalities. Three more captains had returned from whatever they were doing in the valley east of the fortress city.

Captains Rynar, Korsha and Bardorac were still

completely unknown commodities. She hadn't even figured out what species they were since she and Shadowlight hadn't been in sniffing distance of the newly returned captains yet.

Anna weighed the odds. It was more likely Gryton would assign them one of their usual babysitters. Besides, the newcomers likely had a lot of tasks that needed their attention.

Anna continued to chew her food with outward bored indifference, but inside she was smiling. Looks like it was going to be another practice night.

"Honnan," Gryton called down the table. "You will escort Anna and Shadowlight back to their chambers after last meal concludes."

Bingo.

"As you wish, Commander." The incubus didn't sound thrilled, but he was obedient and always did as he was told without complaint.

"And Honnan," Gryton added, a hint of fire lacing his words. "If you attempt anything foolish and Anna is forced to hurt you, she won't be punished, but you will. Understood?"

Honnan grunted an affirmative.

Anna wasn't concerned with him, though. He'd never tried anything before and now that she could assume full gargoyle form it tended to dissuade would-be admirers. Well, all except Gryton. His gaze still hinted that he'd like to explore a physical relationship with her, but he hadn't pushed, and she still hadn't seen a way to use his desire against him, so she just ignored him. Though, Anna hoped she and the kid got away before Romeo got impatient.

Gryton pushed back his seat and stood, pausing only long enough to transfer command of Shadowlight's control collar to Honnan before he marched from the hall.

Honnan took Gryton's seat and broke into an extracurricular history lesson.

Anna sighed. Who would have thought a sex demon would be so interested in dry old history, but he was, and Shadowlight was like a sponge, sucking up every bit of information because it might be useful one day.

A stranger teacher and student pairing Anna had never seen.

Eventually, the hall emptied, and Honnan's lesson about a riot that took place in a small coastal community called Dark Sands came to an end and he ushered them out of the hall.

When they exited, he turned left not right.

Right was back to their chambers. Left was workrooms.

"Why are we going this way?" Shadowlight asked, adding a low growl.

"I need to retrieve something from my workroom and Gryton will have my head if I leave you unguarded to go retrieve it later." Honnan's tone was free of stress, but there was a hint of deception to his scent.

Shadowlight growled louder.

"Damn gargoyles. Can't keep a secret from you to save my life. If you must know, I'm meeting someone. It won't take long, then you can both return to your chambers afterward."

That was all true, but Anna didn't trust him. There was

more he wasn't saying. Shadowlight didn't have a choice. He'd have to follow and there was no way she was letting the kid go alone. So, glowering at Honnan, she followed him doggedly even knowing he might be leading them into a trap.

It wasn't until they took another left, descended two flights of stairs, and then turned right down a dimly lit hallway that Anna recognized the area. A moment later, a draft wafted past and confirmed her fears.

The coiling scent of old blood grew steadily stronger with each step. Shadowlight snarled and Anna instinctively shifted to gargoyle form.

"Stop, both of you," Honnan said with an annoyed huff. "I wouldn't be here if I didn't need something from her. Behave yourself, or I'll order Shadowlight to imprison you in a cage of shadow magic."

It wasn't an idle threat. Since they'd both been training with the blood witch, their mastery of magic had greatly expanded. Unfortunately, Anna had only been a gargoyle for a few short weeks and her training wasn't as advanced as the kid's. If he was ordered to imprison her, he would. Unless he fought the collar. If he did that, they'd lose their advantage and once Gryton learned of it, he'd upgrade the collar again. Dammit.

"Shadowlight, unless we're in danger, just go with whatever he says. We don't want to reveal our cards yet."

"I understand. I don't like it, but I understand."

He continued to growl softly.

As they walked closer to the blood witch's workrooms, Anna's unease grew, her gargoyle nature screaming a warning.

And then a familiar, darkly seductive voice was whispering in her waking mind. *"They mean to enslave you."*

"What? You only figured that out now?" Using a sarcastic tone on Death might not be the brightest move, but it made her feel marginally better.

"Your bravado will not save you or the young gargoyle from what the blood witch plans to do to you."

"She won't risk Gryton's or the Battle Goddess's rage. She can't kill us."

"No, not kill. But she will lay claim to your souls. She plans to bind you to herself and the two demon siblings. Her power will take your souls and twist them in ways that even my sister would hesitate to use."

Sweat trickled down Anna's back. If what he said was true, they needed to escape and tell Gryton.

"Gryton is no savior. Come to me. Now. Before your souls are beyond even my ability to cleanse."

With that slap of clarity, Anna knew they'd stayed too long. They'd been lulled by the Battle Bitch's dark power and let their guards down. They should have attempted escape days ago.

Shit! Shit! Shit!

Anna fisted her hands, but they were already at the door leading to Taryin's dark domain. Honnan shoved the ancient wooden door open with one shoulder and walked through, ordering Shadowlight to follow when the gargoyle balked.

Not about to let Shadowlight face the danger alone, she marched in and shoved her way between the two males and came face to muzzle with the blood witch.

Taryin brought her hands up, the sickly glow of blood magic circling her long elegant fingers.

"Why is the female gargoyle here? I only need the male for the spell."

Honnan chuckled. "Shadowlight, capture and hold the female."

"It's okay Shadowlight. Don't fight the collar until I tell you," she sent along the link.

His trust in her was absolute and he obeyed her at once. He obeyed *her*, not the collar, Anna realized with a bit of shock.

The others in the room didn't seem to notice the difference, so she made a show of snarling and fighting as Shadowlight shoved her into a cage created from his newly mastered shadow and blood magic.

Anna didn't have to fake her displeasure at being locked into a cage while three captains remained outside with Shadowlight, but she needed the captains to think she wasn't a threat.

"Shadowlight, we need to kill or incapacitate all of them. Starting with the blood witch. Lord Death says the blood witch is going to perform some ritual that will alter our souls in ways even he can't cleanse. I don't know about you, but that sounds like a freaking good reason to fight."

"I agree, but I don't know if I can fight the collar and the witch at the same time."

"You won't have to. Just lure the witch next to the cage and then drop the spell when I say. Can you do that?"

"Yes," he said, his voice full of trust and confidence.

Anna wouldn't fail the kid. She'd see the witch neutralized even if it killed her.

"Shadowlight, I require a few drops of your blood," Captain Taryin said. "It won't even be enough for you to miss, but as you can see, I've been working on this one spell for days and it's almost complete. I only need a bit of blood to finish it."

The witch gestured toward the stone worktable at the center of the room. Last time there had been bowls of powders and dried herbs. This time there was a slowly rolling and twisting knot of magic floating two feet above the table. The magic shifted and shuddered and seethed as if the very air caused it pain. It reminded her of a school of fish attacked by some unseen predator.

Watching the seething mass made Anna vaguely nauseous.

"Stay here next to me. Make her come to you," Anna instructed Shadowlight.

In answer, he settled on his haunches and leaned against the cage, alertly waiting but no longer growling.

Taryin had picked up a long-bladed dagger from her worktable and turned toward Shadowlight. Seeing his new posture, she smiled. "That's a good boy. You'll be able to release your Kyrsu from the cage shortly.

Shadowlight's ears swung forward as if curious.

The blood witch had the audacity to pat him on the head, but the kid was on his best behavior and only flashed his fangs, which made the blood witch laugh a second time.

"That's my gargoyle," Taryin said as she brought the blade against Shadowlight's forearm.

"Now," Anna whispered into his mind.

CHAPTER THIRTY-TWO

The cage bars shimmered as they disintegrated into their separate shadow and blood magic components. Anna lunged through the swirling misty remains of her cage, calling on her own blades made of shadow and blood magic.

Shadowlight was half a second ahead of her and his blade-tipped tail stabbed the blood witch. Anna was on her a second later, one of her blades sliding in the back of Taryin's neck, just under the skull.

With her spinal cord severed, the blood witch could only widen her eyes in surprise. Taryin made no sound as she slumped forward against her. Kicking her dead weight away, Anna leaped toward the startled Ninara.

"I've got this one. Honnan is all yours," Anna instructed.

Ninara lashed out with a shimmering wave of offensive magic, but Anna retaliated with her own. Small voids of darkness appeared and shredded her enemy's spells, unraveling them before they could touch her.

She rushed forward, using her wings and tail as weapons like Sorac and Shadowlight had drilled into her. Shredding Ninara's spells, she closed the distance and wrapped her long, powerful fingers around the other woman's throat, squeezing back her cry of alarm.

"The Battle Goddess was foolish to create beings as powerful as Shadowlight and me and think we'd be easy to control." Anna dragged Ninara closer until they were breathing the same air. "We aren't slaves. Why you thought *you* could control us, I have no idea."

She glanced over at Shadowlight to see him slam Honnan into the floor. Not that she was concerned about the outcome. Sorac had already pitted Shadowlight against all his mentors, and Honnan hadn't fared so well in the ring. He wouldn't here either. Anna dragged the still struggling Ninara closer to her brother.

"Ninara, how much do you think Honnan cares? He seems indifferent to most, but I'd say he genuinely loves you." Anna crouched next to Shadowlight and his prisoner. "Shall we find out?"

Anna flexed her talons and broke the skin on Ninara's throat. "I know from Sorac's lessons that beheading kills almost any opponent."

Honnan's mouth opened, and his lips moved, but nothing came out, not even breath.

"Kid, ease up on the grip before you pop his eyes out of his head. Besides, I think he wants to say something."

Shadowlight eased up on the incubus's throat but dug his talons into Honnan's chest until blood pooled around each digit. If Honnan survived, and that was a big 'if,' he was going to bear a gargoyle's talon marks on his pecs for days to come.

"Oh, and Honnan, if I were you, I wouldn't be stupid enough to attempt to issue an order to Shadowlight. I saw him nearly put Gryton through a wall not that long ago and you and your sister strike me as more breakable than Tin Man."

Honnan's nostrils flared and he nodded ever so slightly.

"Are you going to behave?"

Another nod.

"Good, you're going to surrender control of Shadowlight's collar over to me and then he and I are going to imprison you and your dear sister." Anna tapped her blade made of shadow and blood magic against his cheek. "You have my word we won't kill you if you cooperate."

Honnan nodded again. Good. So far, so good.

"Shadowlight, can you make another of those handy cages while I secure them?"

He nodded but didn't release his hold on the other male until Anna had gagged and hog-tied him with layers of shadow magic.

Then she attended to Ninara in the same fashion. Once Shadowlight was finished constructing the cage, Anna dragged her captives over to it and tossed Ninara in. Anna removed the incubus's gag. "No heroics. Just transfer the command spell."

Honnan did, calmly uttering the foreign words she'd come to recognize from all the times she'd heard the spell spoken. When he was finished, Anna gagged him again and shoved him in a cage next to his sister. Shadowlight sealed them in.

"How long do you think that will hold them?" she asked.

"Long enough to get away."

"Good, we need to warn the servants and somehow get them out of here. I'm not leaving them behind—"

Pain exploded in her abdomen. She was suddenly propelled backward, and then her body crashed into one of the workroom's stone walls. Her head cracked against the unyielding surface and her vision darkened until she was temporarily blind.

The pain in her side was intense, a burning agony, unlike anything she'd ever experienced before. Screams assaulted her ears. It took longer than it should for her to understand she was the one screaming.

She forced her lips together. It stopped the sound, but not the pain. She wasn't sure if anything short of death could end the terrible suffering. Anna only hoped there were no guards outside in the hall to hear.

Her hands reached blindly to the point where the greatest agony radiated. Blinking slowly and focusing on her breathing helped to clear her vision. Through her wavering sight, she saw what her hands had already felt.

A long crystalline spear was pinning her to the wall. Its tainted, muddy amber color told her it was forged of blood magic.

She tried to pull the spear from her side, but it was sticky with blood and Anna's grip was too weak. The sound of battle dragged Anna out of her own agony long enough to focus on her surroundings.

Shadowlight was in a battle with the blood witch and he was outmatched. Anna's protective instincts roused even through the waves of blinding pain. Power stirred deep within, giving her renewed strength.

"Should've taken her head," Anna muttered as she hacked up blood.

Not good. This was so not good. Oh, hell. This was going to hurt like a mother.

But Shadowlight was in danger. Roaring in rage and agony, Anna ripped the spear from the wall and out of her body. Crashing to the ground, she lay there for a moment, but her magic bond to Shadowlight was urging her to fight. She gripped the spear and used it as a walking stick to hoist herself to her feet.

The younger gargoyle was still fighting Taryin, but his magic was having trouble breaking past the barrier she'd built around herself. Anna glanced at the blood witch's protective dome of power and then back down at the sickly amber spear in her hand.

Would the witch's shields block a weapon forged of her own power?

Time to find out.

Anna took advantage of Taryin's distraction and took the last few staggering steps toward her prey. While Shadowlight kept her busy, Anna launched the spear with all the force left in her arm. It struck, impaling the witch in the center of her back.

Shadowlight struck from the front. His powerful blow spun Taryin around.

As Anna collapsed to her knees, she smiled at the blood witch's shocked expression.

"Got you again. Bitch."

Shadowlight reached down and grabbed the blood witch and dragged her farther from Anna.

"Wait." Anna's call came out more of a whimper than a shout, but she forced her voice to steady. "Take the bitch's head. I don't want her coming after us again."

Shadowlight nodded and reached down. There was a brief struggle and then came the wet, ragged sound of tearing flesh, snapping bones, and the pop of cartilage. He'd just beheaded the witch with his bare hands.

That he'd had to do that himself would have upset Anna more if she wasn't bleeding to death.

A moment later a hulking shadow was standing over her and then Shadowlight gathered her broken body up in his arms.

"Anna?" Her name came out a sob.

"Going to be okay, kid. I'm not dying here in this place." Anna patted his cheek, leaving bloody smears behind. "Call shadows to hide us and then take me back to my room."

He did as she asked, running back to their chambers as fast as he could. The bumping and jolting was a fresh agony, but Anna locked her jaws to prevent any sound from escaping. She needed to give Shadowlight as much time as possible to free himself of the collar and then escape.

Anna might have control of his command collar, but she didn't know what would happen if she died and he was still wearing it. Probably nothing good for him.

When they reached their chambers, Lanya and her husband rushed forward and helped Shadowlight carry her to the bed.

"You need to go," Anna said weakly as she looked up at the ceiling. "All of you. Go. Leave me."

"Go?" Lanya said. "We will not leave without you."

But to Anna's relief, Lanya's husband was already rushing to pull a large sack out of Anna's wardrobe. It was the go-bag she'd been putting together for their escape.

She'd been worried the servants would find it while cleaning. Guess that answered that question of the family's loyalty.

The father ordered his two children to pack a cloak and change of clean clothes and whatever other food and medicine was already in the chamber.

She was glad he understood what was coming. Her gaze returned to Lanya who was trying to slow the blood pouring from Anna's side.

Fighting past the pain, she sought calm. "Lanya, when I first came here, I was sent by the Mother's Sorceress. She gave me two medallions. They would allow me to return to my home once I found Shadowlight. I buried them a day's travel outside the city." Anna closed her eyes against the pain still ravaging her body and then focused on the memory and exact location where she'd buried the two medallions.

She explained the location in detail to the two servants. The entire time Shadowlight knelt beside her, his hands pressed against her wound as he shared power with her. He was trying to heal her, but she knew enough about how their strange magical link worked to know that while he might be able to heal her, it would take days. They didn't have the luxury of days. They probably didn't even have hours. Someone was bound to notice that there were three captains missing.

And this wound was bad, really bad. It felt like there was still a part of the blood witch inside her, feeding on her. While Taryin might be dead, apparently her evil magic didn't die with her. This reminded her of what the Riven had done to her when she'd first met Shadowlight. And yet, as horrible as the Riven attack and consequent taint had been, this was somehow worse.

She wasn't at all certain she could survive this even if Shadowlight had days to heal her.

"Shadowlight, you and the others need to go now before someone discovers what we did."

"I won't leave you."

"You must. I'm dying."

"*You are,*" agreed that beautiful, familiar voice inside her head. "*The blood witch infected you with her spell. It's not as sophisticated as the finished weaving would have been, but it is still killing you. Worse than killing you. When it is finished, your soul will be destroyed along with your body.*"

Anna's eyes widened at Death's words.

"*You can't have her, neither can the blood witch. I won't allow it.*" Shadowlight's grip on her tightened.

The poor cub. She'd promised that she wouldn't abandon him. Yet like everyone else he loved, she was breaking that promise. She was dying.

Worse than dying if Lord Death was to be believed. But Shadowlight might live. That's all Anna could hope for now.

"Shadowlight, I can't be saved. You need to go. Escape for me. Help the human family escape."

Shadowlight growled and shook his head. "I won't leave you. You wouldn't leave me."

Damn stubborn gargoyle!

"Actually, you're both incredibly stubborn," Lord Death said with a hint of humor. *"But of the two, I think the cub is mildly less so. Perhaps it's time I talk to him. He might listen now that you are dying."*

"No. Wait!" But Lord Death was already gone, and she feared he was talking privately to the kid.

CHAPTER THIRTY-THREE

Shortly after they'd started out, Gregory had found a game trail. They'd followed its snaking path along the valley for what he estimated was close to six hours when they came upon the cliff Daryna had described. As promised, it provided an excellent lookout for them to study the Battle Goddess's fortress.

From here, Gregory could look down upon the foot traffic coming and going on the road. And yet being on the opposite mountain slope, there was minimal risk of exposure to the enemy. When dawn came, they would move down the slope and infiltrate the city under the cover of shadow magic. With luck, they'd locate Anna and Shadowlight and possibly Gryton, then be gone before an enemy had time to raise the alarm.

That was the plan.

The soft crackle of a radio drew Gregory's gaze to where Major Resnick and Captain Stanton were discussing something amongst themselves. Resnick frowned and then glanced up at Gregory and Lillian.

"Alpha recon team was scouting a secondary exfil route in case the primary is compromised when they found another valley where the main canyon branched an hour back." Resnick paused and then frowned. "They report the valley is full of what looks like thousands of statues. Rough count of at least ten thousand."

"Those aren't statues," Daryna said.

"We didn't think so. We've seen how the gargoyles can take on the likeness of stone when it suits them. I figured this might be something similar." Resnick said

Gregory's unease grew. "There are very few species besides gargoyles who can master that magic."

Daryna nodded. "Yes, but as I've said, the Battle Goddess has been studying her brother's soldiers. And she has found a way to raise a large army that only requires the resources of one a tenth of its size."

"She conscripts them and then what?" Lillian asked, thinking aloud, "turns them to stone and then only wakes them when needed? Or are the soldiers not truly alive at all?"

"Your first guess is correct. The Battle Goddess raises, trains, and then enchants her soldiers, so they are in a state that is neither alive nor dead. When she has a large enough force to crush her enemies, she has her captains awaken and command them."

Daryna fell silent. The others around her just stared in disbelief. Gregory didn't blame them. The news came as a surprise to even him. It seemed his enemy had changed her methods since the last time he'd been born into the world.

Lillian growled softly at Daryna. "You knew this but didn't bother to tell us?"

"The sleepers are not our immediate concern. It takes substantial spell work to wake them." Daryna shrugged and Gregory thought Lillian was going to take her by her shoulders and shake her.

Instead, Lillian just sighed and asked, "Anything else you haven't told us that we should know about?"

"Likely many things, but we don't have half a year to get up to speed so I will fill you in later. Now, I think we need to concern ourselves with getting Anna and Shadowlight out and what to do if they've been corrupted and don't want to come with us."

Gregory merely nodded and hoped they'd all return safely to Earth and have nothing more immediate to concern themselves with than a lengthy and boring debriefing where Daryna told them everything else they didn't yet know.

"Daryna if you withhold further information from me, there will be trouble." He glowered at his other half. "But for now, my other half is correct, we need to go over the plan one more time in case anything goes wrong."

Resnick nodded. "If no one else has been withholding information, we should—"

Lillian cut him off. "Major Resnick, while we're telling the truth, there's something else we haven't told you."

Gregory knew what she was going to say. He could have stopped her or deflected the conversation, but he didn't. It was time to get this shame off his chest.

"The one you know as Commander Gryton is Gregory and Daryna's son."

Neither Resnick nor the other soldiers under his command said anything, though their faces were far from neutral. Resnick was the first to master speech after Lillian's statement.

"Thank you, Lillian," he said and then speared Gregory with his gaze. "Now one of the Avatars had better start talking."

Gregory glanced up at the cloudless sky overhead, stars bright against the darkness. Dawn was still a few hours off. Now was as good of a time as any to explain about Gryton, he supposed. "It's a long story, one I only learned of myself a few days ago..."

CHAPTER THIRTY-FOUR

During an awkward two-hour stint, Gregory laid out what he knew about Gryton and how he'd come into being. Daryna filled in details from what she'd gleaned from their son's memories when she was helping him to learn control.

"You helped make him stronger?" Icy venom dripped from Resnick's words.

The human had many uncomfortable questions and underlying them all was a simmering rage. Resnick's anger wasn't misplaced. Gryton had killed many innocent lives in his bid to return to the Magic Realm recently.

But the fact remained, Daryna *had* reached Gryton on some level, and with more parental guidance, he might be groomed into a powerful ally against the Battle Goddess. And a not so small part of Gregory wanted to give his son a chance to redeem himself.

"Gryton will have to answer for every life he's taken. And, if he so much as ponders double-crossing us, he's dead and neither of you will raise a hand to protect him. Or the alliance is over. Do I make myself clear?"

"Yes," Gregory said. "I will destroy him myself if he can't be saved. I've already had this discussion with Daryna."

"And you?" Resnick asked Lillian.

"You can take him out with my blessing if he hasn't held up his end of the bargain and protected my brother and Anna from the worst this place has to offer."

"You?" Resnick asked as he stared at Daryna.

"Gryton has never been given a chance to become other than what he is now. But if he is given a choice and directed down a different path, he will take it. I was in his mind and know he is capable of more than just cruelty and war."

Resnick grunted doubtfully. "If he isn't salvageable?"

"Then we will see his spirit is free to return to the Divine Ones."

"We agree, then," Gregory said softly. Before he could say more, the radio interrupted him.

Captain Stanton answered in a hushed tone. While the humans relayed some bit of news, Gregory looked out from between the two boulders he was sheltering behind, not trusting that someone within the fortress wouldn't be able to hear or see past his illusions.

Resnick called Gregory's name. "My men found something you might be interested in."

Looking away from the fortress, Gregory's ears flicked forward.

～

The Divine Ones had a hand in this new development. Gregory could feel it. This family had been guided to him. Or more accurately, they'd been fleeing one of the Battle Goddess's patrols when Alpha team had seen the family's ill-fated escape attempt. As the soldiers had watched from their hiding place, they'd seen the family get overtaken and captured by the patrol.

Amid the shouting and screaming, the human soldiers had only recognized two words: Shadowlight and Anna. The human family, whoever they were, might have knowledge. Resnick, his men, Daryna, and Lillian all agreed with Gregory's assessment.

The major ordered his men to follow the patrol until they could get there.

The trip didn't take long. Once there, a subtle sleep spell targeting the patrol dealt with the enemy soldiers. Then he and Daryna wove spells so Resnick and his men could understand the human family while they were questioned.

It was Daryna who recognized the mother as River's servant, Lanya.

Together they listened to the woman as she explained how Anna and Shadowlight had saved them. In turn, she and her family had loyally served the two new arrivals. Her story concluded with how Anna had been mortally wounded and the young gargoyle wouldn't leave her side, but even then Shadowlight acted to protect the family by ordering them to flee the city before an alarm was raised.

The servant's story made it even more urgent that Gregory act now. He glanced up at the sky, which was coloring pink with the first hint of dawn. It would be better to wait until the sun was high in the sky and the worst of the fortress's citizens asleep, but they were out of time.

Even if he couldn't heal Anna, he wouldn't leave her to die in that place. Certainly not with a blood witch in residence.

Gregory had thought he and his Sorceress had eradicated the entire blood witch coven eons ago, but it seemed that at least one still lived. He'd correct that mistake if Shadowlight and Anna hadn't already managed to destroy her.

When they were finished questioning the parents, Resnick ordered Alpha team to escort them back to the portal. They'd be returning to Earth for their own safety, but also for the knowledge they had of the Battle Goddess's domain.

CHAPTER THIRTY-FIVE

Shadowlight had ordered the servants away almost four hours ago, wanting them to have a chance to escape before guards learned something was amiss. As soon as they were gone, he'd used shadow magic to hunt down every last drop of Anna's blood so it couldn't be used in dark spells. He may not be able to save her, but he would do that for her.

Once all trace of her blood had been dealt with, he'd jumped up on the bed and curled around her body, mantling his wings to keep her warm. It was the only thing he could do for her. He'd already shared blood and power with her.

Lanya had dressed the wound the best she could before fleeing with her family. Shadowlight would have cloaked everyone in shadow magic and made his escape with them, but he'd been warned that if he tried to move Anna, she'd bleed out.

He couldn't fly with her for the same reason, and

Captain Taryin's spell was somehow preventing Anna from embracing the healing stone sleep. All he could do was wait for her to heal enough that moving her wouldn't kill her.

In the time since he'd first shared blood and magic with her, the terrible belly wound had slowly begun to knit itself together, but that wasn't the greatest danger. The blood magic was eating away at her spirit. His power was countering Taryin's spell, to some degree, but not enough.

Anna was running out of time. He might be young and inexperienced, but he knew what death felt like, and this power would be her death, and it wasn't going to be a clean one. This was the Riven all over again, only worse because he wasn't sure if gargoyle blood would save Anna this time.

"Come to me, my gargoyle. Let me at least save her soul."

Death had been whispering to him since shortly after Anna lost consciousness. Shadowlight knew Death never lied. If he sought out the Lord of the Underworld for aid, Anna would die. He didn't want her to die and leave him. She still might die here, but at least if he stayed, she still had a chance.

"Child, her only hope lies with me. Please return home."

"I can't. The collar—"

"Will not hold one such as you."

Boots thudded against stone in the hall outside. Someone was running swiftly toward his location. A moment later whoever it was rattled the latch. Thankfully, Shadowlight had already barricaded the door with a hastily put together spell, so the door didn't admit the newcomer.

Reaching out with his magic, he learned it was Commander Gryton. His first instinct was to fight the fire elemental until it occurred to him that Tin Man might be able to help heal Anna.

Outside, Gryton cursed. A moment later a hot wave of magic vaporized the door leading out to the hallway and the commander sprinted inside. He crossed the outer room and then the inner bedroom door crashed inward.

Gryton took one look at them and compressed his lips in anger.

"Why are you still here?"

The barked question wasn't the one Shadowlight had been expecting.

Striding over to the bed, Gryton looked down at Anna and cursed louder, then he swiftly checked Shadowlight over for injury. Finding none, he returned to examining Anna's belly wound.

Gryton glanced over his shoulder, scanning the outer room. "We need to hurry. Others will discover what you did to the blood witch and the twins. Ninara's second in command is already seeking her. You and Anna need to be gone before then."

Confusion swamped Shadowlight. "Why are you helping us?"

"Because I've been tasked with protecting you and the hybrid since shortly after she came here to rescue you," Gryton said as he wove his own powerful wards at the entrance of the bedroom.

Shadowlight glanced down at Anna. Even in gargoyle form, her skin was a sickly washed out shade. "Why are you helping us? Is this another test?"

With his back to Shadowlight, he couldn't read Gryton's expression, but he could smell his concern. The commander ignored his questions while he continued to build his protective spells.

"I'm helping you because we're family and I swore I'd help you and the human, or die trying." Gryton glanced over his shoulder again. "Likely it will be 'die trying' since you don't have the survival instincts the Divine Ones gave a rock."

Shadowlight's ears flicked toward Gryton and then flattened against his mane. This had to be another test.

Gryton finished the spell work and walked back to the bed to look down at Anna. "She's dying, and you won't long survive her if you don't do as I say."

When the commander reached for Shadowlight's collar, he snarled a warning.

"Don't bite the hand that's offering you aid, cub." A sharp slap delivered to Shadowlight's muzzle accompanied the words. "I'm going to release the collar, so you don't have to waste your power breaking free."

Shadowlight didn't fight, but he continued to growl as Gryton felt around the collar, delivering little surges of magic into the metal. Then suddenly, between breaths, the weight of the collar fell away and Shadowlight blinked up at Gryton in surprise. The commander had kept his word. Why?

"If you run now, you have a chance to escape the fortress before anyone else knows what's unfolded. With your training, you might even make it to one of the other kingdoms who would offer a gargoyle shelter."

"I won't leave Anna." Shadowlight sprang back up on the bed and crouched over her. If the commander thought he was going to just run away and leave Anna to die, Gryton had another surprise coming.

"Anna will be dead by noon, her soul dragged back to the blood witch for an eternity of torment."

"The blood witch is dead."

Gryton laughed. "No, she is not. Already she is restoring herself. You left her with two powerful victims to feed upon. Ninara and Honnan are no great loss, but the blood witch will rise even more powerful than before. Only the Lord of the Underworld can save Anna's soul."

Shadowlight glanced down at Anna and looked at her clammy skin. "I can't lose her. Lord Death will kill her." He'd already lost everyone else; he couldn't lose her, too. And, yet, if he didn't go, Anna would pay the ultimate price for his cowardice. "Are you certain there is no power here that can heal her?"

"Yes," Gryton snarled. "I would save her soul if I could, but even that is beyond my fire magic. After she dies, her soul returns to the blood witch. Taryin will be able to summon her corpse and mend the dead flesh to create the perfect slave to keep you in line."

Snarling, Shadowlight gathered Anna in his arms and leaped back three steps, as if putting distance between Anna and Gryton could somehow deny the truth of his words.

"Her only chance lies with Lord Death. At least that way, even if her body dies, her soul will return to the Spirit Realm to be reborn one day. Take comfort in that, cub, and do what's right. If I had done that when I was first born, maybe I'd now lead a better life than the one I find myself in."

If this was a test, Shadowlight didn't care if he passed or failed. He couldn't risk Anna's soul.

Sobbing silently, he reached into his own being and sought that power which linked all gargoyles to their liege lord.

Just the briefest of touches was all it took. Already the powerful spell that was a part of his very soul began to expand, spreading out over his body and Anna, too.

Shadowlight glanced up at Gryton one last time. The commander was summoning new spells. Lethal battle magics this time instead of wards of protection.

"What about you?" Shadowlight asked in the last few moments before the spell would activate and pull his body back to his liege lord.

"Me?" Gryton laughed, "I shall be alone again. A natural state for me."

Shadowlight held out his hand. "Come with me."

"No, Death and I have never seen eye to eye," Gryton paused and then grinned. "And, cub, if we ever meet again, don't assume we will be on the same side. Trust no one. You'll live longer that way."

Gryton's voice faded away and so too did the room as the spell flung Shadowlight and Anna far from the Battle Goddess's kingdom.

PART FOUR

*L*illian was climbing over a large outcropping of stone as they made their way back to the overlook peak when a strange yearning sensation flowed over her. Her wings spread and her muscles bunched as if to propel her up into the air. It was unlike anything she'd ever felt before.

Gregory's wings shifted restlessly. He must have felt it, too.

"What, by the gods, was that?" Lillian asked as the feeling slowly receded. It took another ten thunderous heartbeats before she could convince her wings to fold tight to her back again.

"A gargoyle just returned to Lord Death," Gregory said as he closed his eyes and tilted his muzzle to the sky. After half a minute, he glanced back down at her. "Shadowlight and Anna just journeyed to Lord Death this night. May they find him ever merciful."

"My brother is gone?" Lillian felt dismay and a new

kind of fear because while she was glad he wasn't still trapped as a slave to the Battle Goddess, she wasn't sure if Lord Death was much of an improvement."

Major Resnick circled around in front of Gregory and looked the tall male in the eye. "You're telling me Anna and the kid are no longer down there?"

"Yes."

"You're absolutely certain?" Resnick asked, disbelief clear in his voice. Lillian didn't blame him. The humans had to take what the magic wielders said on faith.

"There is no one down there to save."

Still looking unhappy, Major Resnick got on the radio. "We're aborting the mission. I repeat mission aborted. We're falling back to the secondary site."

"What will happen to Anna and my brother now?" Lillian asked with growing dread. Gregory had wanted to avoid meeting Lord Death until he'd had a chance to better understand all the changes in Shadowlight and Anna. Now it was out of their hands.

"I will go before Lord Death and learn what has become of Anna and Shadowlight. If they have been granted mercy, I will beseech the Lord of the Underworld to return them both to their families."

That was more 'ifs' than Lillian liked, and Gregory hadn't said what he'd do if Lord Death decided to keep them. Lillian refused to believe anyone the Avatars considered a friend would be so cruel as to kill two innocent beings who had no control over what fate had unleashed upon them.

"Lillian, Daryna," Gregory gestured toward the human

team already making their way back over the treacherous ground. "It's time we returned to the Mortal Realm."

Lillian was devastated to be leaving without her brother but consoled herself with the knowledge they weren't exactly leaving empty-handed. They'd learned that the Battle Goddess was building an even greater army than they'd expected. They'd even managed to save one human family. That had to be worth something, even if it didn't soothe her fears about Shadowlight and Anna.

A deep, reverberating tone issued from somewhere within the city. It took Lillian a few seconds to recognize it as a horn. One really big-ass horn by the sound of it.

Gregory bumped his muzzle against Lillian's flank to get her moving. Yep. Time to go.

The human soldiers took the lead, Lillian followed close on their heels while Gregory and Daryna brought up the rear.

They'd only just clambered down from the rocky ground surrounding the overlook when Lillian heard Gregory call Daryna's name.

Glancing over her shoulder, she spotted Daryna running back in the direction they'd just come. Gregory dropped to all fours and raced after her.

"What the hell?" Major Resnick took the words right out of Lillian's mouth.

Lillian turned and gave chase. Behind her, the humans did the same. She leaped over a boulder in her path and on the other side Gregory had Daryna pinned down. The Sorceress was using magic, attempting to toss him off.

She ran to Gregory's side and then locked her jaws around Daryna's throat. Gregory was too damn gentle when dealing with his other half. They didn't have time to waste if Daryna was planning a double cross.

"Behave, or I'll tear out your throat. That would be one way to take back my soul and my magic." Lillian tightened her grip and gave Daryna a little shake to reinforce her words. *"Do you understand me?"*

"Yes."

"Good. You will remain calm and explain to Gregory why you were attempting to get captured."

"I wasn't trying to get captured."

"Could've fooled me."

"Gryton is in danger. The Battle Goddess is breaching his shields even now." Daryna started to fight again.

Lillian bit down hard enough to draw blood. *"Rushing off and getting yourself captured won't help Gryton. Besides, how can you be certain this isn't just an elaborate trap set for the Avatars?"*

"It's not. I can feel Gryton's agony," Daryna whispered, her eyes growing distant as she turned her head in the direction her son lay.

Crap. Shadowlight and Anna escaped the Battle Goddess's clutches and suddenly Gryton was getting tortured.

Lillian released Daryna and looked to Gregory instead. "Gryton must have helped Anna and Shadowlight escape."

Suspicion still hovered in Gregory's expression, but he nodded.

Lillian turned her focus back to Daryna. "If Gryton helped Shadowlight, then he deserves our aid. I don't like to be indebted. We need a new plan. If we just rush in blindly, we'll probably get someone killed, maybe even Gryton."

Reason returned to Daryna's gaze. "You're correct. We need to prepare. They now will be on alert, hunting for Shadowlight and Anna. They will not know for certain that the gargoyles went to Lord Death."

"This is madness," Gregory grumbled.

"He is our son," Daryna countered. "We must save him."

"She's right," Lillian said unhappily.

"Fine," Gregory agreed. "There is the blood witch to deal with as well."

Major Resnick join them. "Ah, hell. We *are* going down there, aren't we?"

CHAPTER THIRTY-SEVEN

He'd always known his life would end in fire as his power raged out of control. Though, he'd also thought it would be in battle against his Avatar parents or the Lord of the Underworld. But, no, it was the Lady of Battles that wanted him dead this time.

That the Battle Goddess would be so foolish as to exterminate him in her own kingdom just reinforced how unstable she truly was.

"When I die, I'll take out your kingdom—cities, towns, temples, and army. All of it razed down to the bones of the earth." Gryton said, his voice strangely calm.

Perhaps this had always been her plan.

He fought against the chains, only to realize they'd melted away long ago as the demigoddess continued to pour a vast amount of her magic into him. Even now a torrent of magic held him pinned to the altar, no other physical restraints were required.

"You won't," the Battle Goddess countered, her voice sounding like it came from far away.

Gryton would've laughed if the pressure on his chest had allowed. As it was, he could barely draw breath. Simple suffocation, unpleasant though it was to experience, wouldn't kill one such as him.

However, the amount of power she was pouring into him, that would eventually overwhelm his control. Even now, he could feel his fire magic seeking to slip his control. Only the knowledge the Sorceress had shared with him in her few brief lessons allowed him to maintain mastery over his magic this long.

Soon, even that wouldn't be enough, and his destructive power would cascade out of control. The force would be enough to destroy the Battle Goddess's domain. Perhaps even destroy this entire world.

Lord Death and the Avatars would be able to curtail some of the damage, but certainly not all of it.

"Do you think my death throes will obliterate the duality curse that holds you here?" It wouldn't. She had to know that.

Gryton hoped the demigoddess would come to her senses. If he could reason with her, he might be able to survive a little while longer.

"No. The duality curse is woven from pure Spirit Magic. The Divine Ones had to sacrifice their Avatars to create it. It will take a far greater death than yours to break the spell."

"Then why sacrifice your army?" He'd shed no tears over many of them, but Vaspara, Sorac, and a few others had been fair to him.

If it was in his power, he would spare them. Unfortunately, if the Battle Goddess didn't stop force-feeding him power, the choice would be out of his hands.

"You are almost ready," the Battle Goddess whispered into his mind. She didn't stop the power transfer, although it was less than it had been.

Gryton turned his head and studied all the captains where they circled the altar, looking on with neutral expressions. Only Honnan and Ninara were missing, devoured by Taryin's magic to give her life once more.

Interestingly, the blood witch wasn't watching him as he glowed like a living ember, his armor melting in rivulets off his body. No, the blood witch's gaze was assessing the Battle Goddess.

"*My Goddess,*" Gryton whispered along a private link. "*You exhaust yourself to destroy me, but for saving me from Lord Death all those millennia ago, I will offer one last word of advice: look to the blood witch for your next betrayal.*"

"*She is loyal.*" But the Battle Goddess looked at the witch with narrowed eyes.

"*So too was I, once,*" Gryton agreed. "*I betrayed you to save family. The blood witch will betray you, not in the name of honor, but ambition.*"

"*Lies.*"

"*I've never lied, not even when I helped Shadowlight escape. You ordered me to protect him from those in this kingdom who would do him harm. I did that.*"

"*Your gilded words will not save you.*"

"I didn't expect them to," Gryton said aloud.

"Very well. Since you were honest with me, I shall be honest with you." The Battle Goddess knelt next to him and he could now see her features through the waves of heat and fire bleeding off his skin. Her features were weary with strain.

"You don't look so very well, my lady."

The Battle Goddess laughed. "You're no longer as handsome as you once were either. I can see your soul shining through your ravaged flesh and bones."

"Sounds lovely."

"It does have a strange beauty to it, but that will not save you." She sat and stroked a finger down his chest. "When your body is ready to surrender, I shall transport you to the Sorceress's hamadryad tree. She will sense danger and the Avatars will come running. The harsh trip to the Mortal Realm will shatter your willpower and seconds after that you will become a mindless, raging elemental that will consume the world. When all is done, you will rise to take your place in the sky in a binary dance with that system's sun."

Ah. So that was her plan.

"The flesh and blood Avatars will not have time to react and will find themselves back in the Spirit Realm, and safely out of my way for the time I need."

Sudden understanding struck Gryton. "You always planned to use me."

"Yes. Had things gone as planned, it would not have come for several seasons yet. Shadowlight would have been fully trained when I sent you to the Mortal Realm to destroy the Avatars. Once they were out of my way, I would send Shadowlight and his Kyrsu to crush my brother's army."

As long as she was talking, she wasn't pouring as much

power upon him, so he'd keep her entertained because he sensed something she did not. "What about your plans to enslave the Avatars?"

She jerked back, her eyes narrowing in rage like he'd slapped her. "Plans change."

"Did you know my mother captured me when I was in the Mortal Realm? She knew me. Knew I was her child. The one thing she had been waiting an eternity for. What do you think the Avatars will do to you in retaliation when they leave the Spirit Realm and are reborn one day?"

"You lie. The Avatars would kill you the moment they recognize what you are. They know their duty."

"Actually, they didn't kill me. At first, my father was shocked, and his initial gut reaction was to destroy me; though, even he came around and didn't swat me out of existence. I came here to free Shadowlight and his pet human. I lived up to my end of the bargain. The Avatars are honorable. They will avenge my death. That pleases me."

The Battle Goddess's howl of rage made him smile.

It also gave him the will to hold on a little bit longer as she resumed pouring a torrent of power into him. While she was distracted killing him slowly, he turned his thoughts inwards.

"Did you get all that, mother?"

"Yes," the Sorceress whispered back to him and he felt a loving caress accompany her words. *"Your father heard it as well and together the Battle Goddess is outmatched."*

"Don't underestimate the blood witch."

"We won't," she promised and then dropped out of the link, but the male half of the Avatars was still with him.

"I may still have to kill you one day, but I will not let the Lady of Battles destroy what I brought into this world."

Ah. Such a loving father he had.

"Gryton, I know you helped Shadowlight before you even knew we'd arrived here. That was noble. If you have a conscience, then maybe there is something more buried deep in your soul that's worthy of salvation."

"You're not the type of father who tells his son how much he loves him, I take it?"

"No," Gregory said with a chuckle. *"But who knows. Maybe one day. Let's live long enough to find out."*

Gryton started to laugh. The Battle Goddess and her captains pulled back in surprise.

Love was a foreign concept to Gryton, but he wouldn't mind living long enough to determine whether he was capable of the emotion. And if he wasn't? Well, he'd settle for razing his enemies to the ground and scattering their ashes to the four winds.

He looked up at the Battle Goddess. *I'll start with you.*

CHAPTER THIRTY-EIGHT

ajor Resnick and Sergeant Maracle flanked Lillian as they made their way across the valley floor and onto the road. Ahead Captain Stanton, Lieutenant Willis, Gregory and Daryna led the way while Corporals Laforce and Brown came last. She and Gregory had expanded their shadow magic to hide signs of the group's passage. Even passersby wouldn't hear their whispered conversation.

"A year ago," the major said in an offhanded manner, "if someone had told me I'd be walking down a cobbled road in the company of a female weregargoyle attempting to rescue an evil demigod to halt an even more demented demigoddess from using him like an arsenal of tactical nukes, I'd say they'd gotten themselves some bad drugs."

"Weregargoyle?" Lillian asked wondering if she should be offended.

"White folk have to label everything," Sergeant Maracle said with a humorous glint in his eyes.

Lillian was still getting to know Resnick's new team. Sergeant Maracle was the unit's closemouthed sniper. Most of what she knew about him was second-hand knowledge from Gran.

No one could long resist Gran's extrovert nature, not even the sniper, whom she'd learned was of Mohawk heritage.

"Oh, come on," Resnick complained. "It was funny. Shapeshifters. Werewolf. Weregargoyle. No? Fine, I'm sorry."

Lillian rolled her eyes and kept walking.

"Major, keep talking and you'll need a ladder to climb out of the hole," Maracle commented dryly.

"What? I said I was sorry."

Obviously still finding Resnick's antics funny, Maracle grinned and muttered a 'you're hopeless' as he sauntered past the major on his way up to the front again.

Resnick shrugged and looked at Lillian. "Well, you're a dryad that shifts into a gargoyle when the mood strikes you, so you can see where the confusion came from."

Lillian snorted. "Weregargoyle has got to go. Scratch it from your vocabulary, or I'm going to bite your ass every time I hear it."

"Fair enough." Major Resnick grinned. "Consider it gone."

A moment later, his jovial look vanished and he groaned. "I have to write a report about this shit with Gryton. I can't even begin to describe how bad my superiors are going to chew me out for this." Resnick continued to mutter to himself. Lillian still heard 'evil shit demigod' and more cursing.

Lillian frowned unhappily. "I'm not happy about this new Gryton angle either, but if we don't do something the Battle Goddess is going to use him to destroy Earth. Mention that in the report."

"There will still be deep skepticism. Hell. I'm here and have seen more weird shit than most and I'm still having trouble swallowing the whole story." Resnick shook his head. "And it isn't that I don't believe the Avatars. It's just so—"

"Crazy?" Lillian added helpfully. "Says the woman who thought she was human until six months ago and now I'm a gargoyle. Hmm...yeah. You've got nothing to whine about."

Major Resnick just shook his head and laughed. "Point taken."

Ahead Gregory suddenly halted and motioned them off the road. The soldiers responded swiftly, and Lillian dropped to all fours a second later. Once everyone was belly down in a small overgrown ditch, Gregory joined them.

With Lillian on one end and Gregory on the other, they spread their wings over Daryna and the humans. Where their wings crossed over, so too did their shadow magic.

Even the most observant hunter would detect nothing. But Gregory still waited until the ten-horse patrol rode past and out of sight before he rose up and signaled everyone back onto the road.

Gregory said once they were inside the city, it would be easier since the city had already been searched and the patrols were now expanding further afield in the hunt for Shadowlight and Anna.

That wasn't to say they would be safe within the city by any means. If they were discovered before they had a chance to snatch Gryton and escape, it would be a no-holds-barred fight for freedom. Lillian shoved that unpleasant thought aside.

The road climbed an ever-steepening slope until they reached the main gates. During the long climb, Daryna and Gregory remained in contact with Gryton, to give him hope so he would not give up.

They moved swiftly into the city and made their way toward her hamadryad in this realm. Gryton didn't have much time, but thankfully, Lillian's instincts told her the tree was not much farther, just north and west of their present location.

As the sun rose higher in the sky, shadows became scarcer, but Gregory and Daryna navigated the strangely empty city with familiarity, finding narrow alleyways and tree-shaded walkways. The city wasn't completely empty, though. They still had to avoid guards on watch and subdued servants going about their business.

"News of Shadowlight and Anna's escape must have reached the servants by now. Why isn't the city in an uproar?"

"The servants are likely too frightened to show themselves while the Battle Goddess is raging." Gregory's ears flicked toward Lillian as he spoke. "And her senior warriors are all within her temple, but I am still on alert for any signs we have been detected."

So far, they'd been lucky. They hadn't been forced to take out further patrols after that first one to rescue the human family. If they'd been forced to take out more patrols, their enemies would soon realize something was amiss.

At last, they made their way through the fortress city and reached its north wall. Beyond that was a sprawling field that gently sloped away from the city's wall. It was a practice yard, Gregory said, but she didn't even give it a cursory scan. Her gaze locked onto the two trees that grew further down the slope.

Hamadryads. One of them was hers from when she'd lived here as a child. The other belonged to her mother. As she drew closer, Lillian saw why they were unharmed from any form of the Battle Goddess's retaliation. A shimmering dome of energy encased the two trees.

"That's the spell Daryna and I created so no one else could easily venture into the Mortal Realm." Gregory rolled his eyes in her direction. "You know how I hate uninvited guests."

"Wait. If nothing can pass that shield, why does the Battle Goddess think she can send Gryton through to Earth?"

Gregory huffed and made a sour expression. "The magic is attuned to me, Daryna and you. Gryton is our son. The magic recognizes him as part of us."

"The Battle Goddess knows Gryton is yours?"

"Yes. It must be why she offered to shelter him. It certainly had nothing to do with kindness toward an orphaned child."

They made it through the practice yard and reached the enormous shimmering dome. Bright sparks of color danced and flared over the surface, shimmering and spinning like the rainbow hues on the surface of the bubble. Only this bubble wouldn't break when touched.

"You said the spell would only recognize us." Lillian kept her voice lowered so it wouldn't carry. "What about the humans?"

Gregory reached over to nuzzle her. "My worrier."

"Well, someone has to, since shit hits the fan almost daily."

"The spell will let us bring others through with us, but there is a little..." Gregory paused as if searching for the correct word.

"Blip in your plan?" Lillian supplied.

"Hmm. Yes. Though it's not a large problem."

"Out with it."

"We must wait outside until Gryton is brought here and shoved through the dome," Gregory explained. "When someone passes through the barrier, it will be noticeable. We'll hide close enough to the dome that we can slip across when they send Gryton through."

Understanding clicked. The swirling pretty bits of color would change when disturbed.

Lillian glanced across the area. "There's not much cover."

"Stealth has served us well so far. We will trust in our magic and hope the Divine Ones give us their blessing."

Ah. It was hope and pray time. Nice and reassuring.

Resnick sidled up next to them, and Gregory explained the situation. For his part, Resnick took it well. "Alpha team reports they and the family are safely back at the portal."

"Good," Gregory said as he scanned the area for hidden dangers. "Have your men go through and then radio back once they reach Earth. The portal will carry the signal while it remains open. However, once the human family and your men go through, I want Gran to close the portal. She knows what to do. We won't be returning home that way and I don't want a patrol accidentally stumbling upon it."

"I'll see it's done."

"Thank you." Gregory scanned the area once more. "The Battle Goddess's soldiers will likely approach there, between those two ridges," Gregory pointed to the narrow gully. "If we move west along the dome's curve, we will be in the tallest hamadryad's shadow and still be able to see them coming while remaining out of their direct path. Besides, it's better to be downwind in case one among them can scent something my shadow magic might fail to hide."

"Hiding in shadows still feels like a piss-poor shelter," Resnick stated as he and his team moved to the location Gregory indicated.

Lillian and Daryna were herded after them. Gregory came last and they settled in to wait.

It still felt strange waiting for the enemy to bring them Gryton. And a not so small part of her felt that they should be looking for him instead of just waiting for the Battle Goddess to finish torturing him.

But Gregory's plan was sound. Wandering around an enemy fortress was a good way to get captured. So, Lillian waited.

CHAPTER THIRTY-NINE

Gregory was the first to hear the approach of the newcomers, but Lillian picked up the sound seconds later. Soon a long line of armor-clad warriors approached. They were led by a beautiful woman wearing a long flowing dress. Her hair was unbound, a floating curtain that shifted with the wind.

She certainly wasn't dressed for battle like the others. Lillian's eyes narrowed. That could only mean her power was such that she did not fear the bite of an enemy's blade. Or other forms of physical damage. That couldn't be a good sign.

"Let me guess: the blood witch?"

"Yes," Gregory replied with a soft hiss. "Don't lower your mental shields during the fight or after, not until we're home. Her power rivals that of the old ones."

More comforting news.

Lillian and the others remained hunched down, but she could detect their shift to readiness.

Shortly before the enemy reached the outer edge of the dome, the woman in the lead raised her hand. The line of soldiers shifted as they moved to the side, parting to allow two other warriors forward. The newcomers held chains and dragged something behind them as they marched toward the blood witch's location.

It wasn't until they were at the front of the line that she saw what they dragged at the end of the chains. If she hadn't known this had to be Gryton, she never would have recognized him.

The black lump of char raised an arm and gave his chains a savage jerk. The guards on either side stumbled but didn't fall.

Gryton still had a little fight left in him. She didn't know how. No one deserved to be, to have had done — whatever had been done to him.

God. Lillian ground her teeth together to stop the snarling growl that wanted to escape. Gregory shifted, and she realized he was holding Daryna back.

Suddenly the blood witch spun around, no longer addressing her soldiers but looking around like she sensed something the others hadn't.

"Move," Gregory ordered as he grabbed Stanton and Maracle and shoved them through the barrier. Resnick was propelled through next. Then Lillian was snatching up Laforce and Brown. She wrapped her tail around Willis just as Gregory shoved them all hard. Together the three of them stumbled through the barrier.

Daryna darted through next and ran past them. Gregory came last. He paused long enough to help Lillian to her feet and then he darted off in pursuit of Daryna.

Lillian dropped to all fours and ran after them. It didn't take more than a second to know they were sprinting toward the section of dome where the blood witch and Gryton had last been located.

Ten seconds later Lillian reached the front of the dome to find both Daryna and the blood witch summoning magic.

Other captains were already flinging balls and spears of fiery power at the dome.

The surface danced and flared with a thousand ripples, each new impact caused the pattern to cascade in a new direction.

So far nothing had made it through the shield, including Gryton. Lillian bounded up to Gregory.

"We need to get Gryton," she said as she watched the shifting bodies on the other side of the dome. "They're dragging him further away."

"Go to the edge of the shield and prepare to drag Gryton forward when I say. Use the chains. Don't touch him directly."

Lillian nodded and leaped to obey, still not knowing Gregory's plan. Whatever it was must require a lot of power because he was drawing down a tornado of cold magic from the Spirit Realm.

He stood with his arms outstretched above his head as more and more power built. Outside the dome, the blood witch was doing the same. Then moments apart they both unleashed their respective powers. The dome shuddered under the impact. Lillian felt her heart drop down to her stomach, but the shield held and absorbed both powers.

Waiting with muscles taut, Lillian crouched, ready to

dart forward and snatch Gryton at Gregory's signal. Daryna joined in the fight and flung a torrent of magic toward the barrier. The Sorceress's movements were a strange, graceful dance, almost like watching a martial artist, but instead of landing blows upon an opponent, her power raced to certain points on the shield, counteracting whatever the blood witch had been attempting.

"Now," Gregory roared and Daryna flung a second vast wave of magic upon the barrier.

Lillian leaped forward as the dome's circumference grew, pushing outward in an ever-widening circle. It expanded faster than the enemy could react, hitting armor clad figures and tossing them away like leaves before a train.

The blood witch was tossed back farther than the others as if the barrier was revolted by the taint of her touch.

But Gryton was now inside the dome. Lillian bolted forward. Remembering Gregory's warning, she reached for the chain instead of Gryton's ember-bright arms. She swiftly hauled him farther from the edge of the dome.

At least until she was brought up short by a new resistance. A glance over her shoulder confirmed her suspicions. One of the soldiers had managed to maintain a hold on his chain and was even now regaining his feet. The warrior was immense, his shoulders broad. Lillian grinned.

The fool had never played tug-of-war with a gargoyle. She bunched her shoulders and thigh muscles and then gave a mighty heave. The armor-clad figure on the opposite end of the chain smashed into the dome. He didn't release his hold, so she gave him another two good bashes.

He still maintained his grip. Was the bastard part tick? He was latched on like one.

Soon he was joined by three of his friends. Lillian glanced over her shoulder for aid, but Gregory and Daryna were busy feeding the dome more power, strengthening the areas where the blood witch's magic was beginning to eat through.

Help came in the form of Resnick and his team. The humans rushed forward, and four of them grabbed hold of the chain and aided her while Resnick aimed at the thick chain links. Strengthened by magic, it wasn't an easy target. Two direct hits only dented the magic-reinforced metal.

But it still gave Lillian an idea and she summoned hundreds of sharp little shards of shadow magic and sent them chasing each other down the length of the chain toward the enemy combatants.

The first roar of pain was rewarded by a bit of slack in the chain. More yelps of pain reached her ears as further bits of her shadow magic found its way inside armor.

Stanton, Maracle and Brown quickly hauled the rest of the chain inside the dome while Lillian knelt next to Gryton. He didn't look any better up close. As she studied him, ash and blackened flesh fell from his body.

"Gryton can you hear me?" Lillian asked as she reached for his manacles. A bit of shadow magic found the closure mechanism and wiggled until the cuff sprang free.

"I can hear you," he said in a voice that sounded as dry, cracked, and abused as his flesh.

Lillian didn't know what to say to him, so settled for the first thing that came to her. "I'm not going to hurt you."

"There is nothing you can do to hurt me more than I already hurt." Gryton suddenly reached out and grasped her hand.

His touch burned but Lillian held on.

"Thank you. Please talk to me." There was fear in his voice.

"Daryna is coming. She'll know how to help you." Lillian hoped it was true.

As if her name had summoned her, the Sorceress was there. She took one look at Gryton and dropped to her knees. Tears ran down her cheeks as she took in her son's condition.

She reached out and shattered a collar that was circling his throat. "My child, I'm going to siphon power from you and feed it into the dome. It will get better soon." Daryna promised.

Lillian held Gryton's hand while Daryna worked. As promised, the power flowed out of Gryton now that there was no collar preventing it. It must have worked like a one-way valve, allowing magic to flow into him, but not escape.

Once Daryna siphoned away a large portion of the power overloading Gryton's system, Lillian witnessed a miracle: his body repaired itself, muscle and skin forming over his bones, hiding the molten core she'd seen shimmering between his ribs only minutes earlier.

Daryna was still working to heal Gryton, but he shoved at her weakly.

"Sorceress?" Lillian unfurled a wing and touched the other woman. Daryna felt different, weaker, less substantial. Even Gryton was concerned, so it must be bad. "You need to stop. You're...fading."

Lillian wasn't sure what else to call the dimming sense she had of the Sorceress.

Daryna ignored her demands to stop and continued to draw power away from Gryton. He jerked his hand from hers and crawled a few feet before collapsing.

Even without the link of skin on skin, the Sorceress continued to draw power from Gryton.

"Stop her," he choked out in a dry, rasping voice.

"I don't know how," Lillian said, looking toward Gregory.

"She's killing herself."

Crap. "Gregory!"

Her bellow got an instant response from her mate; he spread his wings and flew to their location.

Lillian stepped back and stood with the human soldiers to give Gregory room to work with Gryton and Daryna.

"We've got a breach," Resnick shouted.

CHAPTER FORTY

"Breach, breach, breach!" Resnick shouted, and his men took up formation in front of a section of dome where a series of fissures were forming. The blood witch and the other captains were now concentrating their attack upon that section of the barrier.

"We weakened the spell by forcing it to expand," Gregory shouted to Lillian over the increasingly loud hum emitted by the distressed shield. "Once I shore up the Sorceress's power and heal the damages to her body, I'll create a second dome inside this one. But I need you and the humans to hold off the Battle Goddess's soldiers long enough for me to do that. I just need a few minutes."

"You've got it."

Lillian sprinted to join the humans. Standing just off to the side on Resnick's left, she began summoning a new barrage of tiny shards of shadow magic. With a flick of her wrist, she sent them spinning through the air, hunting those closest to breaching the dome. Her efforts were rewarded by new snarls and screams of pain.

When the largest fissure expanded enough for the first enemy swords to pierce the barrier, Resnick and his team started targeting the owners, aiming for anything they could hit through the narrow opening. More screams and roars of pain and the occasional cloud of red spray announced when their bullets found a mark. Not all the blood was red, but when hit, they did bleed. Bleeding was very good in this case.

The fallen bodies piled up, which strangely helped slow the growth of the shield's fissures. Lillian could only speculate the bodies were absorbing some of the magic meant to erode the dome.

Shouting encouragement to her human allies, Lillian called more shadow magic and sent several waves of obsidian shards flying. Soon more bodies were adding to the insulation around the shield.

At least until the enemies figured out what Lillian was doing and started to drag their dead out of the way.

Resnick cursed but didn't stop firing. Soon more bodies took the place of the ones removed.

Lillian sent another wave of shadow magic through the barrier and then glanced over her shoulder at Gregory, Daryna and Gryton. Gryton's recovery was astonishing. He was sitting up, and his skin had regrown over two-thirds of his body. It still had to hurt like a son of a bitch.

When he opened his eyes, she was suddenly staring into his blazing amber gaze. She watched in shock as the rest of his wounds closed before her eyes and he was suddenly whole. He glanced over his shoulder at Daryna and then he looked back toward Lillian and the human soldiers.

His lips compressed, fire and rage burning in his eyes. Lillian began calling more of her shadow magic, thinking Gryton had played them all. But his fiery gaze slid past her and Resnick's team. They weren't Gryton's targets.

He stood, stark naked and fully healed, his only clothing a fine coating of ash. Then before her eyes, the ash transformed into armor, the protective covering growing out of his body. As he walked past her, she realized it wasn't metal at all, instead a material forged of his very magic.

A raging ball of fire appeared between his outstretched hands. With a violent motion, he pushed it away from his chest, sending it speeding toward the dome. The power hit the shield and raced past it to incinerate the first line of enemy soldiers.

More soldiers rushed forward to take their place, and beyond them, Lillian could still see the blood witch working some great spell. She didn't know what it would do but knew it couldn't be good.

Gryton was formidable, but he'd just about died. He couldn't be a hundred percent right now. Lillian doubted if he was in any condition to match spells with the blood witch.

They needed the Avatars back in this fight.

Lillian glanced over her shoulder and found Gregory kneeling over Daryna. He'd slashed open his forearm and was trying to strengthen her body with his potent gargoyle blood.

"I'm beyond healing," Daryna whispered into Lillian's mind.

Lillian jerked in surprise and then glanced down to meet her doppelganger's gaze.

"It is time that you claim what is rightfully yours," Daryna said.

Gregory didn't stir from his work, so Lillian doubted he was aware of what his other half was saying.

"Gregory is strong. He might be able to heal your body enough that we can make it home."

"No." The one word was accompanied by a small shake of her head. *"We must strike now while we're here in the Magic Realm. We have an opportunity to land a great blow against our enemies. But I'm not strong enough. Only the true Sorceress has a chance."*

Daryna was talking about her own ending like she wanted Lillian to do it. *"No."*

As much pain and grief as her doppelganger had caused her, she didn't want to see Daryna die because on a deep, secret level Lillian didn't want to become the Sorceress. *"But you're still alive. Gregory is trying to heal you."*

"Yes. The beloved idiot can't face the thought of seeing even a temporary clone die. He'll also see my death as causing the death of his mate as well. He thinks he can save us both. He can't. And there is only one Sorceress. You." Daryna held up a shaking hand. *"Come, claim what is rightfully yours. Save everything you love."*

"But Gregory—"

"Is wrong this one time. He knows it but can't help but fight for the life he so desperately wants. A life with you as his mate and me

housing the other half of his soul. But our hamadryad only did this so that I could buy you time to save our children. Both of them. Now they are safe. Gryton here with us, and our youngest sleeping back in our hamadryad in the Mortal Realm. My task is complete, and my time is gone. I must be allowed to die now so our soul can return to you."

Lillian went to the Sorceress and then knelt next to her. *"I will try to reason with Gregory."*

"There is no reasoning with him. You should know that."

"Then what?"

"Shape your shadow magic, make it into a dagger and drive it into my heart. Be fast and sure."

Lillian recoiled. *"I can't. I can't take your life!"*

"I am dying. Gregory is just prolonging my life a few hours. We don't have time to waste. The blood witch is even now finishing a spell that will crush the shield protecting us. If you love Gregory and our children, you will do this thing."

Lillian felt herself shaking. The Sorceress's words were true, but what she asked was...was too great.

"The fissure is getting bigger," Resnick warned. "Look out. We've got incoming."

Behind her, one of his men screamed. She jerked up in time to see an arrow buried in Stanton's right thigh. Magic circled the wooden shaft in a sickly swirl. The human didn't have long to live if someone didn't do something. Gryton stepped in and ripped out the arrow. Stanton swore in pain, but just yanked something out of one of his pockets and packed the wound while the others continued to aim at the enemy.

Gryton returned to lobbing more of his fiery balls of magic, but bright light seeped between the seams of his armor and Lillian knew he wasn't out of danger. His magic was still testing the limits of his control.

She knew what she had to do.

Tears running down her cheeks, she looked up at Gregory as a long, deadly dagger appeared in her fist. It shimmered, absorbing all the light that touched it.

"Forgive me, Gregory," Lillian whispered as she drove the sharp tip down into the Sorceress's heart.

"Lillian, no!" His startled gaze met hers and then he whispered, "I could have saved her."

"No, you couldn't."

A wave of power rose up and slammed into Lillian, tossing her back. She hit the ground and rolled a few times before landing belly down. With a grunt, she lifted her head and realized the power had tossed her a good twenty feet from where she'd started.

At first, she'd thought Gregory had attacked her, but then she saw him rolling to his feet an equal distance away from where Daryna lay. He'd gotten slapped by the same backlash of power that had sent her flying.

Above the Sorceress's body, what looked like a small sun flared and grew as it expanded outward. Ropy tendrils of power flared and lashed the air, whipping in all directions.

"Mother!" Gryton called from somewhere behind and to the left of Lillian.

If he would have said more, she never heard. The small but ever enlarging sun was streaking straight toward her. It hit with the force of a train but didn't send her flying this time. Instead, it lifted her up, holding her suspended above the ground, where it circled her with swirling cross-currents of power.

It was hard to think, even harder to breathe. She couldn't see anything beyond the glowing power or hear anything over the crackle of white noise. Then in a heartbeat, the blinding light, pressure, and power vanished.

All the world went with it.

CHAPTER FORTY-ONE

Oh, she hurt. Each individual nerve in her body complained of some unknown trauma. Whatever the cause, her body lay curled on its side and urged her to remain still until her magic had repaired the damage. And yet, her beloved gargoyle must be battling a great enemy, something powerful enough to lay her low.

They were in a battle then. At that understanding, power rushed into her body, a mix of both warm power from the Magic Realm and the colder, cleaner magic from the Spirit Realm. She formed patterns of battle magic in her mind, shaping them into defensive spells and destructive offensive weavings.

But before she sent them on the hunt, she needed to remember just what had happened. Why were her thoughts and memories so strangely jumbled? Confusion lay over her in a way she'd never experienced in any of her lives.

Great Mother, what new foe did they face?

A very deadly dangerous one, apparently.

She stirred and turned her head, instinct guided her gaze to her other half.

Exhaling in relief, she reached for the mind of her beloved gargoyle. *"You are well?"*

"Yes, my love. I am...well." He tilted his head, his ears shifting between uncertainty, shock, and a touch of grief. He didn't come any closer. "And you?"

"I am...confused my—" She halted mid-thought. She'd been going to call him Durnathyne, but that wasn't correct. He was Gregory in this life.

Levering herself up onto her elbows, she glanced around. She'd been face down on the ground. Spitting out a mouthful of dirt, she made a new discovery. She had a muzzle. Glancing down at her body, her eyes grew wide. Oh! She was gargoyle...but that...that was wrong.

And, yet, it wasn't. More memories arose from her consciousness. Yes, because of the Battle Goddess's manipulations, she'd been born as a dryad this lifetime, but the changes didn't end there.

She was gargoyle. Oh, but wait. She'd also been raised thinking she was human. More memories asserted themselves and with them came clarity.

Tearing her gaze away from her body, she looked around.

They were in a vast dome that sheltered two hamadryad trees. Others were within the dome with her and Gregory. Her beloved came forward and pressed his forehead against hers.

"My Lillian, do you remember me?"

She laughed, a great rolling sound. "Of course I do. My heart, how could I ever forget you?"

He rumbled and pushed his muzzle into her thick mane. "You remember you are Lillian?"

Yes. She'd been Daryna in her last life, but then had been reborn and named Lillian in this life. Although, there were a few strangely recent memories of Daryna mixed up with the ones from this lifetime.

Ah yes. Her hamadryad had cloned her body to temporarily house her soul because she was in danger.

Even as her memories began to sort themselves out, she glanced around at the other beings in the dome with her. One was incredibly powerful. She'd felt his magic pulsing against her skin even when she'd awoken and started to search for her other half.

This male was familiar, his power strangely akin to hers and Gregory's. Ah, yes, there was a reason his power tasted of the Avatars.

He was Gryton.

Her son.

By the Light! She and her beloved had begotten a child.

At that moment all her memories snapped back into their proper place and she remembered.

Everything.

Every evil twisted thing the demigoddess had set in motion.

"Beloved?" Gregory's hands came to rest on her shoulders and his mind brushed against hers as he helped her to her feet. "Do you remember who you are?

Lillian welcomed him in.

"I am Lillian. And, yeah, I remember every evil thing the bitch goddess tried to do to us."

With understanding came anger, the need for revenge. But even greater than that was the need to save all she loved. Gregory, Gryton, Major Resnick and his team, she would protect them all.

"Sorceress?" The word was uttered by Gryton. Her son.

"I prefer the name Lillian, but you can call me mother, I suppose."

Well, shit. That was going to take some getting used to, but for now, she had other things to deal with.

Lillian narrowed her eyes. For one thing, she owed the Battle Goddess the mother of all beatdowns for what she'd been about to do to Gryton and all the Earth. If the Battle Goddess had succeeded, she would have killed millions!

Gran, Jason, the pooka and unicorn, all would have died.

Everything she knew and loved destroyed along with millions of innocents.

And among that massive loss, there would have been one other tiny soul.

An innocent she and Gregory had brought into the world together!

Lillian had come so close to losing everything.

The Lady of Battles sought to kill the Avatars and both their children, and she didn't care how much collateral damage she racked up to achieve that goal.

Rage ignited in Lillian's soul, but her mind turned calmer as her anger built.

The Battle Goddess would feel the repercussions for what she'd done.

Narrowing her eyes, she turned in Gregory's arms until he was standing behind her and then she held out a hand to Gryton.

He hesitated at first, distrust shining in his eyes. In the end, he came forward.

When his burning hot hand engulfed hers, she remembered how close she'd come to losing this child before she'd been given a chance to really know him.

Oh, she remembered the many mistakes her doppelganger had made, but even if Lillian could have unmade all those poor choices, she still would have given Gryton a chance to repent for all the horror he'd caused.

And she, in turn, would try to heal him of all the horror he'd endured.

She wasn't blind to his faults; there were many. Lillian had always seen that. So too had Gregory.

"Battle Goddess," Lillian shouted, her magic filling her and flowing out of her as her voice grew in volume. "Never again will you be known as the Lady of Battles. I strip you of your title."

The demigoddess screamed in rage as the chains holding her trapped resonated with Lillian's words.

"As I strip your title this day, so too will I one day return to strip you of your power and then your life. I will send you back to the Divine Ones for your long overdue judgment."

The Battle Goddess fought her chains but stilled long enough to eye Lillian over the distance. With a sneer, she said, "You do not have the power."

"You forget we brought you into being. Do not doubt

that we have enough power to return you to the Divine Ones."

The demigoddess leaned forward and reached out a hand, pointing one long elegant finger at Lillian. "You have your orders from the Divine Ones. You won't break them simply because I've sought to make right a wrong done to me when my twin killed my beloved."

Lillian laughed, a harsh note in her voice. "You have selective memory. Have you forgotten I and my other half have already broken our greatest vow? We created Gryton. Yes, we had to answer for that, as we will have to answer for killing you."

"Gryton was a mistake. The Mother's Sorceress won't willingly break one of the Avatars binding vows by killing me."

Lillian continued to summon power. "You are correct. The Mother's Sorceress wouldn't break that vow. But the Sorceress Enraged will. Especially after you tried to kill everyone I know and love."

"Even a billion lives are but a few grains of sand in the vast universe."

"I do not see it the same. And my children's fates are for the Divine Ones to decide—not a crazed demigoddess made mad and bitter by her own loss."

Far away at the top of her temple, the Battle Goddess turned her head and stared up at the sky, as if looking between the stars to the Spirit Realm beyond. When she glanced back down, she said. "I don't believe you, Sorceress."

"Whether a person believes in something or not never changes the true nature of something. You do not have to believe that I've changed. But I have. I am no longer simply the Mother's Sorceress. I am now also Lillian. And the universe has never seen the Sorceress enraged before, but one day soon you will feel my wrath. But until then return to your prison."

Lillian waved her hand and released the spell she'd been holding in reserve. It leaped forward, streaking out of the dome, and crossed the distance in less than three seconds. When it struck the Battle Goddess's chains, they drew up tight, slowly reeling her back inside her temple.

If she didn't have Gryton and all Earth to protect, she might have taken this fight to the Battle Goddess here and now, but she couldn't allow her need for revenge to override her duty to all those she loved.

The Battle Goddess might be out of her reach, but there were other, lesser beings even now scrambling at the dome of power surrounding them.

"Gregory, if you would attend to the second dome, I'll deal with the riff-raff beating at the door."

"As my beloved wishes."

"I do."

He allowed his hands to drop away from her shoulders and then moved several steps back and returned to drawing down the immense power the spell would require. The temperature inside the old dome dropped by twenty degrees.

Ignoring the chill, Lillian tugged Gryton forward. "Would you like to further your training, my son?"

He arched an eyebrow, but merely nodded and followed.

They halted just behind Major Resnick and his team.

The humans had managed to hold back the flood of enemy warriors, giving her the time she needed to reunite her body, soul, and magic.

With a wave of her hand, a glimmering shield formed around the humans, protecting them from further harm, while still allowing them to continue firing into the melee outside the dome.

"I thank you for your service, Resnick," Lillian said and raised hers and Gryton's linked hands. "But on my order, you're going to need to haul ass and retreat behind where Gregory is creating the second dome."

Resnick glanced over his shoulder as he was reloading, noted where Gregory now stood, and then nodded. "Happily."

While Resnick relayed the order to his team, Lillian called down a raging torrent of power from the Spirit Realm. It swirled in the air just above the humans' heads, lashing and flailing with the violence of a coming storm, but she enforced her will upon the power and it coalesced into delicate threads of magic. They knitted themselves together into a fine webbing.

She fed more raw power into the weaving, spinning out more and more of the webbing. As it grew first to a twenty-foot and then a thirty-foot expanse, she pushed the air around it, sending it floating higher.

"Mother," Gryton said as a group of twenty enemies breached the shield. "While the spell work is pretty, and I appreciate the lesson, perhaps, now isn't the best time?"

Fire rose up and incinerated the warriors who ran toward their position, but an endless stream of newcomers flooded into the dome through the ever-enlarging fissure.

"Mother, we're going to get flanked."

"Nope."

Her spell continued to grow, expanding to fit itself along the underside of the old dome. Once the entire surface was covered, she summoned another wave of magic from the Spirit Realm and fed it into both webbing and dome. The two spells blurred, melting into each other.

"Ah," Gryton said as he glanced away from the battle for a moment to stare in awe at her work. "You're rewriting the dome's spell pattern. I would not have thought that wise."

"For most, no. But I've lived a very long time and know a few tricks others don't."

"So I see," Gryton said dryly.

"It's almost ready."

Gryton summoned more fire magic and flung it at the next wave of armor-clad warriors racing toward them. "I hate to pressure you or question your great wisdom, but nonetheless, we *are* about to get overrun."

He launched three more rapid volleys of tightly coiled fireballs that expanded out as they flew. Some of the enemies were able to dodge or to knock aside Gryton's power and they sprinted forward. Resnick and his team were now on mop-up detail, picking off the few enemies able to get past Gryton's defense.

"Almost done...," Lillian said as she manipulated a small bit of power. The tiny bit of magic spun and twisted in the air above her outstretched hand and then with a flick of her wrist, she sent the trigger spell flying. It adhered itself seamlessly to the dome high above. "There. Resnick, time to go!"

"You heard the lady," Resnick barked, not needing to be told twice. "Move!"

The uninjured soldiers grabbed their wounded counterparts and dragged them behind Gregory, where he'd erected another defensive shield separate from the dome spell he was working on.

"Beloved," Lillian said even as she looked forward to the enemies rushing through the break in the dome. "I'm about to kick the hornet's nest. We're going to need your spell about ten seconds after I trigger mine."

He brought his hand down in a long slashing motion as he finished drawing the last symbol in the air. The individual glowing glyphs were adhered to a circular construct, and as she watched, the last symbol aligned with the rest and settled into its designated spot.

Grinning, Gregory beat his powerful wings and took to the air, propelling his weaving twenty feet above her head. Feeding on his pure elation, she laughed joyously. Working together side by side, summoning vast amounts of pure, untainted power and trusting in each other to hold up their end of the bargain. This was how it was supposed to be.

"I am ready, my love," Gregory shouted over the growing noise as more of the Battle Goddess's army rushed forward, sensing the old dome's growing weakness.

Their enemies didn't yet know it was a trick. The old dome had tinted to an opaque sickly green shade. While it had darkened to such an extent as to prevent Lillian from seeing outside, it also blocked their enemies from seeing within. Only the soldiers running through the breach could see what was going on inside in the seconds before Gryton burned them to ash.

Lillian glanced at Gregory's spell one last time. It spun slowly, awaiting his final command while it cast off a multi-hued light that reminded her a little of a disco ball. She stepped away from Gryton and took to the air. Gregory made it look easy, but Lillian imagined her own attempt probably wasn't quite so graceful.

But it didn't matter. She had a whole lifetime to learn what her gargoyle body was capable of and she would do it with her beloved at her side. "If you're ready to rock, let's do this."

Gregory chuckled. "I very much want to ring the Battle Goddess's bell."

Lillian fought to keep a straight face. "Flight lessons for me, the urban dictionary for you."

Then she reached out to the trigger spell and flicked it with a bit of power. The spell flared brightly like a small detonation and then within seconds the entire web and dome began vibrating. A louder hum emanated from the dome. As the vibrations increased, the sound grew higher in pitch.

It continued to climb to uncomfortable levels, but she could heal a little hearing loss later.

The vibrations increased until the webbing couldn't hold back the force. With a loud shattering and a high-pitched crystalline scream, the dome bowed outward, a great wave of boundless force and raw, burning power raced out in an ever-widening circle of annihilation.

Lillian was blinded by the sudden brightness after the greenish semidarkness inside the dome. Nevertheless, her vision adapted in time to see the shockwave roll over the hapless soldiers in its path.

As the backlash of power expanded further out, it began to weaken and break apart. It was still a great force, but more and more of the soldiers were now surviving the blast, their personal defensive magic strong enough to withstand the hit.

But the spell had done its job and cleaned a huge swath of land, giving Gregory time to erect the new dome. A glance in his direction showed him already releasing it. As Lillian watched, his spell grew brighter and he began to feed it more power during its last growth phase.

Something set all her instincts on edge. Lillian twisted in the air, facing the swirling ash and ravaged ground just beyond where the old dome had stood. Moments later movement in the ash had Lillian summoning a spear of power.

"It's Captain Taryin," Gryton said in warning and summoned a wall of fire. "She's a powerful blood witch."

Lillian had the scent now. Yes, that stench was blood magic. The power of the shattering dome wouldn't have been enough to kill one such as this. Narrowing her eyes, she summoned two more spears forged of shadow magic to add to her arsenal.

An amber-colored mist rose up out of the ashes moments before a female form struggled back to her feet. The figure was badly burned, but already beginning to heal, the blackened skin flaking off to reveal pale pink tissue. All the deaths fueled her power, and she continued to call upon her dark magic, shaping it into a ravaging cloud that she sent flying toward Gregory.

Lillian darted through the air and erected a shield between her beloved and the blood witch. When the two powers collided, a shower of sparks rained down upon the ground. The blood magic spell did not break apart though, continuing to slowly eat away at the defensive shield.

"I'm capable of protecting myself," Gregory said in a dry mental tone while he worked.

"Of course, but your power is better spent fueling the new dome spell."

He grunted in acknowledgment. Lillian returned her focus fully upon her enemy and flung one of her spears at the blood witch. The woman Gryton had called Taryin countered with another wave of her foul magic.

Already Lillian knew this wasn't going to be a quick victory. If she wanted to kill the blood witch, she'd have to take her heart and burn it and once that was accomplished, burn the rest of her body, too. Otherwise, the witch would just regenerate.

Lillian dropped to all fours and charged forward only to have a wall of fire burst into being directly in front of her.

"Damn it, Gryton!"

"There's no time." He gestured, pointing behind him where Gregory's dome spell was even now growing down toward the earth. "Mother, if you get caught outside Gregory's new shield when it forms, it won't go well. For either of us."

Lillian was aware of the dangers, and she also knew she could survive outside the dome in a one on one fight with the blood witch, but Gryton was reaching his limit. She couldn't risk him losing control, but he had that determined look she'd seen on Gregory's face so damn many times over thousands of lifetimes. The one that said he wasn't leaving her side.

Like father like son, apparently.

But Gryton had already sustained colossal trauma this day. She wouldn't expose him to more.

"Beloved," Gregory's voice was suddenly in her mind. *"You well and truly kicked the hornet's nest. But now it is time we leave."*

Fine. Lillian glowered unhappily at the blood witch but backed toward Gregory's position. At a muttered word from him, the new dome spell went through one last expansion phase and then snapped into place, forming an impenetrable shield between them and their enemies.

Pristine and powerful, the new dome shimmered in the early morning light. Two seconds later, the blood witch screamed as she tossed more magic at the shield.

The dome flared with power, its nebulous colors floating and shifting in swiftly changing patterns as the shield voraciously drank in the energy, using the magic to fuel its own defenses.

Gregory dropped down onto the grass next to her, one wing curling around her in a familiar, protective way. "We did not come here to start and end the war with the Battle Goddess in one day. We came to free Anna and Shadow-light. Instead, we have liberated our son and saved the Earth. That is not a terrible day's work. Now we must return home and report all we have discovered."

That slow simmering rage still bubbled in Lillian's soul. She wanted to end the Battle Goddess once and for all. Unfortunately, Gregory was correct. Gryton's power was unstable and to stay and continue the fight might end with their son's death and much of this world's as well.

Gryton deserved a chance to atone. He couldn't do that if he was dead.

"You are wise my beloved protector."

"Some of the humans need healing as well," Gregory added, glancing over his shoulder at Resnick.

Outside the dome, the Battle Goddess's army was rallying, but there was nothing they could do at present. They'd have to create another gateway if they wished to traverse the Veil between the Realms. It wouldn't be easy, but Lillian didn't doubt that with a blood witch's help, they'd one day succeed. It just wouldn't be today. And with luck, it would give her and Gregory time to face Lord Death, mend some fences and get Shadowlight and Anna back.

"Draydrak?" She mentally reached eastward, in the direction his temple lay. *"Old friend, I now know that I and my other half broke our vows in a past life and that we must make amends, but please, don't take my brother from me, or the human he loves like family."*

She waited for a response. When none came, she forged on. *"Dray, I know you might not have faith in my judgment after the breaking of our vows, but Anna and Shadowlight are pure, strong souls, capable of great courage. The Battle Goddess will not have changed that in so short a time. Please let them live to prove that to you."*

Lillian waited a few seconds longer, but no beautiful voice manifested in her mind.

Yep. She and Gregory needed to mend some fences with the Lord of the Underworld before they went to war with the Battle Goddess. In the meantime, she had to believe Lord Death would be merciful.

Speaking of mending fences. She glanced sidelong at

Gryton and studied him for some moments. "You must return with us and own up to what you've done. In return, I promise to teach you how to better control your power so that nothing like what happened today will ever happen again."

"I...thank you." Gryton's expression showed nothing, but she could feel the emotional need he tried to deny.

"Don't thank me yet. The humans are going to want your head on a platter, and I can't say I blame them."

Gryton turned to study the humans and his expression darkened.

"If you promise to behave, I won't let that happen."

"I shall...behave," he said after a rather long awkward pause.

"Good." She was certain he wouldn't betray her. Besides, he had nowhere else to go. It was more likely he didn't know what to do or how to act. She didn't blame him. It wasn't like her long existence had prepared her for a son.

Grunting, Gryton nodded slightly and then stalked over to the humans to help Gregory gather up the injured.

Once the others were gathered around the trunk of her hamadryad, Lillian joined them and glanced at Gregory. "We're going to need to have a long talk about Gryton later."

"I know." He nuzzled at her hair. "But we also need to talk about us."

Ah. Their relationship had changed again, hadn't it? Gregory's fear had come true: he'd lost his mate.

At least in his eyes. Lillian didn't see it the same way. But he was correct, that was a conversation for later.

Closing her eyes, she summoned more power and touched the rough bark of her hamadryad. With a sense of being jerked forward and then falling, Lillian and the others were suddenly pulled back to the Mortal Realm.

Falling back was much easier than going the other direction.

Still, Lillian just stood in the shadow of her hamadryad tree for a few seconds, enjoying the sensation of being home.

"God, I need a beer," muttered Stanton, still holding a hand pressed against his bleeding thigh.

"I second that," Resnick said, but Lillian saw the way he was giving the death glare to Gryton.

Yep. The next debriefing was going to be long and joyless.

As if the thought of a debriefing summoned them, Gran came striding into the glade with several of the joint task force's top brass marching behind. One of which was the tall, now familiar form of Brigadier General Mackenzie.

Oh crap. How the hell were they going to explain about his daughter?

Alcohol was starting to look like a good idea.

CHAPTER FORTY-TWO

After a day-long debriefing, where he and Lillian did a lot of explaining, persuading, soothing and even a good bit of pleading, the meeting ended with a lot of questions still unanswered. But Resnick and his team had seen what the Battle Goddess had attempted, and the major came to their defense, explaining what might have happened if they hadn't saved Gryton. Plus, he was valuable for the intel he could provide.

It was true. No one knew as much about the Battle Goddess's plans as Gryton did. In the end, the humans demanded that Gregory and Lillian collar him. To his surprise, Gryton merely nodded his head, saying that he'd expected nothing less.

After they'd created a powerful spell to stop Gryton from calling on his magic, Gregory had watched somewhat bemused as the male was led away under heavy guard, where he'd be taken to a cell and guarded by both humans and fae.

It wasn't ideal for studying and determining if Gryton was redeemable, but the day had gone better than it could have.

After the debriefing, they returned to Lillian's hamadryad where he gathered her in his arms and folded his wings around her, just holding her while they both gazed up into the hamadryad canopy. Every so often, he reached out and touched the tree, marveling at their miracle. A daughter. He and his beloved were having a daughter.

He was sure he still had a silly grin plastered on his face as they walked back to the house.

If he hadn't sensed Lillian was emotionally and physically exhausted, not to mention hungry, he would have stayed longer.

She'd already returned to her dryad form before the debriefing, claiming that the humans were more comfortable around the more human-looking fae. Gregory hadn't commented at the time, but he was sure her dryad form just felt more natural.

"I want to eat half the contents of the fridge," Lillian said and then glanced sidelong at him. "Then I want a long, hot bath. With you in it."

Gregory halted, but Lillian continued without a backward glance, although, she had to know he'd stopped.

Hesitantly, he said, "You know things must be different between us now that you are again the Mother's Sorceress."

Even as he'd allowed his sorrow to take on the form of words, he forced himself into motion. He caught up with her, but she still didn't respond. "Lillian?"

"Uh-huh." Lillian kept walking, only stopping at the

fridge long enough to grab two plastic-wrapped sandwiches and some bottles of water a blessedly-thoughtful person had left for them.

They continued to their bedroom and Lillian set the sandwiches on the dresser and entered the bathroom. A moment later he heard the bathtub filling.

Seriously? For once he wanted to talk and she didn't? Lillian always wanted to talk. About everything. All the time. He frowned, tempted to just reach into her mind and learn what she was truly thinking.

Lillian glanced over her shoulder and grinned. "Your expression is priceless. Yes, I know we can't have intercourse while I'm the Sorceress. However, I don't plan on being the Mother's Sorceress forever, at least in this lifetime. I told you, once we've dealt with the Battle Goddess and her army, I plan to grow an entire glade of hamadryads, stow my soul in one of them and have lots and lots and lots of sex with you."

Gregory swallowed wrong and started to choke.

"Don't swallow your tongue, you idiot. If you die on me before we have a big-ass family, I'm going to come to the Spirit Realm and chew your ass out." Lillian shrugged and grinned. "And besides, the Divine Ones didn't smite us for begetting a daughter, so I doubt they'll have a problem with us having a family this one time."

That was likely true. "What is the human saying? Beg for forgiveness instead of ask for permission?"

"That's the one." Lillian grinned. "As much as it might not sound like it now, I, too, hold our vows to the Divine Ones close to my heart, but I don't see this as breaking our faith with them. They never demanded we be chaste.

We decided that to honor them. They only warned against the Mother's Sorceress and the Father's Gargoyle Protector begetting a child that wasn't born of Divine will."

Gregory closed his eyes, not because he wanted to deny what she was saying, but because he wanted to reach out and grab Lillian and pull her to him and kiss her until they both passed out from lack of oxygen.

"I know we can't be mates until after we've completed what we were born for, but that doesn't mean we can't still be lovers. There are many creative ways to share our passion without risking a child. We won't slip up this time. Light only knows, we already have Gryton. One of him is plenty for all three Realms to share. We've learned our lesson."

Gregory chuckled, surprising himself. "I shouldn't be laughing. This is far from funny."

"No. Certainly not. We're talking about our life and future happiness." Warm, smooth fingers caressed his cheek and jaw, slowly trailing down his neck to rest on his shoulder. Lillian's warmth brushed against him and then her lips were pressing little kisses along his muzzle.

"If you'd shapeshift, I could kiss you properly," Lillian said with a hint of humor as she stepped back. "But if you're not interested, I'll just go take a cold shower instead of that bath."

Gregory coughed. "The Divine Ones never mentioned a shared bath as being forbidden and they nurture creativity."

"Then let's get creative." Lillian grinned and led him into the bathroom. He shapeshifted into his human form and leaned in for a kiss. Shortly thereafter, Lillian sighed and wrapped her arms around him.

It was much later by the time they stepped in the tub, and far later still before they climbed back out. Afterward, he carried Lillian to bed. She snuggled against him, half asleep when she suddenly jerked awake and sat up.

"There was something I was going to give you, but after the failed mission to rescue Shadowlight and Anna, I wasn't sure if it was appropriate. Then I got thinking, we never know for certain how long we'll live in any one lifetime. Seeing the future was never one of our gifts."

Lillian rolled across the bed. At first, he didn't know what she was after. Pulling open a drawer in her nightstand, she took out a small black box. Gregory's eyebrows drew together in curiosity. What was his strange dryad up to now?

She crawled back to him and sat on her knees gazing down at him with warmth, humor, and love in her eyes.

"This was something I asked Daryna to create." Lillian flipped the lip open. The small box had some kind of hinged lid. "It's a human tradition, and if I was a man, I'd get down on one knee."

"I'm happy you weren't born a male," Gregory said with a bemused smile crossing his face.

"Actually, you'd normally be the one to get down on one knee, but it's an archaic, somewhat sexist tradition, come to think of it, and since we're all about being equals..." Lillian held the box out for him.

He leaned forward and glanced inside. It was a plain gold ring, large enough to fit around one of his fingers if he was in gargoyle form. His breath stilled in his lungs. While he wasn't that familiar with modern human customs, he knew what marriage was.

"Gregory Livingstone, my most beloved gargoyle, will you marry me?" Lillian paused, waiting for his answer.

A soft growly purr escaped him. He reached up and pulled Lillian down for a kiss. It was some minutes later before he was able to answer aloud.

"I suppose I must," he said with a grin, fully expecting to get a rise out of his dryad. "After all, I've knocked you up twice now." Then turning serious once more, he cupped her face in his hands. "I love you more than anything in all the realms. It would please me greatly to hear you call me husband."

Lillian chuckled, and then placed the ring on his finger. "Smart boy. If you'd said no, I was going to shift to gargoyle form and beat you up."

Even as they snuggled together, Gregory knew it was a beautiful pledge that fate might be too cruel to allow them to see fulfilled, but it didn't lessen the moment as he fell asleep with his beloved Lillian, whole and happy, in his arms.

Tonight, he'd enjoy what peace he could find. Tomorrow, it would be back to planning a war and readying for a visit with the Lord of the Underworld. For the first time in all his lives, he did not look forward to facing his old friend. If they were even still friends. Though he hoped so for the sake of Shadowlight and Anna.

*A*nna's low moan of pain woke Shadowlight. It was only then that he realized he'd lost awareness for a few precious seconds. He raised his head and discovered Anna was curled in a fetal position next to him. Her skin held a greyish tint to it and sweat coated her body. Every few seconds a mighty shudder would rack her smaller frame.

"Please don't die," he whispered to her and petted her damp mane.

She blinked up at him, her lips trying to form words.

"S...sorr...sorry," she croaked out at last.

"Don't talk. Save your strength." But what he really meant was, 'don't finish that sentence' because he didn't want to hear his worst fears vocalized out loud. He tried not to think about them even in his own mind.

Glancing around, he started to look for help.

They were on a vast island, overlooking the ocean. Far

below, the ocean crashed against the base of a cliff, sending sea spray high up in the air. He didn't care about any of that.

Anna was dying and needed help.

"Lord of the Underworld, if you can hear me, please help Anna," Shadowlight whispered the words out loud as well as in his mind.

There was no answer, but far off Shadowlight could hear hooves impacting stone. As the sound grew louder, the ground underneath him began to shake. At least he hoped it was the ground and not his body quaking in fear.

He glanced toward the center of the island.

A gigantic form, easily as tall, or taller, than the Battle Goddess, leaped over a low cliff wall and continued to thunder toward Shadowlight's position. Size was the only thing Lord Death had in common with his twin.

He galloped over the ground swiftly, his four powerful legs carrying him over the dangerous terrain effortlessly. When he reached a ravine too wide for his horse-like lower body to safely jump, he spread his wings and sailed over it before landing with a clatter of hooves against stone.

The God of Death pulled up short when he reached Shadowlight's side. Then he stared down at them and rested his hands on the hilts of his four massive swords. He tilted his head until his muzzle was pointed down at them.

"Never have I met two such stubborn souls." Lord Death's mellow voice rumbled above their heads.

Anna tried to push herself to a sitting position, but Shadowlight wrapped his arms and wings around her as if that would protect his friend from Death incarnate.

Though, he didn't think anything he did would protect her from this four-armed god of death.

"Hello, young ones. My name is Draydrak, but you may call me Dray if you prefer."

Shadowlight glanced up. This wasn't precisely the greeting he'd been expecting. With renewed hope, he asked, "Will you save Anna? A blood witch's magic is trying to destroy her soul."

Draydrak stared at them in silence for a moment then he reached down and plucked Shadowlight and Anna up in one giant hand. Adrenaline sent Shadowlight's heart pounding, but he refused to show fear. Anna had taught him not to show weaknesses to an enemy. And while his gargoyle nature told him Lord Death wasn't an enemy, Shadowlight still wasn't convinced he and Anna were safe in his care, either.

"Her soul I can, and will, protect," Draydrak said, cupping a second hand above them and summoning magic. "Saving the human's life? That I cannot promise."

The large hand slowly lowered, trapping Anna and Shadowlight within a cage of interwoven digits, but that was the least of Shadowlight's worries, for the next instant the temperature dropped as a chilled power flowed over them. Seconds after that Lord Death began to sing.

The hauntingly beautiful sound surrounded Shadow-light, soothing and lulling him into a sense of peace. Slowly, his eyes drifted closed and his head grew heavy. Anna no longer moaned in pain and his fears became a distant, forgotten thing.

"Sleep well, young ones," Draydrak sang. "You will need your rest for what is to come."

THE END

None of this would have been possible without, you, my readers. You're awesome! Thank You!

Bye for now,
Lisa Blackwood

ABOUT THE AUTHOR

Lisa Blackwood is the author of the bestselling Gargoyle and Sorceress urban fantasy series. Her work has also landed on the Wall Street Journal and the USA Today Bestseller lists as part of the Dominion Rising Anthology. When she's not reading and writing, she also enjoys gardening and spending time with her horse and her dogs.

At present, she grudgingly lives in a small town in Southern Ontario, though she would much rather live deep in a dark forest, surrounded by majestic old-growth trees. Since she cannot live her fantasy, she decided to write fantasy instead.

BOOKS BY LISA BLACKWOOD

Gargoyle & Sorceress

Dawn of the Sorceress

Sorceress Awakening

Sorceress Rising

Sorceress Hunting

Sorceress at War

Sorceress Enraged

Legacy of the Sorceress

Sorcery & Firedrakes

Scion of the Sorceress

Sorceress Eternal

In Deception's Shadow Series (Epic Fantasy Romance)

Betrayal's Price

Herd Mistress

Maiden's Wolf

Death's Queen

The Prince's Gryphon (forthcoming)

Ishtar's Legacy Series (Epic Fantasy Romance)

Ishtar's Blade

The Blade's Beginning (short story)

Blade's Honor

Blade's Destiny

The Blade's Shadow

First Queen of the Gryphons

The King of the Anunnaki (forthcoming)

The Anunnaki's Blade (forthcoming)

Huntress vs Huntsman (Epic Fantasy Romance)

Master of the Hunt

Night Huntress

Dragon Archer

Soul Mage (forthcoming)